The Challenger

Rowan Rossler

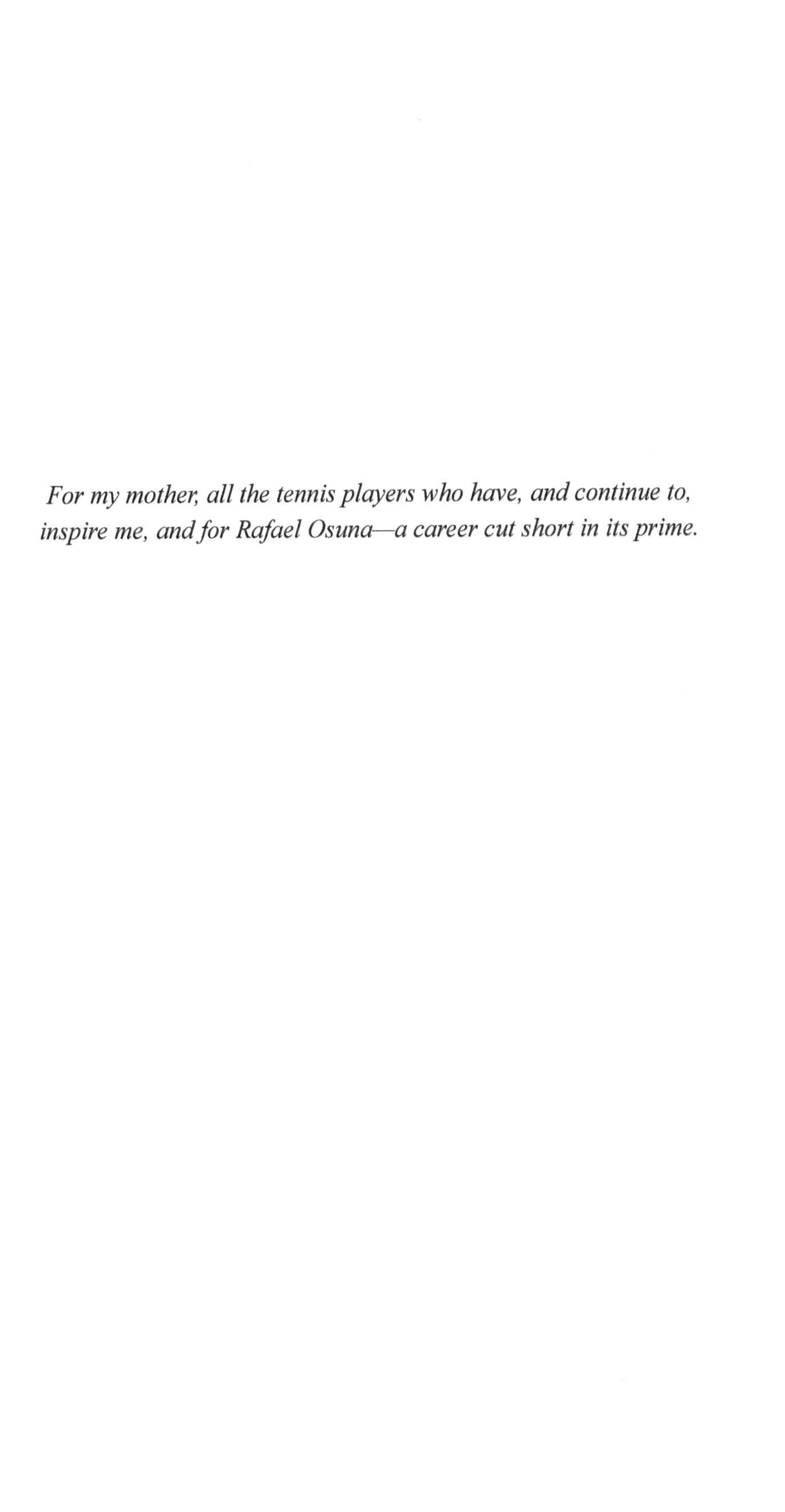

For my mother, all the tennis players who have, and continue to, inspire me, and for Rafael Osuna—a career cut short in its prime.

Challenger

/ˈCHalinjər/

- A person who threatens someone's hold on a position
- The second-highest tier of professional tennis

THE TALENTED TORNADO

DECEMBER

Chapter One

FLYNN

EVERY WOMAN TELLS LIES IN LOS ANGELES. BEING SLIPPERY WITH THE truth is part career strategy and part necessary coping mechanism. The pressure to be beautiful and successful is relentless in the City of Angels, and though my fans consider me both, they don't know the real me. I've been lying for years. Some days I'm better at it than others, and today is a definite other. My anxiety has shot up like mercury in July and I'm fresh out of magic pills, about to lose it on the world's most annoying gatekeeper.

"Can you check again?" I ask Madison, another blonde actress wannabe slumming it as a Beverly Hills receptionist. "I made an appointment a month ago before I went out of town."

She snaps her gum and scrolls through the calendar on her computer monitor, making a big production of it. "I don't see your name anywhere. And Dr. Bradford is booked solid for the next two weeks. You'll have to reschedule."

"Is there any chance he can write me a new prescription without an appointment?"

I dig deep for my most sincere Flynn Dryden smile—the one my fans pay a hundred dollars a pop to see in person—and fight the urge to yell, *Don't you know who I am! I am America's favorite motivational guru. My entire career is helping people.* After playing nice for the last thirty days and smiling through the lovers, haters, and hecklers on my book tour, right now, I just need someone to help me.

Madison's baby blues show the first sign of crumbling when the clinic door beeps open behind me. She straightens in the chair, unconsciously primping her hair. I glance over my shoulder expecting to see a famous producer or agent, not some young guy helping himself to water at the cooler. Only a rearview because he's facing away from us, but damn. He's fit as fuck with skin the same color as the almond butter I smeared on my toast this morning. I can only assume he's a delivery guy. Who else waltzes into a psychiatry office for a drink wearing only a tank top and shorts?

Anyway.

I turn back to Madison and go for the beg as a last resort. "Can you swing me ten pills for now? A courtesy top off. It's an emergency."

"You know we can't do that. Not for Zoloft," she says, loud enough that anyone in the LA Basin can hear. "And according to this," she peers at that godforsaken calendar again, "you're back sooner than you should be."

With an unsteady breath, I ball both fists to avoid throttling her. *Judgment on top of it all.*

"She doesn't care. Get used to it. No one in the system cares."

I whip around, ready to lay into this guy who's mistaken my business for his. But words dissolve like dust on my tongue.

For the love of god.

He's now lounging on the lobby couch with one arm draped along the top and his sneakers crossed on the coffee table like he owns the place. His mouth curls into a rebellious smirk that says, *I dare you to challenge me,* and I plan to, right after I scoop my jaw up off the floor. It's kind of pathetic to stare so openly, but if there were a Mr. USA beauty competition, this smoldering Latino honey would bring the judges to their knees.

"Cat got your tongue?" he asks.

I clear my throat and wish I'd put some thought into my appearance before rushing down here. Some blush to brighten my pale skin or something more inspired than my curls pulled into a simple, messy bun. At least I'm in heels and a dress and not a hoodie.

"I was going to say—"

"That I'm right?"

His eyes bore into mine. Were they angry or just unhappy? Either way, I sense trouble and not the good kind. Why else would he be here?

"No. You're wrong. People do care." People other than Madison, I almost add.

He studies me, gauging my sincerity. "An eternal optimist. How encouraging, señorita."

He rolls the R in señorita and I feel it. Feel his tongue making a single letter an illicit event. I feel it in places where I probably shouldn't. While that sensation buzzes through me, he pushes off the couch and swaggers over, a hip-swaying advertisement for testosterone and virility. I'm 5'10" without heels, the neighborhood giraffe, but I can tell he's grooving on the power of being taller, staring down at me with peepers a shade of turquoise so unreal they might as well have a Crayola label slapped on them.

"Chavez," he says. "Since we're swapping names."

"I didn't know we were."

He fingers a curl that's gone AWOL from my bun with a slow smile. "C'mon, beautiful lady. What's your name?"

"My name is Flynn," I say, swatting his hand away. "And ask before you touch me, please."

His eyes drift over me without landing on any one place, but they still manage to get their point across. "You always wear dresses that short?"

"You're one to talk, Sporty Spice," I flip back. "Not leaving much to the imagination, are you?"

He shoots me a saucy wink. "I got you imagining. That's the first step."

Jesus. How is it even possible to have a mouth made for sin on such a baby face? My mind races back and forth because he looks so familiar. And his name rings a bell. Something about him in general rings all my bells. Curiosity gets the better of me.

"What's step two?" I ask.

The office phone jingles to life, and Chavez steers us away from Madison's chatter to corner me by the fish tank. He raises one arm, boxing me in further by laying his palm against the wall beside my head. Heat radiates off him like a five-alarm fire.

"You tell me," he says, his breath sweet and dangerously close to mingling with mine.

A flush creeps onto my cheeks. He is young and yummy and flaunting way too much skin for eleven in the morning. And if it's possible to smell like male dominance, well, he's got that covered too. Sweet fuckery, where was he last night? My dating app run and gun with Dwayne from Denver imploded into the usual disaster. Nothing sexier than a guy lapping my lady business like a panicky toddler with a melting ice cream cone while I count spiderwebs on his ceiling. I had to fake an orgasm to end that misery, and he passed out believing it was all due to his Herculean efforts.

"Ms. Dryden." Madison's voice jolts us out of our intimate cocoon. Chavez cuts her an irritated look over his shoulder and steps back, taking his body heat with him. "You're in luck," she says. "I just had a cancellation for tomorrow at four."

"Oh, uhm … sure," I reply. "Tomorrow works."

"Flynn Dryden." Chavez says my name as if he's testing out a new language. "My last name also starts with D. If we got married, you'd still be Flynn D. How do you feel about that?"

In my attempt to suppress a laugh, I end up spraying it instead. "How often does that line work for you?"

"You'd be surprised."

"Well, I'm sorry to be the one to crush your odds."

My pushback only seems to amuse him. "Muy tierna y fogosa," he says, working the Spanish accent with a smile. "I like."

Whatever is going on here, I like it too. It's a good feeling, this rarity of being admired by a younger man not clutching one of my books. Our little flirtathon is the first bit of fun I've had in a long while. But like everything good in my life, it's cut short. One of the office doors in the hallway opens and a weeping, expensively tended woman clutching a hairless dog shuffles out.

"Excuse me," she sniffs, sliding past us to make a dramatic exit in her sequined tracksuit.

Following in her footsteps is a burly man of the Scottish Highlands variety, with horn-rimmed glasses and a braided beard held together with a festive red hair tie. He looks surprised to see us.

"Hey, Smythe." Chavez greets the man with a two-fingered salute off his forehead.

Smythe glances at his watch. "You're early."

"If you're late, that's not showing respect."

Funny that I've been coming here for a year and have never set eyes on the Ethan Smythe of Bradford and Smythe Psychiatry until now. Compared to the dashing and impeccably dressed Dr. Bradford, Ethan and his flannel shirt looks better suited to carve statues with a chainsaw than probe my mind.

"Your punctuality is appreciated," Ethan says. "I need to use the little boy's room. Make yourself comfortable in my office." He turns to me with an apologetic smile. "I'm sorry, but no girlfriends allowed."

I arch a brow. As if I don't have anything better to do with my time than hold my boyfriend's hand during his therapy session.

"I'm not his girlfriend," I point out.

Chavez glances over and disarms me with another wink. "Not yet."

Ethan's head is on a swivel, unsure what to make of us. "I'll be back in five. I hope that's enough time to sort yourselves out."

After he leaves, Chavez takes a step closer, erasing the distance between us. My body hums with a strange energy.

"Looks like our time is up, Miss Flynn. I left my phone in the car but how about I do my thing and you leave your number with her?"

He tilts his head at Madison who, to give credit where credit is due, can certainly act like she's busy. Chavez must think this is a slam dunk, judging from his confident smile.

Not so fast.

"How old are you?" I ask.

"Old enough to know what I'm doing."

"And you're assuming I'm single?"

"Fortune favors the bold, right? I'm all about taking my chances."

He curls his fists to reveal the words *FEAR* and *LESS* inked across his right and left knuckles. Hand tattoos are not on the top-five list of what I'm looking for in a man, but gah, his mouth. It brings to mind dirty kisses in the rain that go on forever. With lots of tongue.

Perhaps I search his dreamy face too long for his liking.

Maybe he has no clue I'm processing multiple layers of rationalization.

Or maybe it's a game for him after all.

"But hey," he says, dropping his hands as if I've personally rejected them, "if you're one of those chicks who likes to play hard to get, I'm out. I don't have time to chase women. Leaving it up to you."

No time to chase but lots of time to put on one hell of a show with his insouciant strut down the hall. Molded onto a butt built for serious thrusting, his canary-yellow shorts are the equivalent of an amber traffic light.

Slow down and proceed with caution.

Madison watches him go with a snorting laugh. "Unbelievable, huh? Some guys think they're God's gift to women. He probably figured since you're old he could—"

"Old?" I interrupt.

"What I meant is, he's only twenty-five."

"How do you know?"

"He's plastered all over the internet," she says, emphasizing *internet* in the event I need a refresher on this marvelous invention. "Supposedly he got kicked off the tour for anger management issues."

Madison is now zero for two in keeping client information confidential, although the bubble of familiarity I feel with Chavez now makes sense.

"What's his band called?" I ask.

"Not *that* kind of tour. The tennis tour. He's a tennis player. Chavez Delgado." She shrugs. "I guess he's a big deal. Or he was."

Hearing his name and tennis sends a spasm through my right elbow. A ghostly reminder that at one point in my life, I knew who all the top tennis players were. I don't track the detailed comings and goings of the sport anymore, but you have to be living under a rock not to have heard of Chavez. I couldn't make the connection because the context was out of place. Who expects an infamous tennis star to slum it in a shrink's office with Enya warbling over the speakers?

"Just so you know," Madison adds, "he asked for my number last week, but I didn't give it to him. It's your call if you want to leave yours."

I'm more than a little interested to see where a future conversation with Chavez might lead, but there is no way I'm picking up Madison's sloppy seconds. Plus, I've made a vow never to date tennis players. It's too personal—a reminder of the scars, inside and out. And I've got enough on my plate. Like the reason I came here in the first place, unshowered, without makeup, in a dress crumpled from lying on the floor overnight.

All that and Chavez still called me beautiful.

A dark feathering sensation begins to choke my throat. I shut my eyes and tell myself, *Breathe, Flynn.* Don't forget to breathe.

"You okay?" Madison asks, genuinely concerned.

No, I'm not, although I should be. I sell books by the truckload and host events streamed live into ten different countries. I am my own freaking industry. But like I said, every woman tells lies in Los Angeles. So I tell Madison I'm fine, and no, I won't be leaving my number because I'm already seeing someone. And I get the hell out of there before another lie leaves my lips.

Chapter Two

I stumble out of the elevator onto the rooftop parking lot and need a hot minute to center myself. To think about what just happened. Thirty-two years on this planet and never, not once, has any man made me orgasm without me intervening. How did Chavez spark an immoral glow between my legs with one rolling R when Dwayne from Denver couldn't find my G-spot last night even if I'd supplied a flashlight and a map? And Chavez isn't even my type! My go-tos are available and instantly forgettable men, not indifferent hot messes who are more famous than me.

But, fuck.

Our exchanges crackled hot like flames on bone-dry kindling, and I bet his twin pillows of lip pleasure would know what to do down south.

And he had smiled so charmingly.

I steal another glance at the elevator. My chaotic thoughts tumble like socks in a dryer.

Do not go back, I tell myself. *You did the right thing.*

Flynn Dryden Truth #1: Every decision brings you closer or takes you farther away from your goals. Nothing would come of Chavez other than another night of wishing for something different. I would be just another number to him.

End of story.

Except his story piques my curiosity.

I rummage through my purse for the phone and turn my back to the sun for shade. Madison's gossip might sound believable to an untrained ear, although no tennis player gets kicked off the tour for displaying emotions. They can be penalized, fined, or, at worst, defaulted from a tournament, but if every player who ever threw a racket got the boot, no one would be left playing. So, what naughtiness has Mr. Delgado been up to? Only one way to find out. I type his name into the browser, navigate to images, and start to scroll.

My heart rate stumbles and falls flat on its face.

Lord have mercy.

I understand now why I had trouble recognizing him. The flowing, shoulder-length locks he rocked for years are gone. His shorter haircut makes him look younger than twenty-five, but the endless shirtless pictures are deeply troubling for a breathing woman of any age. Jeez. Six-pack. Forearms corded with muscles. With a smile that lights up the world, Chavez is a blueprint for freaking perfection. Except no one is perfect. And a mile-long Wikipedia page covers every high and lowlight of his career.

Florida or Monaco comes to mind when people think of tennis players. Or the great academies where young prodigies get groomed into superstars. No one thinks about the son of Mexican immigrants who taught himself tennis on the public courts of Fresno, California, a city better known for cultivating almonds than tennis stars. With his blistering lefty game and charisma of the gods, the lore of Chavez grew, as did his fanbase and the pressure to succeed. After a long drought of bankable American male tennis stars, the expectations seemed to derail him when he turned pro. A few sources cite his father, Rodrigo, as a questionable coach with no tennis background and no control over the volatile personality of his son. Whatever the case, Chavez flirted with the top twenty now and then but never made it any higher.

The personal section of his Wiki is where it gets interesting.

An engagement went up in smoke at the tender age of twenty-four, and seven months ago, something else went down that he still refuses to discuss. Whatever happened precluded his decision to step away from the sport. The timing feels strange, considering he was in the midst of his best pro career year and tipped as a contender to win Roland Garros.

Huh.

I chew on my thumb, mulling it all over. I have always loved mysteries, and leave it to Chavez to be tall, dark, gorgeous, *and* intriguing. He threw me off in a way almost no man does by exposing me for who I am—a conflicted disaster with the opposite sex. But I've honed my confidence front to the point it's a second skin most people rarely question, including my BFF June Allison. Her name and number suddenly pop onto the screen, and I curse quietly. I completely spaced on her picking me up for brunch.

I start speed-walking toward my Escalade parked at the far end of the lot. "Hi—"

"I'm late," June says, steamrolling over the rest of my words. "Malibu traffic was grim, but San Vicente is moving at a good clip. I should be there soon."

Unchangeable as her British accent, late is her permanent state, only this time I'm grateful for it. "Oh, no worries," I say, "I had an errand I forgot to mention. Let's meet there instead. I'm just around the corner in Beverly Hills, and someone should be on time to meet Vandana."

Vandana Hillman is part three of our bestie crew. High-strung is a polite way of saying she vibrates at a frequency that would make most dogs yelp, although she's been much better since her old life blew apart. Still, Vandana is our ringleader, the queen who expects her subjects to do as told and show up for brunch at noon on the dot.

"I can feel the poor lass pulsing from here," June jokes. "Yes, you arrive on time and spare me the grief. I'll be there at quarter past at the latest. Do you fancy a mani-pedi after?" she continues. "I'm in dire need of both."

I'm only half-listening now, distracted by the sun in my eyes and the lewd thoughts of Chavez spooling across my mind. He strikes me as the type who would push me against a wall and take me down without hesitation. If my best blouse ripped in the process, who cares? And if I wasn't wet enough, he would spit in his hand, tell me to spread 'em, and slather me up. Most definitely not a romantic, but his laugh sounded kind, even under all the bravado.

"Are you still there?" June asks.

After walking in a daze across the lot, what's in front of me finally registers.

What the hell?

A flutter rises in my belly, staring at what has to be the mother of all coincidences.

"Uh-huh," I say. "I'm here."

"You sound a little preoccupied, and there are a million slow dimwits on the road today, so ta ta for now, while I focus. See you in a few."

"Yeah," I say slowly. "Bye."

Despite the heat, goosebumps pebble both arms. I tuck my phone away, feeling out of my element for a second time. Three hundred parking spots to choose from and Chavez picks the one beside me? I take a good hard look at the yellow Ferrari gleaming like a buffed M&M in the sun, and yup, the custom plates say it all.

TORNADO

The Talented Tornado.

A sportswriter nicknamed Chavez after a natural disaster because he swept over his opponents and left behind a path of destruction, just like the real thing. If the internet whispers are true, tornado refers more to his demeanor than his play in the past few years, but the pressure of not living up to all the hype cannot be an immediate concern for anyone driving around in this flashy beast. A Ferrari is beyond my pay grade, but we would look good in it together—top down, my curls whipping in the wind.

Señorita.

The fiery melody of his voice thrums through me, somehow more powerful even in absentia. I mentally sift through our charged conversation and latch onto the one tidbit niggling at the back of my mind.

Let it go, Flynn.

But I can't.

And intel gathering is hard to resist when the opportunity stares me in the face. I glance around for potential witnesses, feeling like a second-rate spy. Careful not to brush against anything and trigger an alarm, I peer through the tinted driver's side window. Not that I expected a Big Gulp in the cupholder or candy wrappers littering the floor but talk about immaculate. And go figure, he was telling the truth. Slowly cooking to death on the caramel leather dash is his cell phone.

But the Lotería card dangling from the rearview mirror on a yellow ribbon is what sends ghost fingers walking up my spine.

El Corazon.

My legs start to tremble. The sun feels hotter on my skin. I am not particularly superstitious, but the image of a bloody arrow slicing through a heart—a real one, not one of those soft and round Valentine's Day affairs—once unraveled my future. And no pill has managed to piece it back together.

"Excuse me, Miss? Is that your car?"

I shriek and stagger back, thumping hard against my car door. A security guard, all attitude and beefy arms with olive skin and dark features of a Middle Easterner, peers at me over the rims of his lowered sunglasses. Where did he come from? I pump up a smile because I can see it in his eyes—a pretty woman in business casual scoping out a Ferrari does not add up.

"Hey," I say, clearly not enough of an answer for him. Caught red-handed and flat-footed, my mind blanks. "My, uh, boyfriend wanted me to check if his phone was in the car."

"Boyfriend, huh?" The guard rubs his goatee, unhurried. A clock puncher welcoming any distraction to make the day pass quicker. "I see his car here all the time. What does tornado mean?"

"It's his nickname. He's a tennis player."

His eyes voyage over me. "You two serious?"

Sweet Jesus. Mr. Small Talk *and* making a move. I need to get out of here. Too many emotions swirl through me, and I can only name a few of them. The El Corazon card doesn't actually infer trouble in the Mexican game of Lotería, although I forever associate it with distress. If I needed another sign to stay far away from Chavez, the void cracking open in my stomach is pretty damn clear.

Suddenly all thumbs, I fumble for my keys buried deep in my purse. "I've got to run," I say, doing my best to sound breezy. "But you can check him out online. The Talented Tornado."

The *beep* of my car unlocking and the lights flashing on deepen the line between his scraggly brows. "Aren't you going to get his phone?" he asks.

I brush off the idea, and hopefully him too, with a wave of my hand. "Oh, I don't have the keys. I'll text him. He's busy right now."

I yank the door open, hoist myself inside, and slam it shut. Frowning, the guard tugs a phone from his breast pocket to snap a photo of my license plate. Seriously? Give a man a uniform and he's suddenly all that? Is he going to narc me out to Chavez? Good thing I didn't leave my number.

I push the starter button and the car roars to life. I feel woozy and borderline nauseous, and the guard staring at me as if I'm a criminal isn't helping. The truth is, seeing that damn card has stirred up a hornet's nest of memories. And if I start thinking about the past, it will smother me like cold river water. But history has a way of creeping up on us. And to prove the point, my phone, dumped on the passenger seat face up, flashes with an incoming message.

Unknown number: Flynn, I'm getting closer! Soon we will be together.

I feel the old anxiousness like a cold hand on my neck. A stalker started harassing me during my speaking tour last year. Before that, I believed only three people knew the truth about me. But this guy, and I know it is a man, also knows. His choice of words radiates familiarity. Whatever technology is available for tracking texts back to a specific phone or location has not worked on this guy, and the police couldn't do much twelve months ago when he first surfaced. They advised me to save every text as evidence, but when the stalker suddenly went radio silent, I erased them all in the hopes of erasing him. Nothing for months, and now this is the third text in as many days.

I punch the gas and the guard leaps out of the way, shouting at me as I swerve past him. My face is ashen in the rearview mirror and the color slowly returns on the drive down Santa Monica Boulevard. The temptation to ignore this situation is huge, but I have avoided things for far too long.

The irony of this does not escape me.

Flynn Dryden has made a career out of encouraging people to face their truths, but the last thing I want to do is face mine.

Chapter Three

"Over here, babes!"

Vandana waves at me from across the tiled courtyard, looking every inch the style icon in a couture jumpsuit, ankle boots, and fur shrug. She recently split from her husband of six years and is now involved with a gorgeous French yacht designer named Morgan. She leaves tonight for several months of "finding herself" in Monaco, which apparently will involve endless, amazing fucking on yachts bigger than my house.

No one ever said I wasn't the teensiest bit jealous of her.

We embrace tableside, and I'm caught off guard by her double air-kiss.

"So good to see you," she gushes. "You look great."

"June's running late," I say. "In case you were wondering."

She takes a seat, smirking. "Quarter past?"

Vandana and I call June the Quarter Past Queen because she inevitably is always that late.

"Right on time in her world."

She laughs and runs a hand over her immaculate blowout, oblivious to the tension humming under my skin. I debated bowing out from brunch, but Vandana and June are my only real friends and Baxter's is our favorite restaurant. The West Coast homage to the French Quarter in New Orleans is the place to be seen—unless you are a nobody, in which case, you will be seated as such. Four Asian ladies crammed in at a nearby table for two have ice in their glares, none too pleased that Vandana has commandeered the best table in the house, which seats eight. Her reign might be on temporary hiatus, but for now, the queen of public relations still has all of LA's hot spots under her rule.

"So," she says, pressing her hands flat on the table. "Tell me everything. I heard nothing but rave reviews about your book tour, and I loved that shift dress you wore on *Good Morning America*. It brought out the green in your eyes."

"Thanks. And yeah, so far, so good. Sold a gazillion books. My hand has finally stopped cramping from all the signing."

"June didn't want me to say anything, but we snuck in to watch you speak at UCLA. You really know how to work a crowd."

"What? You should've told me. I had comps for that."

"Please," she says as if she'd ever be caught dead accepting a freebie. "We *loved* being undercover spies. Everyone around us was gushing." She pats my hand with the dazzling smile no man can seem to resist. "We're so proud of you."

I know Vandana means well but embedded in her praise is a hint of amazement that I've managed to pull off a career so convincingly. And she might think I missed the judgment in her raised brow when she clocked my haphazard bun and rumpled dress and said I looked great, but I felt it. Around her, I inevitably feel like the tomboy younger sister with scuffed knees, too weird to be asked to prom.

But I love my friends and accept their flaws. If I could change anything, it would be telling them the truth back at Stanford when we first met. Unfortunately, trust was in short supply at eighteen, so I ran with my initial story and never changed it, not even when it went into print. Fast forward twelve years, and I still hide behind the same lies.

But no one can hide forever.

"Oh, lookey who's here!" Conrad, who's been waiting tables here since the original *Top Gun* premiered, swans over to greet us. Ruggedly handsome as a man and downright beautiful as a drag queen, you never know who he will be on any given shift. Today he is six feet of male diva, with ash-blonde hair in a forties pin-up swirl. "How are my favorite ladies today? Rumor has it you're back on the high seas, Ms. Hillman. The chef can whip you up a mango salad, but I'll be fully dressed while serving it."

Conrad's impish smile is hard to resist, but Vandana nonetheless waves a warning finger at him. She's slowly coming to terms with her recent scandal, but every blushing, squirming moment is a reminder she too, is human.

"Cappuccinos to start?" he asks sweetly.

"Make it three," I say. "June will be here. Eventually."

"Ah yes. The Brits always bring up the rear. Maybe that's why I like them so much. Ciao, ciao." He whirls on one heel and sashays off to a new group of devoted clientele who enjoy his abuse as much as we do.

Vandana sips her water, eyeing me over the rim. I wonder if she's made a deal with the devil because her French manicures never chip.

"You sounded weary when we spoke the other night," she says. "Are you still thinking of taking a break now that the tour is over?"

The tilt of her head and dreamy gaze can be deceiving like maybe she's thinking about her next Instagram post, but you don't become a PR superstar merely by being a stunning bon vivant. It's a people business, and she reads people better than anyone I know. She'd caught me at a low point after the first text from the stalker landed and clearly filed our conversation under "to be reviewed at a later date."

Before I can reply, angry squawks erupt from the hostess desk and we turn to watch June muscle her way past the small mob of influencers pacing like caged tigers in the waiting area.

"I'm not jumping the queue!" June fumes. "My friends are over there. Now, if you'll excuse me."

All the men, in their pastel button-downs, dragged here by their girlfriends, sneak a look at the blonde and buxom Brit bombshell who's just lit up the room. In an oversized blazer, strappy heels, and nothing else, June struts over like the female James Bond that she is. She dumps her handbag on the table and whips off her sunglasses to reveal eyes a shade of ice blue I've only seen in Argentinian glaciers.

"The bloody traffic," she grumbles. "You'd think it might let up just a smidge midday." She kisses both of us on the cheek and sits in her usual place, between Vandana and me. "How are my dolls? Both looking fabulous as always. Have we ordered yet?"

Conrad hustles past our table with two plates of steaming omelets and can't resist a dig. "No, but we're open until eight so take your time."

June catches Vandana and me smiling and says, "Piss off, the lot of you. I'm here, aren't I? With time to spare. And is it just me or is he getting cheekier every time?"

"I think at that age he's considered 'seasoned'," I say.

"More like salty," she mutters. "Anyway…" She reaches for my hand and then Vandana's. Never one to be overly emotional, she looks a little lost trying to overcome several at once. "I'm beyond gutted today," she confesses. "This is truly abysmal. I feel like we just got you back, Flynn, and now Vandana's leaving."

Our brunches are legendary and never missed unless duty or an emergency call. We swapped the usual Saturday for Thursday to accommodate Vandana's departure, but knowing one of the few steady things in my life will soon vanish is discombobulating.

"You two have to come and visit," Vandana says. "The yacht Morgan found me has—"

"Six bedrooms," June and I say at the same time.

Vandana rearranges herself in the chair with the tiniest pout. "Fine, so I may have mentioned that."

June, always the one to stroke Vandana's fragile ego, assures her we'll be there in no time. I nod in agreement, though I have no desire to visit Monaco. It's the size of a stamp, expensive, and from what Vandana relayed, a perpetual parade of arrogant billionaires. Not my scene. But we indulge Vandana because that's what we do, and she's still talking about her epic yacht when our coffees arrive. I'm about to doctor mine with cream and sugar when my phone rings. I scan the screen in the dark of my purse, surprised to see Dr. Bradford's number. Maybe he can fit me in today after all.

I swivel in my chair and answer quietly. "Hi, this is Flynn."

"Miss Dryden? It's Madison from Dr. Bradford's office."

"Hi," I say, carefully. It sounds like she has me on speaker. "What's up?"

In the background, Chavez shouts, "Since you didn't leave me your number, I had to track you down."

"He insisted I call you," Madison whispers.

"Don't pretend you're not on the make here," Chavez grumbles. "I just gave you two hundred dollars. Hand over the phone."

"Do you want to talk to him?" She asks me like I'd be a fool to say yes.

"A deal's a deal," Chavez says, losing patience. "You have my money. Give me the phone. And take it off speaker." After some commotion the line quiets to a private connection. "Hey Miss Flynn," he says. "Long time no talk."

It all happened so fast, and I find myself trying to wrap my head around what is going on. "You paid her two hundred dollars to call me?" I ask.

Out of the corner of my eye, June, taking a sip of her cappuccino, spews foam all over the table. Vandana stops stirring hers like she's frozen in amber.

"A man's gotta do what a man's gotta do," he replies.

"I thought you didn't chase women."

"First time for everything, right? And be flattered that I am chasing you. It's a rare event. I'm only here for a few more days, so we should hang out."

"You want to hang out?" I repeat.

"Yeah," he says. "As in, do something together."

I pause, think about it, and decide to test my theory. It's just an inkling I had. "Since Madison turned you down last week, what makes you think I'll say yes?"

"What?" The phone muffles as he blasts Madison. "You told her I asked you out? That's some major bullshit and you know it."

She defends herself in a small voice. "I didn't want her to feel like she had to leave her number."

Yeah, nice try, scammer. I believe that like I believe the earth is flat.

"You still there?" he asks me.

"Yes. I'm curious to know how this ends."

Vandana grows more curious, her dark brown eyes brimming with questions. An out-of-the-blue man ambush has happened to me exactly never.

"It ends with you taking my number or giving me yours," he says. "Pick one."

Hmmm. A mini dictator. Am I surprised? Not really. He bristled hard when I asked him how old he was earlier. Mr. Fearless did not like that at all.

"Hold on, okay?" Half the time I hang up on people when I try to multi-task on the phone, so I turn to June and make the motion of writing. She scrambles in her Stella McCartney bag for a well-chewed Bic pen and a business card and hands both to me. I tell Chavez I'm ready for his number, and he reels off his digits.

"Don't be shy, all right?" he says. "Time is of the essence. I leave town next Tuesday."

Five days. Longer than any of my relationships. I need that pleasant reminder like a root canal at midnight. "Thank you for the call, but I have to go. I'm in the middle of brunch."

"Adios, Miss Flynn. And just so you know…" His voice drops, and I can feel the warmth of his smile through the phone. "I'm still thinking about your legs."

My cheeks glow pink when I hang up, and the look of shock stamped on my besties' faces is priceless. They're always weighing in on my love life, or lack thereof, to the point I don't tell them much anymore, to spare myself the grief. But neither of them ever had a man throw down money to call them.

After a beat, June clears her throat. "We're not going to sit here and pretend that call didn't happen, are we?"

"I met this guy today," I say, casually.

"And?" Vandana spins her finger in a circle, meaning, *more, please.*

I share a few details of the Chavez run-in without dropping his name and switch up the location to the dentist. They don't know I'm seeing a shrink. No one does.

"Is he hot?" June asks. "He sounds spicy."

I bring up his photos and hand over my phone. "You tell me."

June zooms in on one of the photos and whistles under her breath. "Are you kidding me? He's famous."

At the whiff of celebrity, Vandana leans forward, practically foaming at the mouth. "Who is it? Gimme, gimme, gimme."

June hands off the phone with a whistle. "Now I know what zero body fat looks like."

Vandana thumbs through the images with a frown. "Since when do you date tennis players?"

"We're not dating," I say, mildly annoyed. "I met him like, an hour ago. Not even."

"How old is he?" June asks.

"Twenty-five."

"Christ, love," she moans. "He'll be able to fuck you to the moon."

"That's a seven-year age difference," Vandana says, handing back my phone.

I gaze at her coolly. "Meaning?"

"I'm not judging," she says, when she totally is. "But considering you've struggled with any relationship longer than a week, a young guy traveling the world most of the year doesn't strike me as the best choice for … hanging out."

"Whatever," I grumble, for once not wanting her to be right. "He's not my type, anyway."

June lays a hand on mine in solidarity. She's faced her share of Vandana's relationship opinions, whether she's wanted them or not. "For one night, a strapping, athletic sex god can be anyone's type. Who cares if he's *twenty*? From what I recall, he's a beast on the court, and I've always said a caveman would be good for you. You're so in your head all the time. Thinking. Analyzing. Writing. Half the time *we* don't know what's going on with you. Why not give him a go? He's clearly interested and look what happened over here."

She gestures at Vandana, who prefers not to be corrected or reminded that she didn't follow her own rules and is now better off for it.

"Babes," Vandana says, and here it comes—another lecture or well-meaning story to prove I'm chronically inept with men. "Don't flip out on me. Just listen. My friend Lorraine, the sports agent with a big nose? We had lunch last month. Her colleague used to represent him and was dumped with no warning earlier this year. Said he's a handful and not in great space. 'Bit of a disaster' were her exact words. Men on a downslide can be ugly."

As if Vandana knows what it's like to date a man on a downslide. Perfectionism was practically written into her SoCal, platinum-spoon-in-mouth contract. She's gone from debutante, to wife of one of Hollywood's most in-demand assistant directors, to the budding girlfriend of a Monaco kazillionaire who could buy Spain and still be flush. *Down* isn't in her vocabulary. And right now, I don't need another one of her knocks. I want to bask in the glow of a famous hottie tracking me down and paying good money for the opportunity.

It's not like anything will happen.

"There's no hope in hell I'm calling him," I say, bringing the topic to a close. "But how else was I supposed to get him off the phone?" I wave Conrad over, and he flips me the finger in response. "I don't know about you two, but I'm calling it mimosa o'clock."

Chapter Four

I'M BACK HOME IN THE LATE AFTERNOON AFTER SURVIVING THE dreaded Costco snarl. As I unload supplies in the driveway, my neighbor Sally cracks open her front door and waves at me like the queen used to do from her carriage. Meaning, *I acknowledge you but don't want to engage.* She's a half-blind retiree who refers to me as nouveau riche and leaves handwritten notes in my mailbox if Lizzo is blaring too loud or the smell of my grilled salmon drifts through her window. If anything, I'm an enigma to her—a writer who can afford a Tudor-style home in a classy neighborhood and travel the world, all without a husband.

The person I have to thank for all of my bounties is my agent, the notorious Nathaniel Lenard. He hustled to get my debut memoir, *Pieces of a Pisces*, into the hands of Oprah, who touted it as a tour de force. With her anointment, sales went through the roof. My story of loss and rebirth graced the New York Times bestseller list for fourteen months and launched me as a writer. Soon my email inbox was overflowing with readers desperate for advice on how to turn their own lives around, and Nathaniel smelled the opportunity like a bloodhound.

Instead of writing the mystery novel I had stuck in my head, he insisted I capitalize on my newfound fame. *The Ten Truths of Flynn*

Dryden was my follow-up, an inspirational guide on how to make your dreams come true. My world has never been the same since. Nathaniel spun my success and girl-next-door appeal into Flynn Dryden, motivational guru for the next generation.

The market needed a fresh face, and I was it.

But all the attention created a whole new cycle of anxiety. I'd written my memoir to get that monkey off my back, so the irony of it is laughable, should one find humor in this kind of thing. Four books later, the pressure is on for number five, and I'm not feeling it. I've already ignored several calls from Nathaniel, but as I toe off my heels in the foyer and haul grocery bags into the kitchen, the ringtone I've assigned him, a shrieking alarm—you do the math—goes off. My agent always calls, never texts, and if he had his way, I'd be locked in a tower writing eighteen hours a day. Such is the case when you make someone a shit ton of money.

After having five hundred sweaty shoppers crowd me already today, all I want is to zone out with a beer, but I have to deal with the devil sooner than later.

"Hi," I say.

"Are you sitting down?"

"I just walked in the door. What's up?" I ask, pretending I don't hear in his voice how he's about to explode with glee.

"First of all, who loves you the most?"

"You have a wife and three sons who adore you, not to mention half of New York's literati. Isn't that enough?" Not in the mood to prop him up, I grab a cold Stella Artois from the fridge and wander into the great room.

"I'm still working on the other half, who clearly have no taste, so no, the mission is not complete," he quips back. "But sugar, listen up. I just got off the phone with an exec at Amazon Studios. They want to make a movie about you."

A wave of illness rolls through me. The last thing I want is my life on the screen. "Really?"

"*Pieces of a Pisces*, coming soon to a theatre, I mean, TV screen, near you."

"What does that mean?"

He clears his throat. "Am I missing something, Flin Flon, or are you not comprehending the biggest news of your career?"

I sink into my marshmallow of a sofa, swallowed alive by purple velvet. Neither of us is sure how or why Nathaniel started to call me by the name of an obscure town in Canada, but it's stuck. "What I meant is, how involved am I in this?"

"As much as you want to be. An executive producer credit for sure. I can't guarantee sole screenwriting credit. The Hollywood vultures like to mutilate scripts with ten other writers."

The ceiling fan spins above me in slow, lazy circles. Another bird of prey hungry and ready to pick at carrion. "Do they know I've never written a script?"

"Number one," he says, "do not say that out loud. And number two, do not tell me you are saying no. This is the big time. I've worked my ass off to get you here."

A sly, Manhattan dealmaker who favors polka dot bowties and actual newspapers with his morning Earl Grey, Nathaniel is both lauded and feared. No matter what packed New York eatery we lunch at, the waiter whisks us to an available window table, and I slowly get hammered on buttery Chardonnay as a rotation of publishing bigwigs stop by to either fawn, grovel, or dish on the latest deals and scandals. He can operate on four hours of sleep and is, right now, guaranteed, in a Zegna suit chewing on a number two pencil with a sprawling view of midtown just beyond his tasseled loafers that are propped on the Louis XVI table he uses as a desk. He took a chance on me and leverages that to his advantage at every opportunity.

"Give me the holidays to think it over, okay?"

"Uh-oh," he says. "Christmas is your Bermuda Triangle. What state will you be in when you resurface?"

"It's not so bad anymore," I lie, wishing for the umpteenth time I had never told him.

"You're welcome to join us in Manhattan. As long as you don't mind Marla fangirling you," he adds, chuckling. "My wife worships you."

"Being worshipped is overrated."

"Says no one," he lobs back.

I drain half the beer and burp quietly. We can play this game forever if I let it go on. Nathaniel always has the final answer. The thing is, he has hustled hard, and we've been through so much together. But I can't deny what's accumulating inside me.

"What if I don't want to do it anymore?" I blurt out. "The motivational stuff."

The lengthy silence has an uncertain quality to it before he asks, "What *do* you want?"

I stand and start to pace, the need to assert myself requiring physicality. "I'd like to try my hand at fiction. I have a good idea for a mystery."

Nathaniel makes an indeterminate sound of someone trying to understand and failing. "Not that again. Sugar, we are so close to Flynn Dryden becoming a global household name. Write mysteries when you're sixty and your glory days are behind you. I know it's been a wonky year, but take the holidays to decompress. Let me organize a spa day. Or I'll send you a beefcake gigolo wrapped in a bow."

"Oh, God. No, thank you!" I rub my temple, dreading what else he has up his kinky sleeve. "And not to cut this short, but I just got home from Costco and my mind is mush. The movie sounds interesting. Keep all the balls in the air, and I'll touch base after Christmas. I promise."

He breathes a noticeable sigh of relief. Odd, given he's the very definition of the Teflon Man. "Please call me if things get rough. Even on Christmas Day."

We say our goodbyes, and I guzzle the remaining beer, once again feeling torn. My last tour was a flying success, and I have my choice of any deal coming down the pipe. To walk away from it all is borderline insane. The easier path is to keep on keeping on. But as I like to tell an auditorium full of enraptured souls, Flynn Dryden Truth #2: Old ways won't open new doors.

Maybe it's time I follow my own advice.

Phone in hand, I wander back into the kitchen to find my purse.

When I was in Costco, I almost took out a family of four, my cart weaving as I scrolled through more half-naked photos of Chavez. I pluck the business card inked with his phone number from my wallet and place it face up on the counter.

The tennis off-season is ridiculously short—a few weeks at the end of the year—and play ramps up at the start of January. If Chavez leaves town in five days, it means he's playing in one of the lead-up tournaments to the Australian Open. Five days. If I call today, maybe we meet tomorrow, at best. What can happen in four days, aside from nothing?

I undo my bun, shake out the curls, and brace both hands on the counter. Opening new doors means stepping through them without knowing what waits on the other side. I spent eighteen years on one side of a door I thought was perfect. And then the couple I believed were my parents told me they weren't. Betrayal cracks your insides into a million tiny shards. They cut and bleed and the hemorrhaging never end because you can't reverse that wrong. And their lies created a domino effect of more lies, but it all leads back to that damn El Corazon card.

It set everything in tragic motion.

I grip the countertop to stop my hands from trembling. Feelings I can't pinpoint creep around my heart. Chavez is an omen in the form of an unopened door, but there was something about him. It's hard not to be enchanted with an unforgettable face. So I ignore the rumble in my belly and dial his number, secretly hoping his phone goes to voicemail. What Gen-Xer answers their phone anyway?

"Hi," a female voice answers. "This is Domino's Pizza."

"Oh, uhm…" My heart sinks. After all that, he gave me a BS number?

"Just fooling with ya! This is Chavez Delgado's answering service. He's indisposed right now and—"

In the background, Chavez shouts, "Hey! Would you stop answering my phone? Goddamn, you are a pain in the ass."

In a sing-song voice, she says, "Oh Cha-vez, it's a wo-man."

"Get outta here, mocosa." After some heated Spanish between them, he says, "Hello?"

"Hi." I let out a breath I didn't realize I was holding. "It's Flynn."

After a pause long enough to crush my remaining confidence, he says, "Hey."

"Did I catch you at a bad time?"

"Nope. I'm just surprised to hear from you. Figured you'd make me wait at least a day."

"I didn't want your good money to go to waste."

"Hold on a sec Miss Flynn." The phone muffles as he says, "Back off, you barracuda! That's my torta. Yours is in the kitchen."

"I ate it already. I'm still hungry."

"Make yourself another one."

"I want you to do it," she whines. "You're so good at making at them."

"Carmelita, por favor, vete!" he says, his voice a shade darker. "This is a personal call."

"Fine. Let your sister starve," she says, and finally, my chest opens up. They're related. Nothing is more soul-crushing than calling up a guy only to find him getting his groove on with another woman. Been there, done that.

"Sorry about that," Chavez says, circling back to me. "I gotta lock my food down whenever she's around."

"Do you two live together?"

He laughs at the proposition. "If I was into bloodshed, maybe. My sister looks after my place when I'm on the road. I had to show her a few things today to bring her up to speed."

"That's nice of her to offer."

"Carmen's great," he admits. "She's familia. I love her, and some days I want to kill her. Do you have any brothers or sisters?"

"No, I'm an only child."

"I figured that. You give off that vibe."

"What vibe?"

"Someone used to doing their own thing."

My heart skips a beat. He said it so offhand, like I'm another overachieving LA superwoman not struggling with isolation wearing me thin. His voice shifts deeper after a shuffling sound, giving me the impression he is now lying down.

"You ever been married?" he asks.

Jeez. He's hitting me from all sides. "No. You?"

"Almost. But I got out of that in the nick of time."

My question is a throwaway because I'd read about his tumultuous relationship with Sofia, a pretty Mexican American woman he was engaged to for over a year. They split up eighteen months ago. Digging around online for the reasons why made me feel dirty.

"Madison told me you were seeing someone," he says, "but I doubt you'd be calling me if that was true."

"She's a hot bag of lies, that one."

He bursts out laughing, and the sweet sound is one I could listen to for days. "Tell me about it," he says. "I swear I never asked for her number. I'm not into blondes. But I am a sucker for curls."

I had a suspicion his earlier cockiness was the practical armor we all carry around. But the softer, gentler Chavez still affects me the same way. Something is doing the jitterbug in my belly. He was also the first guy in forever who, when I told him my name, didn't follow up with, *Isn't Flynn a boy's name?* And I'm digging his Miss Flynn schtick. It makes me feel dignified.

"Anyway," he continues. "I'm stoked you called. You free for dinner tonight?"

"Tonight?" I'm so surprised, it just slips out.

"Yeah. Text me your address and I'll pick you up at eight."

My shoulders tense, yet at the same time, I feel something inside me give a little. His forthrightness is refreshing, but there are unwritten rules in my life and guarding my privacy is number one. I registered my house under a false name because in LA, anyone can Google your name and *boom*, your address pops up. Chavez is someone I probably do not have to worry about, but I hate having to worry about it at all.

"But if you're one of those women who eats a carrot for dinner," he adds, "we're probably not going to get married after all."

His out-of-nowhere joke makes me laugh, and it feels damn good to laugh. Chavez makes me feel all sorts of long, lost things. And my stomach is as empty as my social calendar.

"Sure," I say. "Where do you want to meet?"

"That's not how it works. This is a date. I'm picking you up."

I bite back a smile. A date? It sounds so official. "I'm in Hancock Park. If that's not convenient…"

"Nothing's convenient in LA," he says. "That's why we're all in cars. I'll see you at eight and dress up in something nice, please. I'm not into fugly or Birkenstocks."

"What are you going to wear?" I ask, throwing it back at him.

"Don't worry. You'll like what you see."

Like there is any doubt of that.

"Anything else?" I ask.

After a pause that feels loaded, he asks, "Were you snooping around my car earlier? In the parking lot?"

My stomach jumps. Oh, shit. "No. I don't even know what kind of car you drive. Why? What happened?"

"It sounded like someone was trying to case it."

"So, I'll see you at eight?" I confirm, eager to switch gears before the guilt squeezes a confession out of me.

"Yeah," he says. "And eight means eight, so don't make me wait. I hate that shit."

Chapter Five

At 7:55 p.m., Chavez and his Ferrari California rumble into the neighborhood like a bat out of hell. I knew he would be early, and I'm waiting at the head of the driveway, chill in the air be damned. My black jersey cocktail dress is first-date approved—sexy, but without body parts spilling out everywhere. (Not that I have body parts to spill.) The ring of feathers on each wrist might be overkill, but if I've learned anything from Vandana, it's safer to be over-dressed.

Chavez peels into my driveway with his high beams flashing, cuts the engine, and steps out to admire me with a full head-to-toe.

"Wow," he says. "You look amazing."

I've done a complete one-eighty from this morning, with ringlets in loose, wild mode and enough bronzer to fool anyone into believing I'd just arrived home from Hawaii instead of Cleveland. And he kept his end of the bargain up, too. His beautifully cut dress pants and serious thread-count shirt hug him in all the right places. He had that Prince almost-facial-hair thing going on earlier, and I have to say, I prefer his face freshly shaven.

"Thanks," I say. "You clean up pretty nice, too."

"You want to grab a jacket?" he asks. "It's freezing out here."

"I'm good. Ferraris have heated seats, right?"

I will suffer through goosebumps as any vain woman would to avoid spoiling the effect of my dress. Besides, I will be wearing far less if tonight goes as planned.

"It sure does, mamacita. And I hope you like Mexican food. I know the owners of Heroica, and they could swing us a table this late in the game."

"Nice. I've been dying to try that place."

The heels of his brogues ring hard off the concrete as he rounds the car to open the passenger door. My Escalade squats like a guardian troll in the shadows next to us, and he takes a long look at it.

"Is that your ride? Or do you have full-time security?"

"It's mine. Why?"

"Why is a skinny little thing like you driving around in a tank?"

"I like it. It makes me feel safe."

He's quiet for a moment, surveying the front yard. "Safe. Is that why you have razor wire on your fence?"

"I live alone," I explain, the clip in my voice meaning, *Let's not start with the third degree, please.*

He smiles while pretending not to notice my dress riding higher while I navigate myself into the low-slung seat. "You might not after tonight."

His salacious wink makes me laugh. This guy has no shortage of confidence. Chavez slides behind the wheel and shuts his door, a rush of cold air following. The El Corazon card spins lazily on its ribbon like a dead man from a noose. A sharp taste rises on my tongue.

"What's with the card?" I ask.

"It's from a game called—"

"Lotería," I finish.

He glances at me in surprise. "You know it?"

"Not the rules, but I have seen the cards before."

His gaze flickers to the laminated image. "My Abuela, my grand-mother, gave it to me. I was going through a rough patch and..." He trails off, a muscle around his mouth twitching. After a moment of heavy silence, he clears his throat. "Anyway, it's a reminder of her. She passed away earlier this year. We were close."

"I'm sorry to hear that."

I look sidelong at Chavez. An unspoken understanding hovers in the small space between us. He swallows hard and palms the stick shift. The *FEAR* inked on his hand is very close to describing the sensation rushing through me, and I should not be thinking of how his fingers would feel cupping my ass when a net of nostalgia still tangles over him.

"I like the feathers," he says quietly.

The tats, the car, his taking control of the entire evening … My skin tingles with something raw and unmentionable. Danger, yes, but it also feels bizarrely fated to be together in the tight confines I had spied on nine hours earlier, adrenaline pumping hard in my veins. One thing is for sure: after years of shoe-gazing fanboys and Vanilla Avenue, Chavez is a hard right down Unexpected Street.

A wrong turn never felt so exciting.

AFTER A MONTH OF LONELY NIGHTS IN SILENT HOTEL ROOMS, AN upscale taco bar crammed with hipsters talk-shouting over Shakira and her hips that don't lie is the perfect shot in the arm. My toes refuse to stop tapping.

"This place looks funky," I say.

"There's a private room in the back," Chavez shouts back. "It's quieter."

He flags down a middle-aged man sweating hard in frayed cords and a Ramones T-shirt, and they hug like old friends. It's impossible to decipher the rapid-fire Spanish flying back and forth between them, but Chavez introduces him as Mateo, the owner, who smiles and waves at us to follow him through the crush of bodies. Chavez and I look pretty fab, and when a wolf whistle cuts through the thrum of music, he tightens his grip on my hand and adds in a shoulder check and wink combo. Beyond the bustling kitchen is a private room, heavy on gothic flair with wooden floors and Renaissance tapestries hanging from golden spindles mounted high on the wall. What comes to mind is a chamber in a castle, only much better smelling.

"Whatever that is," I say, inhaling the thick scent of charred meat, "we need to order it."

"They make the best pork tamales other than my Mama's," Chavez says.

"Can you share the recipe?" I ask Mateo, who's busily dimming the lights. "I love to make tamales."

"I'll have to ask the boss. No promises," he says with the shrug of a man who knows his place in the pecking order. "In the meantime, what would the lady like to drink?"

I order a classic margarita, no salt, and whatever Chavez wants is communicated with a simple meeting of the eyes. Mateo leaves us to settle into our comfy velvet seats, two of eight fancifully carved wooden chairs circling a tabletop of white marble. Chavez unfurls a napkin and drapes the square of linen onto my lap. He smells divine, the signature tang of Aveda product wafting from his hair.

"You make tamales?" he asks.

"I'm more of an advanced recipe follower than a legitimate chef," I admit. "But I enjoy cooking. It's relaxing."

He strokes the feathers on my wrist with a thoughtful expression. "A beautiful cook and a former tennis player. How did I get so lucky?"

It's already toasty from the candelabra that's lit up and glowing in the corner with more white candles than I can count. But the heat blooming between my boobs has nothing to do with that. It sounds like some equal-opportunity online investigation went down.

"How do you know I played tennis?"

"Ah, busted," he says, and fuck me, is he beyond adorable with that embarrassed smile. "I downloaded all your books from Amazon today. I'm only forty pages into the first one but so far, super impressed with your writing."

I feel my pulse pick up. Chavez reading my work feels stranger than when Oprah and all her accolades did. And I didn't peg him to be a reader.

"You still play?" he asks.

"Three or four times a week. When I'm in town."

"You wanna hit together sometime?"

How a person plays the game of tennis is a window into their soul. I would love to play with him, but there are other things I want to do more. "When are you back in town?"

He never answers the question because Mateo reappears with our drinks. Much to my dismay, a large bottle of San Pellegrino and two glasses land with my amber margarita. There goes my game plan of drunken debauchery to end the night.

"You didn't order a drink?" I ask.

"Nope," he says. "I don't drink. I mean, I did the ten-year-old thing of chugging beer and pretending it was fun, but I'm not into altered states. This," he says, pointing to himself, "is enough for me. No additions required. But don't let that stop you from getting tipsy."

Mateo rattles off another diatribe in Spanish with Chavez either nodding or making a sign of no with his hand.

"They're going to whip up something special for us," Chavez explains. "Any allergies?"

"No allergies. I eat everything. And maybe what's on your plate, too."

I knock him with my elbow and he smiles, understanding my dig. "Nice try," he says.

And then finally, we are alone. The door shut tight behind Mateo, the decibel level manageable, and Chavez raising a glass after pouring both of us water. He is also a believer in eye contact during the toast, but the trouble is, I cannot stop staring. For someone who's been crawling through the relationship desert for what feels like an eternity, Chavez bathed in candlelight shimmers like the world's sexiest mirage.

"Salud," he says. "Gracias por venir."

"Salud por una gran noche," I reply.

His smile falters. "You speak Spanish?"

"Un poco."

I clink his glass and savor the burn of reposado sliding down my throat that almost, but not quite, delivers the same hot thrill as his stunned expression.

As it turns out, hoarding food is the least of our concerns. Thank God for the giving properties of jersey, because this mama's belly swells into second-trimester territory after being served a banquet fit for six.

"Oof," I say, setting down my fork. "I am stuffed."

Chavez polishes off the last tamale and licks his fingers. "Was I right about how good these are?"

Everything was good, including how easily our conversation flowed. Mind you, I've mastered the art of keeping people talking about themselves. Chavez tried to lob a question out here and there to get me talking, but a strategically placed hand on his thigh did wonders to distract him. Still, he didn't back down from asking about my family, forcing me to reveal a slippery half-truth—that my parents are deceased. A conversation-killing topic if there ever was one, we circle back to tennis and his upcoming season.

"It's going to be interesting," he says. "I'm playing a few Challenger events to get my game back without the media breathing down my neck."

The Challenger tour is the second tier of professional tennis, where juniors cut their teeth before graduating to the major leagues or where pros recovering from injury will ease back into the game. But for a fit player coming back to the tour who could gain entry into the major tournaments through qualifying matches or wildcards, this route is highly unusual.

"What does your father think of this approach?" I ask. From what Chavez shared earlier, their long-term coaching relationship involved plenty of head-butting and differing opinions.

He takes a swig of water and stares beyond the table. "He's not coaching me anymore."

"Who is?"

"No one, right now. Still looking."

"How do you feel about going on the road by yourself?"

"Not great," he answers. "I've never been on my own."

The glimmer of uncertainty in his eyes speaks volumes. To be a pro tennis player these days requires the fortitude of a gladiator. The globetrotting and time changes, along with being fit and match ready, is hard enough when some days peeling yourself out of bed is the biggest challenge. I played on the ITF Tour (the entry-level tour for all young tennis players) and experienced a taste of the grind. It is not for the faint of heart. As a solo warrior battling conditions, expectations, and mostly yourself, having a team around you, even a small one, can make all the difference.

Mateo sticks his head in to see how we are faring, and Chavez indicates he'd like the bill. I glance at his Rolex, surprised at the time. Three hours have slipped away like nothing.

"It feels like I've been talking all night," he says, digging for something in his pocket. "Which sucks because I want to hear more about you. But I've got practice tomorrow at nine and need to get you home."

"I'm in no rush," I say. Hint, hint.

He stands abruptly, his attention elsewhere. "I'll be right back. Sit tight."

His disappearance gives me time to think about strategy. Do I invite him in when he drops me off? Do we make out in the car? He had his arm around me half the night, fed me morsels of tender meat from his fork, and let my hand roam free on his thigh. Something has to go down.

He keeps my hopes high when he returns, holding my hand as we wind through the pumping crowd to more chaos outside. Third Avenue is the usual Friday night madness of bar hoppers, with cars jamming the street in both directions. Chavez releases my hand to whisper something to the valet, and as he does, a woman storms out of the restaurant and beelines straight for us. With long black hair hanging to her nipped waist and blazing eyes that make Frida Kahlo look happy, she lays into Chavez without a hello.

"All of a sudden you're too poor to pay the bill? The little man in his big house?"

I saw her earlier on my way to the restroom and figured she was one of the staff, up until she gave me the evil eye. From the set of his jaw, Chavez is none too thrilled with her presence either. I have seen alligators exchange friendlier glances.

"Did you slap another GPS tracker on my car," he says, "or is this a coincidence?"

"Don't flatter yourself," she scoffs. Her sour expression turns to land squarely me. "Your big-time date didn't pay the dinner bill. If he's promised you dessert, you better get your wallet out."

"Sofia!" he hisses. "Beat it."

Oh, shit. Nothing like running into a pissed-off ex. And that's what Chavez was up to with his disappearing act. He should have said something to me.

"I can pay," I tell him. "It's not a problem."

He glares at me as if I've offered to strip naked and panhandle. "Yeah, it is a problem. You're not paying. I forgot my wallet and I'll settle up later."

It's how her hand absently runs down the drape of her hair, how her lips purse and how, ever so subtly, she pushes her magnificent chest forward. Sofia loves every bleeping minute of this.

"Your Mama know you're out with her?" she asks, addressing me with a vague motion of her chin.

"Spare her your jealous gossip," Chavez grumbles. "You know she's not doing well."

A cold smirk spreads on her face. "Seems to run in the family. I hear you're seeing a loco doctor."

His jaw twitches as he curls and uncurls the fingers of his left hand like a boxer dying to throw a KO. Sofia stands with her back straight, daring him to cross the line. She is itching for a confrontation.

"Mateo said you had tonight off," Chavez says. "Don't you have anything better to do with your time than chase after something that's no longer yours?"

Her gloves come off with that comment, an unleashing so bitter I taste it. "You were never mine. A ring on my finger means nothing when you're a malinchista."

Something in his face changes for the worse, and I feel blackness in my heart witnessing it. That word is a sword plunged deep into his soul. He takes a menacing step closer to her and a huddle of smokers nearby swivel their heads our way. Everybody loves a front-row seat to a juicy meltdown.

"Always the mouthy one, huh?" he spits out. "Pushing your luck."

Before fists start to fly, I reach for his arm. The valet has rolled up with his Ferrari and it is time to skedaddle.

"Let's go," I urge. "The car's here."

It's as if he's forgotten I'm here, and my touch jolts him back to reality. "You don't call the shots, all right?" His aggression startles me, and then he yanks me off the sidewalk and tries to stuff me into the car. "Get in," he says, pushing against my resistance.

"Thank you and thank you, but I can get in without your help." I rip my arm out of his grip so violently that a few feathers from my dress death-spiral to the ground. "Or I might walk home."

We are now the focus of everyone milling outside and the wide-eyed valet has clearly decided not to get involved with a domestic. Chavez needs serious schooling in manners, and I would love nothing more than to teach him a lesson and hightail it out of here. But my Louboutins are not built for trekking. Chavez is one wrong word away from losing it, and he is probably the kind of loose cannon to track me all the way home.

Fuck! Now there's that, too.

Why did I let him pick me up?

Tears of humiliation threaten to fall, but I will not crumble in front of Sofia. I drop like lead into the car seat, slamming the door so hard that the aftershock rattles up my elbow to the small bones in my neck. Chavez crushes his door too, and we squeal away in a very illegal U-turn with horns blaring at us while the smug mug of Sofia in my side mirror eventually gets smaller and smaller until the night swallows her whole.

Chapter Six

CHAVEZ

WITH THE RAGE SLOWLY FLOWING OUT OF ME, I'M NO LONGER SEEING death stars and I can deal. Not so sure about Flynn. She's sitting there all rigid with a pissed-off set to her jaw and every fricking right to be mad. Que pendejo! What was I thinking? Smythe says I'm a textbook example of unresolved childhood anger, but I know I can't keep being angry my whole life.

"Hey."

"Hey what?" she asks.

"I know that wasn't cool."

"I think I hear a sorry in there, but maybe I'm mistaken."

"Listen—"

"No, you listen," she interrupts. "Don't *ever* talk to me like that again."

Ay Yi Yi. I'm deep in the penalty box and the only Hail Mary within my pathetic reach is if the Chavez shit show gets his act together. Last-minute Christmas shoppers are clogging up the streets like a cardiac arrest and I weave past a Corolla slug to pull over after the next light.

She immediately asks, "Why are you stopping?"

"Can I explain?"

"No. I need you to take me home. Now."

Finally, she looks at me. Her pupils are greener than center court at Wimbledon, but I can tell they are still seeing red. The clock is ticking on my ability to turn this around. Now is the time to pick my words wisely. And get them out, fast.

"I can say sorry a hundred times, but it boils down to the same thing: I fucked up. I took you to a restaurant owned by the family of my ex. She wasn't supposed to be there. You think I'd put you in that situation on purpose? On a first date?"

She digests this, holding my gaze in case I crack, like my voice just did.

"For your future dates," she says stiffly. "I suggest someplace else."

Future dates do not sound like they involve her, and I feel a pinch in my heart. Hostile Chavez is a dismal shell of who I know I can be. This is the time to dig deep for strength and resilience, but I'm suddenly overcome with all the things I need to change and don't know how.

"I know. I know," I say. "It's just…" I lean on the steering wheel, out of steam and excuses. "It's complicated. My family knows her family. We go way back. We support each other. That's how it goes with familia, right?" I'm praying she'll understand this mess and the muscles around her mouth twitch like I've struck a chord. Then I remember she told me her parents had passed and I'm like, fuck. I can't catch a break to save my life. "Look, I'm useless at managing my self-control. What can I do to make it up to you?"

She studies me for three long seconds. "Is that why you're in therapy?"

"Pretty much."

"Why did you ask Madison to call me?"

"Why do you think?"

"What changed from you being the guy who doesn't chase women?"

She asks patiently, like she can rephrase the question ten more times if I'm still not getting it. But some things you keep close to your chest. You don't go around spilling your guts on everything.

"Maybe I had an epiphany," I say. "Stuff like that happens in therapy."

Smythe did ask me about Flynn; what the deal was between us. I told him the truth like I'm supposed to do. That we'd literally just met and the fire in her turned me on, and she had a pure and radiant face that could make angels weep. Smythe might dress like a redneck but stupid, he ain't. He grilled me on why I left her in the dust as if I didn't give a shit. At first, I thought it was a trick question because he should know about the walk-away: deny a woman and she becomes a starving puppy scratching at your back door. It's in the dude playbook because it works.

Except it didn't work with Flynn.

And since Smythe and I spent most of the sesh talking about different approaches, when I found out Flynn took off without leaving me her number, it was time to put words into action.

I ended up two Benjamins poorer, but with the riches of this gorgeous woman sitting in my car.

I'd say I got the better end of the deal. One I need to salvage.

"What about you?" I ask, flipping the script. She's had me talking all night. "Why are you in there?"

She shifts in her seat. "This and that. Life. Work."

"You haven't murdered anyone?"

"Not lately. But don't tempt me."

The frosty authority is still there but a first hint of a smile creeps onto her lips. My groveling is miles away from over, but a ray of light does wonders for confidence.

"You don't make a very convincing criminal with these," I say, and lean forward to brush my thumb across the freckle constellation dusted high on her cheekbone. She read me the riot act earlier for touching her without asking but mellowed out over dinner, so I feel it's the right move. And she doesn't pull away or say no. Her skin is like glass, smooth and flawless. The idling twelve cylinders create this deep, sonic rumble that feels like an invisible force pulling us together. Her eyes find mine, and I breathe in the lavender lotion buttering up her skin. I am so ready to step in and taste her sweetness, but it's time to think long game and end this night on a high note.

"Think about how I can make it up to you while I drive you home, all right?"

A man never knows if he is truly forgiven, and she's giving me nothing other than a flutter of her lush lashes, so I ease back into traffic and keep my mouth shut. Out of the corner of my eye, I catch her glancing at the Lotería card again. Something in her expression from earlier made me think it held meaning for her, but I doubt she grew up playing Mexican bingo like my family did. My Abuela, Valeria—bless her soul—loved the game and also loved me. She was the one who stepped in with kind words when I called it off with Sofia. Our mothers went off the deep end, and I was in a dark place, nothing clicking. Valeria gave me that card as a reminder not to give up—on love, tennis, any of it. It's kind of what the El Corazon card means. That whatever you're longing for will eventually show up.

I miss Abuela so badly and had to choke down my heart when Flynn first asked about the card. Nothing worse than bawling when you're trying to be a baller.

And speaking of that, I'm trying to keep my thoughts from sliding into the gutter. I need to focus on the road and not those milky inner thighs screaming at me to look. I doubt she'll invite me in, and even if that miracle happens, it's not the right strategy. But I'm praying for some action. The urge to kiss her is like the need to breathe.

When I pull into her driveway, I jump out before she has time to shut us down. She doesn't kill my offer to walk her to the door, but the mood gets killed somewhat when all her security lights pop on like watchful eyes. The air seems colder doused in their brightness, and her warm body pressed against mine would be the perfect solution.

Fingers crossed.

Framed in the tangle of scarlet bougainvillea arcing over her doorway, she looks at me and smiles. I smile back. Fuuuck. She's so pretty. Tall and graceful, and everything soft where it should be. And so smart. Smart enough to kick me off her doorstep.

"I had a nice time tonight," she says. "For most of it."

"Me too. A real nice time. I'm sorry about how it ended."

After a beat, she tilts her head. "Should I give you another chance?"

"It would save me from having to pray every night."

Both her brows shoot up in surprise. "You pray?"

"On my knees."

She laughs and it sends a ripple of excitement up my spine. "I might need photo evidence of you being submissive."

Hallelujah. This social disaster finally breaks in my favor. It is time to bust a move, except this is what happens when you've lost your mojo. A woman as ripe as the sweetest melon stands in front of me and I can't even connect the dots.

Get with the program, hombre.

I shake off the cool air pressing on my shoulders. "Tell me if I'm out of line here Miss Flynn, but I really, really want to kiss you."

A vein on the soft white of her throat pulses and her smile turns shy. "Sure."

That front door of hers looks sturdy enough to take both of us crashing hard against it, but my instincts tell me to go slow even though she's shivering in that scrap of a dress and I could warm her up big time. I cup her face in my hands. Feel her breath draw in. A light switches on in my brain when we connect and it's like the night turns into day.

No need to pray, after all. Flynn is willing and eager and has the tempo dialled just right. Like playing on a new court for the first time, with kissing, I have to explore the lay of the land and get a sense of things, adjust, and feel out the new environment. The art of it is to build up to tongues and not get choked by some snake right out of the gate. She tastes like sweet tequila, and I'm behaving, or trying to. But when those arms of hers decide all that uptight shit is no longer necessary and can be wrapped around me instead, I'm all in. I plaster her against the door, and for a woman who was one step away from ditching my ass minutes ago, she's now a destroying force.

Jesus.

My poor dick's been on a yo-yo all night and it snaps back to attention with her body grinding hard against mine. I almost give in to her warm tongue, but I love how she whimpers and clutches me tighter when I pull back.

"You can…" She falters and catches her breath. "You don't have to stop."

I fist my hands into her soft mess of curls and bring our foreheads to touch. "I want to keep going," I whisper. "That's not the problem."

"Problem?"

In those teetering heels, her eyes are level with mine and spooling across them is a story, something she's trying to tell me without words. A vulnerability that makes my heart fold in on itself. Never mind she has glued herself to my hard-on. Or maybe it's the other way around.

"You want me to lose my cool right here on your doorstep? I'm about fifteen seconds away. What are you doing tomorrow?"

She searches my face. "I thought you had practice?"

"I'll be done at noon. Why don't you swing by for lunch?"

"Where?"

"My house."

"You have a tennis court?"

"And a pool. Bring your bikini. And your tennis gear."

"You want to play with me?" she asks.

"If you don't mind playing with fire."

Her smile keeps going, and I am tempted again to cross over her threshold and dive headfirst into her all-night buffet, but my thoughts start to spin at an unsafe velocity. Smythe keeps telling me I need to be mindful of triggering moments. My dick so swollen it needs its own zip code is not a moment, technically, at least not in the scope of his world. Although I'm very mindful of what it does mean. And it's times like these when pulling back the curtain is a necessity, so I'm not howling for the wrong pussy under the spotlight of a cold moon.

"You mind me asking how many guys you've slept with?"

She jerks her head in surprise. "Where did that come from?"

"More than a hundred?"

"God, no!"

"Less than fifty?"

She disconnects from my embrace and crosses her arms. "Sorry, but I am not having this conversation."

"Okay. So more than fifty but less than a hundred. I'm at eighty-three, so you know."

The sound of her laughter carries high into the sky. "That's some meticulous record keeping. You sure it's not eighty-two or eighty-five?"

"I know how to count."

"And you felt compelled to tell me this because?" She isn't putting her foot down too hard, like maybe she's curious about where this is all heading.

"Clearing the decks, so to speak," I say. "You need to know what you're getting into, and the same goes for me. The other part is that I like even numbers. I've been holding at eighty-three for a while. I'm in no rush but wouldn't mind tapping out on an even number."

"Tapping out," she deadpans.

"The way you say it doesn't sound romantic. When you find the person that does it for you, you call it quits is what I mean. You stop chasing. You've been there, right?"

"Of course."

Someone told me when people look up and to the left, they're fibbing. Flynn's gaze is way up and so hard left the Democrats are saying wait up. A babe like her had to be pinned down a few times or else the world isn't making sense, but maybe her past boyfriends were all culeros not worth remembering.

A man can only hope.

For now, I count my lucky cajones she is one of those rarities who rolls with the punches and doesn't hold onto anger for time eternal. And her not even blinking at my numbers is a stone cold miracle.

"I better hit the road, Miss Flynn," I say because she's got goosebumps everywhere. "See you tomorrow. I'll text you my address when I get home."

She walks with me back to the car and that role reversal has to be a good sign. I risk one last kiss, a quickie on her cheek, and fold myself into the car as dignified as the current situation allows. I punch the engine good and loud to give her a sense of how she's got me feeling. When I roll down the window for a final goodbye, she has the strangest smile going on.

"What's so funny?"

"Nothing," she says. "Just that I'd never slap a GPS on your car."

"Because you aren't a crazy woman, I hope."

A beat passes, and there it is again, that story in her eyes. I'll read every goddamn page until I figure it out. But my last five days are coming up fast. Where was she six months ago when I had all the time in the world?

"I'm not like most women," she says.

Ain't that my new reality? Her not being like most women worries me because I can't endure any more heartbreaks. I say goodbye, slam into reverse, and on the drive home, all I can think about is the tightness of her small breasts still burning a hole through my John Varvatos shirt and how unsettled she sounded telling me her truth.

Chapter Seven

FLYNN

Brentwood Park is where the Hollywood elite hides out, so I was surprised when Chavez texted me last night with an address smack in the middle of this exclusive community. Sprawled over half a block, his Spanish modern is more castle than casa, a moat and a drawbridge the only things missing. I park in front of the four-car garage, grab my tennis gear from the back seat, and take a deep breath.

I'm ready for this, or at least I think I am.

I am having a lot of second thoughts this morning.

The idea of hitting with firepower like his is intimidating, and so was his aggression last night. Rudeness on that level is a hard pass for me, but then came Chavez, the one-man kissing machine. The permanent dent his erection left on my womanhood had to be hammered out in the bathtub last night with some serious self-love, and I crawled into bed half-blind from a different kind of intensity. I slept deeply for the first time in forever and woke up punch-drunk, the air thick and stale, the fragments of my dream slipping away, like Hamilton in the rapids so many years ago. I haven't dreamed of my first and only boyfriend in a long time, and it usually leaves me shot to pieces when I do.

But this morning, I feel like a pile of rusty nuts and bolts swept into something functional for the first time in forever.

As long as the butterflies in my belly do not take over and fly away with me, I should be fine on the court with him. My adoring public would never think of me as ruthless, but I didn't cream through competitors by being the nice girl. I trained with men to hit hard and flat with pace. I added ten pounds of muscle to put juice behind my serves. I can still outhit any woman I play, but Chavez will be an interesting test.

I punch in the security code he provided me on the gate next to the garage, shoulder it open and freeze.

Good God.

It's like I'm in Jurassic Park, surrounded by swaying palm trees and lush green that goes on forever. The size of his yard makes me feel like an ant in comparison. A sign (an actual sign!) that says, *tennis court,* points me in the direction of a flagstone path winding through the trimmed grass. The crisp *thwack* of tennis balls hit hard and precisely echo into the hills long before the spectacle of a shirtless Chavez in motion comes into view. A pit bull of a man pummels forehands from the other side of the court, and Chavez defies the rules of geometry with the angles of his returns. His speed is deceiving—how quickly he gets into position to drive the ball deep. He's got good hands for a young player and floats on the court like a dancer. But when his hitting partner executes a gossamer drop shot that spins just out of reach, bye-bye ballerina and hello frustrated understudy.

"I said rallies to my forehand!" he yells. "Why am I paying you?"

"It's called mixing it up," the guy shouts back. "You think Arlo will hit to your forehand all day?"

"You and he can…" Chavez gestures at his crotch to finish the sentence.

"Promises, promises. And you better watch your mouth," the man adds, pointing his racket in my direction. "Looks like your company has arrived."

Chavez spins around and a smile wipes away his scowl. "Hey. How long have you been here?"

"Just arrived. Please, keep going. I'm happy to watch."

Happy to drool from the sidelines. Jesus. Adidas will be hard-pressed to find a better wall of muscle to advertise on. And if I'm not mistaken, he's commando under those shorts.

"Nah, it's time for a break. Come in." Chavez opens the chain-link door and swats my entering behind with his racket. "Cute outfit."

My favorite Lacoste tennis dress matches the color of his eyes, and I might have chosen it on purpose. With a break in the action, the other man strides over, peeling a camo headband off a shock of bristly black hair. His features suggest he might have Central American roots, and he has at least a decade on Chavez, although both shop at the same tight short store and have the blessings from Jesus in the sculpted legs department.

He waves his arm forward and dips into a gracious bow. "Buenos Dias, señorita. Python the Great."

"Hi, I'm Flynn. Nice to meet you."

"He's my hitting partner," Chavez explains. "With a great hearing problem."

"Ex-partner," Python corrects. "I'm officially retired as of next week."

"Might be a decision you regret. In with the old, out with the new. Flynn used to play competitively."

The challenge in that statement draws a smile from Python. "You don't say?" He turns to me and winks. "It's only the third time he's mentioned that."

"You can retire today if you want to, old man."

Python grins as he packs up his bag. "Same time tomorrow?"

"I got a bunch of shit to do before Christmas Eve. Let's say ten."

Despite the insults, the respect and love between these two are evident as they engage in ritualistic hand gestures that end with a high five and a bro hug.

"Good luck out there," Python says to me. "The best way to piss him off is the short and wide serve. Gets him every time."

Chavez rolls his eyes. "If you could get it in the box, dude, maybe I'd bother."

Python flips him the finger and he's off, whistling down the path. Once he's out of earshot I ask Chavez, "Why is he retiring? He's like the Energizer Bunny."

"He's retiring from me. Moving back to Peru."

"Was he part of your team for a while?"

"Five years. But whatever, I'll find someone else." He scuffs his shoe on the court and looks past me to the cabana and pool across the atomic-green lawn.

"Nice digs, by the way," I say. "What a beautiful property."

"Thanks. As I said, fortune favors the bold. I took a risk and it paid off."

I glance at him. "How so?"

"A friend of mine plays basketball with some big-time investor. We were shooting the shit one day at the gym, and he asked if I wanted to put some money into the next deal this guy had brewing. No idea it was Leostrata. I put in a mil, cleared forty and bought this place with cash."

Leostrata is the Pink or Beyoncé equivalent of the tech world. One word and everyone knows the biggest IPO in the history of the stock market.

"Congrats," I say. "Good timing. Who was the guy brokering the deal?"

"Dallas Evener. No promises, but I can let you know when his next deal is," he offers. "A mil is his minimum."

"I'm not asking for me," says the woman who parks her money in mutual funds and promptly forgets all about it. "One of my friends works in the start-up world, and finding money is her full-time job. A warm intro never hurts."

"If you want, I'll hook you up, no problem." He pops the lid off a fresh can of balls, and I never tire of hearing that satisfying *whoosh*. "Want to get into it? I'll make you lunch after. The specialty of the house."

"Let's do it."

I unzip my racket bag and test the flex of my fresh strings, mentally filing the name Dallas away for tonight. June and I plan to connect before she leaves for Vancouver to spend Christmas with her mother, a widow who moved from England to Canada to be closer to her only child. June wanted me to come along because she knows the holidays are my dark time, but being alone is often better.

Chavez pockets two balls and hands one to me. "I'll dial it back. Make it fair."

"You scared I might beat you?"

He laughs and flashes me his knuckles. "As a reminder."

"Then play to win," I say. "Give me everything you got."

CHAVEZ STARTS EASY IN THE WARM-UP TO FEEL ME OUT BUT THROWS IN vicious lefty spins and deep, knifing volleys once we move to the baseline. I have to use more of my knees, bending low to absorb his power and pace. But he needs to adjust too. My heavy, flat shots push him beyond the baseline he prefers to crowd, and when we start practicing serves, I scoop him with a couple of short and wide ones. After a testy glare, his response is three aces whizzing past me and leaving nothing but a vapor trail.

"One set?" he asks, with a confident smirk.

"Game on."

In the end, I hold all my service games, only to get crushed in the tiebreak. We shake hands at the net, and I can tell he's impressed I didn't die like a dog in the street. The fact he's breathing hard gives me a little thrill.

"You're a hustler out there," he says.

"Footwork is my greatest asset."

He leans on the net with a slow, broad smile. "I don't know about that."

The day is warm for December and carries on its breeze the deeply sexy scent of his exertion combined with coconut suntan lotion. A faint embarrassment gnaws away at my insides. Me in the bath last night, under a blanket of lavender-scented bubbles, cursing the eighty-three other women who had made it farther with him than I had.

Chavez playfully walks his fingers up my arm. "Time to get wet?"

A chill seeps into my bones despite the heat. I never said anything yesterday when he brought up the pool, and he obviously hasn't gotten that far in my book.

"Uhm … I've never learned how to swim. But I'm happy to dip my legs in."

"Oh," he says, blinking in surprise. "Whatever. We can shower and be done with it. But I'd still like to see you in a bikini."

We stroll to the cabana and Chavez gives me a rundown of the famous Old Hollywood names who once owned this mansion. After showering, I wriggle into my bikini, and the usual triangle number feels like a lot less fabric with the anticipation of his eyes roaming over it. I hop onto a daybed facing the pool and sink into the softness of fat, feathery pillows. I'll feel the effects of our hitting tomorrow, but for now, I'm content to dream of a manservant running me drinks and the latest hot script to read. It's hard not to fantasize of the movie-star life while lounging in opulence that makes the most deluxe resort look like a Detroit backyard.

"They came with the place, in case you were wondering."

Chavez emerges from the shower in a fresh pair of shorts, toweling off his hair. He's referring to two stone cherubs at the far end of the pool, water arcing hilariously high from their dinks.

"I wasn't judging," I say.

"Everyone judges me for those." With a rueful smile, he heads for the wet bar, which I noticed is decently stocked for a non-drinker. I bet this is the hub whenever he throws a party because, with seating for twelve and a jumbo TV over the fireplace, where else would you want to hang out? "Water for my heavy hitter?" he asks.

"Yes, please."

He joins me on the daybed with two chilled Perriers. The cold bubbles go down easy, and our silence is companionable, but it's hard to think of activities such as speaking with our shoulders and thighs touching in the shade. A water droplet runs down his chin to ping off a torso so ripped I could coax some high C notes out of it if I had a mallet.

"Are you excited about Australia?" I ask.

"Yes and no." His thigh starts jittering imperceptibly against mine. "I'm starting over from scratch, in a way. But on the flip side, this time I can do it right."

"What wasn't right before?"

The question is a roundabout way of addressing the thirty-odd YouTube videos of his now infamous first-round debacle at the French Open last year. I watched three of them this morning, different angles of a visibly agitated Chavez losing it on the umpire after an overrule and accidentally hitting a young fan in the chest when he drilled a ball into the stands. The ump defaulted him immediately. He left the court in a hail of *boos*, incurred a fine for skipping the press conference, and went dark for seven months. Whatever happened on the court is something he hasn't shared with me yet.

"What are you doing for the next little while?" he asks. Trying, like he did last night, to make the conversation about me.

"I've decided to take some time off. Not sure what the next step is."

He glances over. "You don't want to write anymore?"

"Oh no, I do, but…" I pause, unsure how to describe my vastly uncertain future. But I believe Chavez might understand part of my struggle in the long dark hours. "Do you ever get tired of the pressure? That it's only you out there?"

"Yeah," he admits, picking a piece of fluff off the daybed and flicking it away. "It can be a drag. But I got into tennis because team sports never appealed to me—relying on others for my success. This is what I wanted, and I still want it. I know I have a Grand Slam in me. Several."

"You sound very motivated. Maybe a couple of months on your own might do you good," I say, trying the Vandana approach and finding a positive spin. "Gain some perspective without input."

"I need someone," he counters. "But a regular coach might not cut it. My problem is I get way too deep into my head. Shit gets squirrely, and there goes my game. I thought Smythe might step up to the plate and help out, but he's not down with remote sessions."

"For a small monthly fee, you can call me."

The words spill out before I can stop them, and my face clouds a fraction. Now is not the time to be flippant or glib, not when he's opening up. Chavez hijacks my apology while it's still forming by reaching for my water bottle with a smile curling on his lips. He sets it on the ground next to his and faces me. Looking into the endless blue of his eyes is like being in a fever dream.

"I hope your kisses are free, Miss Flynn," he says softly. "Or else I'm going bankrupt."

He lifts my chin with a gentle push of his finger, and everything I'd told myself on the drive over—the logic, how I decided I'd act and what I'd say—melts away as his mouth finds mine. He smells like soap and sin and makes a case for never wanting a kiss to end. That's how damn good it feels. Never breaking the kiss, he nudges us lower, slowly becoming horizontal. His skillful fingers ply my tense back muscles, working them into submission. Each deep stroke dissolves my willpower until a warm liquid light funnels into my sweet spot. I arch against him, a helpless pin drawn to the magnet of his irresistible body. Sensing surrender, he pushes his erection against my dampness, and the ache of wanting spills out in a low, desperate whimper.

"God, that feels amazing."

"I want to do everything with you," he whispers back, lips humming on mine.

His hand roams north, seeking unchartered territory. The exquisite burn of my nipple tweaking between his fingers floods the part of my brain that is supposed to think straight with a rush of arousal. Later this afternoon, when I'm sitting across from Dr. Bradford and telling more lies, I'll rethink why I do what I do now.

But sometimes, there is no good reason other than pure need.

"Wait," I say and wedge my hand between us, my hand flat and pressing back on his chest.

He chases after my mouth with a mewling sound. "What's up?"

"Nothing. I, I want to kiss you with me on top."

He searches my face. And yes, I want to say, this is what you get with a woman who has slept with fifty-five men (give or take, I'm not in there with a calculator like he is) incapable of getting her off. Being on top gives me an advantage. I can finger myself more easily and clock if he's getting weird about it. And I need to be more careful with him. He's trained to read the body language of opponents across the net —all the little things that give someone away.

He'll know if I'm faking it.

Chavez stretches flat onto his back and says, "No complaints here." Maybe he thought I would sit on his thighs or his belly, not plunk myself down onto his stiff jewels. He jerks beneath me as a startled laugh slips out of his mouth. "Woah, woah, woah. Go slow, mamacita. I'm already struggling here."

Hands steady and holding my hips still, it makes no difference because he swells like a balloon into my spreading thighs. His glistening satin tip pops out from the waistband of his shorts a second later and my mind trips all over itself. Do I plunge and go? Ride that beast bareback into the sunset with a yippee ki-yay? No, we need a condom. But...

"Flynn, baby," he whispers. "Don't think about it. I'm with you. Just go. Hold onto my hands."

His fingers flower open, and when mine intertwine with them, he locks us together like tent stakes hammered into granite. Oh, no. No, no, no. I need my hands. One of them, at least. But it's too late. There is no chance for backward, not as we slip into a sweet, bucking rhythm that Chavez dictates with every upward drive of his hips.

"Ride me," he mutters, a command if there ever was one. "All the fucking way."

His eyes are dilated, wet and ready for it all. And forget about removing clothes. Who has time for that pesky step? We move together until the world shrinks, the sun disappears, and only darkness exists. In a warm haven where the line between exquisite pain and pleasure blurs into infinity, I feel my control breaking and lust burning through me like wildfire, the blood thumping in my ears. Tension funnels lower and lower, my back arching in anticipation.

Holy shit, is this happening? We're not even having real sex. The kind that involves penetration.

"Hang on," he says, his voice sounding far away and somehow so close. "I'm almost there."

His eyes flutter shut, and he crushes my hands to the point of pain. His relentless, vicious strokes devastate my clit until the destroying course of nature rips through me like a strike of hot lightning.

"I can't hold on," I cry out.

The speed of it.

The force of it.

Jesus Christ.

My feet burn and curl. The flash of light behind my eyes blinds me before I shatter into a thousand blazing white pieces. Shuddering waves slam me senseless, and I think one of us is screaming or moaning, or maybe it's all in my head. I'm only dimly aware of his face crumpled in agony, his body tight like glass. And those two cherubs have nothing on Chavez because he's unloading a pool's worth of love onto his dark torso with deeply savage thrusts.

Finally, the bubble in my brain pops, and it's not me screaming, but him.

Fuuuck!

And everything cuts to black.

Chapter Eight

There is no before without an after. No sunset without a sunrise. No crashing out of heaven with any degree of delicacy. Not with scorched wings and adrenaline coursing through me so violently I'm seeing double. Chavez's chest heaves like a bellow beneath me, and he's a man searching for answers, his eyes dazed and deeply confused when they land on mine.

"What the hell just happened?"

"I'm … I'm sorry."

"For what?" he asks, incredulous. "That was the hottest thing ever." He frees my hands, still clamped around his, smears his love juice until it's worked into his skin, and says, "You gotta lie beside me, Flynn. Please."

I slide off him with the grace of a cow on ice and land with a soft *thud*. Limbs like jelly, I lower into the space beside him, and he snugs me close until the drumbeats of our hearts play as one. It's been a long time since anybody held me this fiercely and it triggers strange, conflicting feelings. The prospect of a new and very different future shimmers somewhere on the horizon, but I shut my eyes as a way of shielding my heart.

Peace is something I'm always chasing and never expect to find.

I'm not getting my hopes up.

MY EYELIDS FLUTTER OPEN, HEAVY FROM A SLEEP THAT WENT ON TOO long. Chavez snoozes lightly beside me, the wall of his back ridged with muscles. A heady primal scent that exists only in the afterglow hangs between us, and I feel like I've slipped off earthly chains and woken up a profoundly changed woman—dissolved into something bigger and more powerful. With nothing but the sound of tinkling cherubs, my mind drifts like a balloon until I notice the shadows of the trees stretching long over the pool.

I jolt upright with the taste in my mouth fouling.

Dammit! Dr. Bradford.

Nothing in the cabana indicates the time, so I bum-slide off the daybed and rummage for the phone in my bag as quietly as possible. But with the deep silence interrupted, Chavez rouses from his slumber. His half-lidded eyes brighten on me with an adorable smile.

"Hey," he says, voice groggy with sleep. "What's going on?"

"Nothing. I have to be somewhere at four." I find my phone and curse softly at the screen. Three-thirty.

His smile dims. "What about lunch?"

"I'll have to rain check," I say, searching for where I left my dress.

"Can you come back later?"

"No. I'm seeing my girlfriend tonight before she leaves for Canada. The one who does start-ups."

He wipes the cobwebs from his eyes and sits up, silently watching me yank the found tennis dress over my head and tie my hair into a messy bun while jamming my feet into my sneakers.

"Slow down, Miss Flynn. It's all good."

He stands and wraps me in a gentle embrace. The touch of his hands eases the tightly wound sensation humming inside me, and I hug him back, a bit desperately, burrowing my head in the dark comfort of his shoulder. Neither of us seems to know what to say.

Chavez strokes my tangled curls and whispers, "You all right?"

"Yeah," I say. Because how do you tell a person that a fog in your soul you never thought would lift clears with nothing more than their touch?

He pulls back and studies me in the late afternoon light. "What are you doing the day after tomorrow?"

I freeze, as old emotions wash over me. "It's Christmas Day. Aren't you spending it with your family?"

"Christmas Eve is my family's deal. Why don't you … I mean, if you're free, some, uh, friends of mine are having brunch on the twenty-fifth. Be great if you came along."

Christmas? With him? Something flips inside me. "You sure I won't be intruding?"

"I leave soon," he says, a solemn quality to his voice. "I want to see you again if you're cool with that."

He hugs me again, and there is something unspoken, an undercurrent running between us that is impossible to ignore. Our time together isn't finished and where it goes from here is anybody's guess, but for now, I'll take the two of us locked together in the safety of each other's arms with the warm glow of knowing someone wants me.

I AFFECTIONALLY CALL JUNE'S MALIBU HOME OFFICE THE SANITARIUM. Some designer hoodwinked her into paying a hundred grand so he could splash white paint around and indulge his glass and chrome fetish, but the real madness lies in how much time she spends here. She's been at work since six this morning, and reminding June they have internet in Canada and that she doesn't have to work right up until her flight leaves, is futile because Putin will move to small-town America before she'd ever call it quits at a reasonable hour. Not much can tear her attention away from her latest deal, some tech thing I don't fully understand, but the retelling of my afternoon tryst captures her full attention.

"The pool cabana?" June whoops with laughter. "Bloody fucking hell, girl. That is some of your best work."

"He said afterward that it was the hottest thing ever."

"I bet he did." June smiles. We've been friends long enough for her to pick up on the vibe. "This lad has potential, by the sounds of it."

"What do you think of the brunch invite?"

Her eyebrows raise in an, *are you serious,* look. "Making time for you on Christmas Day this early in the game? That is a man crushing hard."

"A man who leaves for Australia on Tuesday," I add.

"He won't be there forever."

I'm lying on her white-leather sofa in my second therapy session of the day. With the static in my mind dulled from the pills I squeezed out of Dr. Bradford this afternoon, I can focus on tactics. Or lack thereof.

"Don't tell her I said this, but Vandana might be right," I say. "Dating a guy who is never around is a dead end. Look what happened with her and Derek."

"Their marriage was already on the rocks," she reminds me. "We need to approach this thinking from a fresh perspective." June leans back in her chair with the ever-present Bic pen in her mouth, mind as sharp as the lapels on her Phillip Plein blazer. "You planned on taking some time off. Why not travel there with him?"

"I can't just invite myself along," I say, astonished at her suggestion. "Australia is not a vacation for him. He's getting his career back up and running. I also don't want to be *that* girl," I add. "Hanging around, waiting to spend time with a guy."

"Flynn," June says—and for someone who insists she would be a train wreck as a mother, her approximation of one is note-perfect. "You don't hang around *anyone.* Look, I know it's your life, and I'm no great shakes since dumping my ex, but Vandana and I are concerned. You talk about men, and you shag a fair lot of them, but you don't have relationships. Maybe it's time to try a new approach." She crosses her stilettos on the smoked-glass desktop with a scheming smile. "Here's the deal. After your Santa Clause shag, throw the question out there. Hey, I was thinking…" She pulls off a decent rendition of my SoCal accent before switching back to her posh Brit drawl. "You know the best time to ask a man for anything is after an orgasm. It's a guaranteed yes."

I look at her sideways. "Tell me that is not how you raise money."

June makes a *pffft* sound. "I'm not swallowing anything, including my pride, for money. Ever."

The money talk suddenly triggers my earlier conversation with Chavez. "Oh, hey, speaking of cash. Are you still looking for some? Chavez mentioned this guy he invested with for *Leostrata*. Turned a million into forty, which, as you know is, like, insane."

June shoots me a wary glance. "He's not talking about Dallas Evener, is he?"

"Yes," I say, before it dawns on me why his name sounded familiar. "Oh, shit. Is he the one who screwed you over?"

"The one and only. Dallas is the last person I will ever talk to."

"Is he still a major slimeball?" Most of the venture capital guys are, according to June.

"Yes, and the most successful wanker of them all," she grumbles. "Not one to leave a penny or a pussy unturned if it means a buck. If you know what I mean."

"Ewww. Well, scratch that idea," I say.

June heaves a sigh. "My companies always need cash, but I don't need a dirty dick in my face to make it happen."

The full scoop of what went down between her and Dallas years ago escapes me, but I know it wasn't pretty. June's had a tough run with men. Her father never supported her entrepreneurial dreams. An early boyfriend screwed her out of a Kickstarter deal that went viral. And a string of questionable dates ended with a quickie marriage Vandana begged her to reconsider. She didn't. And it all went downhill fast.

"Anyway," she continues. "You hardly said a peep about the book tour at brunch. How did it go this time around?"

I sit up and my legs tremble as I cross them. This tour was the straw that broke my back. "It went okay. I mean, all the extra security made me more paranoid."

"But no sign of the stalker?"

A mutinous lump expands in my throat. I should tell her about the texts. I need to tell someone. But the small, stupid, scared girl inside of me says if I don't breathe a word of it, maybe it will just go away.

"So far, so good."

June studies me. A stone's throw away, waves crash on her sliver of multi-million-dollar beach front. I can taste salt in the air, heavy and sharp, as much as I can taste her scrutiny. She and Vandana don't know who I was growing up in Santa Cruz. The painfully introverted girl with a rotation of friends who swiftly moved on from the local weirdo who spent most of her free time talking with imaginary people in her bedroom. Instead, they know what I told them.

"I hope you're not putting up a classic Flynn front," she finally says. "That whole ordeal last year was misery for you. I thought about you alone on the road, and I'm glad you're home safe."

Safe? That is a moving target I can never land on with both feet. And even if Mr. Stalker died a slow death right in front of me, it wouldn't change a thing. He is not the underlying problem.

A *ping* draws June's attention back to her computer screen and her outcry is pure frustration. "A four-hour delay on my flight? Crikey. Who flies at one in the morning?"

"I can still drive you to the airport," I say.

She slams her laptop shut and wags her finger at me. "I have the perfect plan. We grab a G&T and shoot a round of pool while we plot when and how you will shag the tennis star ... for real ... before he leaves. Australia is a given after that. What do you say?"

June is a lethal pool player, and by that I mean a shark of the great white variety. Her side hustle during our Stanford years was luring unsuspecting guys into betting on games and making out like a thief. I don't mind getting bulldozed because watching her bank the most ridiculous shots is worth the price of embarrassment.

I pull on my jacket and remind her that Christmas and Boxing Day are my limited windows with Chavez. June packs up her Chanel tote and throws down the ultimate challenge, channeling Flynn Dryden Truth #3: Crush your habits.

"Two days is a lifetime in Vandana years," she says. "Time to take a page out of her book and make her proud."

EVEN THE CRICKETS ARE ASLEEP WHEN I STAGGER OUT OF THE Escalade at midnight. It's a fool's game to try and out-drink June. But after Chavez texted me at the start of my pool game beatdown, our brief exchange left me feeling bulletproof and swilling one too many forty-proofs.

CD: Hola. Trying not to think about you and obvs working, right? Ha ha.

FD: Hi.

FD: I liked hitting with you today.

CD: I liked a lot about today.

At that point, June saw the goofball smile on my face and poked me in the belly with her pool cue.

FD: What should I bring to the brunch?

FD: And what should I wear?

CD: Nothing. I mean, bring nothing, ha ha. Wear a nice dress, please. You have beautiful legs.

CD: Make that beautiful everything.

The soft night breeze feels like a whisper of silk on my skin, and I sway drunkenly in my driveway, remembering.

I'm with you.

Yes, Chavez, you were.

How could I not submit to him so completely? I've been a woman in search of a miracle and desperate enough to kick Mother Teresa and her dog to the curb to find it. He drove our erotic bus to newfound destinations, and my jumbled brain can't pinpoint what his special sauce was. It left me breathless and desperate for more. I glide along the walkway to my front door, pleasantly buzzed and excited about Christmas Day for the first time in years.

Once inside the house, I drop my bag in the foyer. My throat is raw from a few too many vape hits offered by the drunken couple playing next to us in the bar, and I stumble into the kitchen for a cold shot of OJ.

I do not notice it at first.

But in the wedge of light thrown out from the open fridge, whatever sticks to the sole of my shoe is blindingly white to my eyes, rimmed red from the long night. Was I dragging toilet paper around all evening? Classy. I bend over to dislodge it, and a brutal head rush sends me crashing to my knees. The spinning room takes far too long to settle, and I ass-plant, hoping to speed up the process while looking like a first-class idiot attempting to pull my shoe off.

What the hell is this?

I yank the envelope off the piece of gum I must have stepped on at the bar and hold it up in the light. Plain white, without a stamp and bearing no address, shoved through my mail slot by someone other than the US Postal Service. I feel it immediately in the pit of my stomach: defeat. Cold as acid. The eerie quiet of my house pulses louder than my freaking-out heart. I rip the envelope open and unfold the single sheet of paper shaking in my hand. Three words and the entire heavenly day spirals into a soul-deadening hell.

I found you!

Chapter Nine

December twenty-fourth technically happened, despite my choosing to forget it. Chavez picks me up at my house for Christmas Day brunch completely unaware that I spent the past two nights at the W Hotel in Hollywood, shivering in the dark, alone. My home security system caught the stalker in the act the other night, although a baseball cap and bandana shrouded his features. But it was him. And his intrusion has left me skittish and unsure how to tackle this. The best way to ignore my life is to focus on Chavez.

"Everything okay?" I ask him.

"Yeah," he replies distractedly. "Why?"

"You're driving thirty miles over the speed limit."

Traffic is light on the 101 heading east, and we are making good time, enough not to warrant hauling ass.

He backs off the gas with a sigh that holds the weight of the world in it. "Lots on my mind today."

"How did yesterday go?"

We had texted back and forth, the only bright spots in my day, and he sent me several photos. The fake silver Christmas tree his mother dumps a bed sheet over after the holidays wind down. A crowd of heads at the church during midnight mass. A dining table heaving with brightly colored savory dishes. All of them left an ache in my heart.

"The usual family stuff." He reaches for my hand. "I really wanted to see you. You look beautiful, by the way."

I took extra care with my hair and makeup this morning to make the right first impression, although who his friends are is still unclear to me. I asked Chavez earlier if only to memorize names, but his rant after a car cut us off allowed him to duck the question. What I do know is they live in Echo Park, a neighborhood east of downtown and home to Dodger Stadium. After leaving the freeway, we cruise past modest homes with gently failing front yards of cracked concrete and weeds. But the newer Craftsman house at the end of the block has a tidy square of picket fence wrapping the yard perimeter and well-tended blooms bursting from the flower beds on either side of the porch.

"This is very pretty," I say.

"They look after the place," he says. "As you should with your home."

He parks behind a dated Honda Odyssey, and beside it lurks a scary looking Ducati motorcycle I would never feel comfortable on, even wearing the bright pink helmet dangling from one of the crossbars. Today's brunch crowd is eclectic, to say the least.

Chavez takes my hand, and his body language feels a little guarded when we enter the house without knocking. Most homes in LA lack a proper entrance foyer, and as soon as you step through the door, you are smack-dab in the living room. Or, in this case, the dining room. With a table set for four. Huh. Chavez led me to believe a small crowd of twenty-somethings would be mixing and mingling, but it is awfully quiet in here.

He casually dumps his keys onto the table and calls out, "Hola."

I grew up in a middle-class house like this—nothing over the top— with rooms that could use some brightening. But we never had box-store pleather furniture crammed to one side of the living room to accommodate a life-size nativity scene.

Sweet baby Jesus, literally and figuratively.

In complete contrast to the scent of something fatty and welcoming in the air, a forty-something Latino woman limps out of the kitchen wearing an apron over a shift dress and a frown that looks permanently welded into place. She has the handsome features and carriage of aristocracy, which might explain why she looks at me like I am a commoner infiltrating her turf.

"Dios mio," she mutters.

On her heels is a tall Latino man, buff for his age and greying slightly at the temples. He startles to a stop at the sight of me, and I'm developing a complex from all the staring. In the vacuum of silence, I scan the room to determine why Chavez tightens his grip on my hand as if we're behind the eight ball. Why I failed to notice the silver Christmas tree until now is a mystery, but the cluster of framed photographs on the side table brings it all to a dreadful certainty. Every single photo is of Chavez. As a boy, a teenager, a junior tennis player holding trophies.

And the man standing in front of me in a tacky reindeer sweater with battery-powered lights blinking on and off has eyes that are an unreal shade of turquoise like I have only seen once before.

Oh, God. No.

"Mama, Papa," Chavez says, confirming my worst nightmare. "This is Flynn. Flynn, these are my parents, Gloria and Rodrigo."

Their blank faces say it all. Chavez, who I might kill in a moment, did not tell them he was bringing me.

I smile through the lurching drop of my stomach. "Merry Christmas Mr. and Mrs. Delgado." And then, stupidly, "Thank you for having me."

Gloria ignores me and asks Chavez, "Quien es Ella?"

Before he can tell her who I am, a third stranger wanders out of the kitchen. Younger than all of us, with an arresting face framed by a blunt cut of pinkish hair, she carries herself with a, *you want a piece of me?* attitude. Her romper looks thrifted and should not work with white cowboy boots, but she's owning it, like the cigarette tucked behind one ear.

Her eyes narrow on Chavez, and with one hip jutted out and her fists parked at her waist, she says to no one in particular, "What the actual fuck is this?"

"Carmelita," Rodrigo warns, and I realize this spitfire is Carmen, the infamous sister.

"Don't Carmelita me," she huffs. "You said only familia today. Why does he get away with everything?"

She points to her brother as Exhibit A, and Chavez responds like a grumpy grizzly. "I'm not getting away with anything. Flynn isn't some random."

Carmen rolls her eyes at this news. "So, you aren't shitting the bed yet again?"

Gloria points a warning finger at her daughter. "You will not curse in my house." Her judgement then falls on my dress hem—the wrong side of North—and her stark disapproval stirs up a cluttered saga of horrible memories. I want to say I'm just here for some eggs, lady, not to be put on trial for a double homicide because that is how her scrutiny makes me feel.

Both cheeks aflame, I extricate my hand from Chavez's with a brittle smile. "You know what? I left something in the car. Can you come outside with me?"

Carmen smirks and makes a face at him that says, *have fun*. Chavez breathes hard in and out of his nose but maintains his composure. Barely.

"We'll be right back."

Despite meditation, yoga, journaling, and every other New-Age remedy flogged on Tik Tok, stress still swamps me. I bolt straight for the car and lean onto it, trying to gather my bearings as the footsteps of Chavez loom closer. I don't trust myself to say anything objective. When our eyes finally meet over the roof of the Ferrari, his face is tense but determined.

"Flynn," he starts. "Listen—"

"Open the door, please. We'll talk inside."

It's like a never-ending Groundhog Day. Us in his car again, with me feeling like an alien in a world where I don't understand the rules.

"I know what you're thinking and you're right," he immediately says. "I should have told you."

"Really?" I ask, with the faintest lift of my eyebrows. "Because for a minute, I wondered if you had any clue how I might feel meeting your family on *Christmas*. Without any advance notice."

"I thought—"

"For the love of God, Chavez!" I shout. "You did not think, and you cannot be that brain-dead." I scrounge in my purse for my phone, the shrill in my voice ratcheting higher. "I'm not going back inside. I didn't even bring anything because you said *not* to. I'm calling an Uber."

I take deep, gulping breaths that do nothing to stop my hands, my entire body, from shaking. Seeing my distress, how dark and wild it is, briefly silences Chavez.

"Please don't go," he finally says. "It's going to look worse if you leave."

I stare at him in disbelief. "Your mom looked at me like I was a stripper. I don't think she's going to mind one bit if I leave."

I can't even muster baseline empathy for him right now. Gloria's reaction to me weighs like a dead thing on my heart, and he can't understand because he doesn't know that I fear a mother's rejection like I fear death.

"Oh, here we go," Chavez mutters as Carmen slips out the front door and struts on over. She raps her knuckles on his window and motions for him to roll it down. He cracks it an inch.

"What do you want?"

"Feliz fucking Navidad, you dumbshit," she says. "Like maybe I can help you salvage this disaster?"

"See ya. Nice knowing you."

The window edge rolls up to bite her skin, but she refuses to budge. "Mama prays every day you and Sofia will get back together. She is having a heart attack in there."

"It's not my fault she's in denial," he protests.

"Of course, she's got her hopes up. You never bring women home, and then you drop her on Christmas?" She glances at me, and I feel like she's seeing something that's not there. "Why don't you take the whipping from this nice lady and then man up, get your ass back inside, and explain yourself."

"He doesn't need to explain," I butt in. "I'm leaving."

"No, you're not," he says, quiet urgency in his voice. Back at Carmen, he turns borderline hostile. "Have *you* explained that I'm the only one supplying grandkids?"

Her face stills like someone cranked the anger tap off. Until now, I didn't think twice about her woven rainbow bands stacked five deep on her wrists. Or her pretty face devoid of makeup and the unmistakable current of wayward sensuality in her eyes. Guess I know now who straddles the Ducati.

"Have you said anything?" she asks, sounding hollow, the vim stripped away.

"Right," Chavez mutters. "Why would I bear your cross?"

"Because there is someone on this earth other than you, Chavelito."

"Are we getting into that?" he asks immediately on the attack. "All right, then who's paying for your education? Some fucking mystery man?"

She laughs bitterly, and I know it's not the first time they've gone down this path. "Now I have to bow down to you? The man with all the money? If that's the case, you're no better than Earl."

It's like she flipped the same Sofia switch that was activated the other night. Chavez pounds the window so hard with his fist I feel the rattle in my teeth.

"Don't you *ever* say that!"

After a sticky silence that could trap a jet mid-take-off, the set to her jaw loosens. "I've dealt with your mierda my whole life. It's always about you and your drama to prove yourself. It's like you don't know how to live without it. Even Papa threw in the towel, and he's the patron saint of patience." Her gaze lands on me and something in her expression tells me she would never do anything as dubious as stick around for a man who's treated me like Chavez has. But then she says, "Do me a favor and stay. Make him face reality for a change. And Mama makes the best tamales."

She stomps off and leaves us in a silence that could smother a million shrieking girls at a Dua Lipa concert. I still can't believe how badly I got suckered.

"This is pretty awesome," I say. "Best Christmas ever."

Chavez side-eyes me. "Now you're going to ride my ass, too?"

He can sit here all day if he wants to, acting all wounded. He's got some explaining to do. "What exactly is going on here?" I ask. "Because there is something, and I get the distinct impression it involves me."

He hesitates and the pause conveys the answer. But he still dances around it. "I wanted my parents to meet you."

"I need more than that, Chavez."

He rakes a hand through his hair, cornered and frustrated and not happy about it. "What I wanted to ask, at the right moment, which I guess is now, is if you'd be interested in coaching me."

I stare at him, unblinking. I don't know what I was expecting, but it wasn't this.

"My dad isn't coming back," he continues, "and Python doesn't want to travel anymore. I know most of the other coaches, and I'm not interested in working with them. I got more into your book yesterday and you're smart up here," he says, tapping a finger to his forehead. "That's what I need."

Holy Toledo. He is serious. "I have never coached anyone at tennis. Let alone someone at your level."

"It's not like you're reinventing the wheel," he counters. "You coach people all the time—on stage, through your writing."

"It's not tennis," I remind him again. "And you're trying to rebuild your career. That's a huge deal. It requires commitment. Time and travel."

"You said you've got nothing going on for the next while. And you've played," he adds, before I can interrupt. "Fuck, you can still play. You hit harder than some of the junior guys."

Somewhere in Vancouver, June is laughing. Chavez is asking me to come to Australia, but with completely different intentions than what she predicted. Did I misread all the signals? I thought cabana-gate was pretty defining, but instead of a Santa shag, I'm deep in Echo Park at a job interview slash parental vetting session. I sink my face into my hands, overwhelmed with swirling emotions.

Don't lose it. Stay strong.

"Look at me, Flynn." Through the screen of my interlaced fingers, his eyes carry the same dark intensity as his voice. "Tell me what went down between us at my place wasn't real."

My hands lower so our eyes connect. "Of course, it was real," I whisper. "Why do you think I'm here?"

"You and me both then," he says, gentler, as he squares himself to face me. "I like you, you seem really cool, and it's fucking hard to make any relationship work when I'm on the road all the time. I know I probably sound crazy, but I go with my gut on a lot of things and my gut is telling me something about you."

I cut him a sharper glance. "A coach-with-benefits arrangement? Is that your vision?"

He shrugs like it's not a bad idea at all. "That's one way of looking at it. But I am being serious," he adds. "Can we try? Two weeks in Oz is all I'm asking for. We can always ditch the coach part if it doesn't work out. And you can always ditch me, too, if I don't work out."

Rodrigo and Gloria suddenly appear in the living room window, pulling back the curtain to investigate what evil spell the she-devil is casting on their only son. Chavez glances from them back at me with guilt riddling his features. He's played both sides, and neither very well.

"It's important that my parents know what's going on," is how he frames it. "I wanted them to meet you today in case you said yes."

The thing is, I have agreed to nothing. I can drive away in an Uber and ghost Chavez until he gives up on me. But if I stay in LA, I'll have to deal with the stalker. And the loser knows where I live. I can't handle the idea of reopening a can of worms with the police and getting everyone involved. The security and constantly looking over my shoulder sound exhausting already. Avoidance of pain is a form of pain itself, but if I'm halfway around the world, maybe that is enough distance to have it all go away. But will it? I don't know. My spidey sense tells me to use caution, but where has that gotten me lately? Maybe this is a solution on a silver platter.

Chavez and I lock eyes, and a certain tension digs into my body. I hate feeling conflicted, but I've had too many months where I've felt nothing, and that was worse.

"So, the plan now is to go back in there and tell your father I'm replacing him?" I ask. "Somehow I don't see that improving the situation."

The tiniest opening is all Chavez needs to run with it. "I'll work on my mother," he says. "You talk to my father. He always wanted to be a writer." About to open his door, he adds one last thing. "Do me a favor and eat whatever Mama puts on your plate, all right?"

Chapter Ten

I feel like I'm having an out-of-body experience. From high above, I watch us walk back into the house and see myself bracing for the shit to hit the fan. I already won a preliminary award for sucking the life out of a room, so why not grab gold by sticking the proverbial finger in their eye with the coaching announcement? But then some other Flynn, a mystery girl, expertly handles Gloria when she asks, "What do you know about tennis?" And after I explain my credentials, I watch Rodrigo become visibly relieved that someone will be taking the reins on his son's career.

Chavez must think this is all fine and dandy and normal—me about to uproot my life and join him on the tennis tour. I certainly give him no reason to think otherwise, floating around in my dissociative state. He happily steers his mother into the kitchen to help with last-minute brunch preparations, leaving me with Rodrigo (and a very curious Carmen) to talk tennis in the living room.

Carmen makes herself comfortable on the sectional and both boots land on the coffee table with a *clunk.*

"He must be paying you a fortune," she says. "No other coach will touch him."

Rodrigo eases into a plaid Laz-E-Boy lounger that's seen better days and *shhh's* her, annoyed. A soccer game plays silently on the TV angled toward his man chair, and behind him, Virgin Mary in the nativity scene judges me with her solemn gaze.

"It's true," she insists. "You know how stubborn he is."

"We haven't talked salary yet," I admit. And now that I think about it, payment in a coach with benefits arrangement has a disturbing undertone. Carmen pats the space next to her, encouraging me to take a seat. I keep a respectful distance, both hands crossed over the expanse of thigh she's stealing a look at.

"My son can be challenging," Rodrigo starts. "But—"

Carmen spits a laugh. "You think?"

"Go help your brother in the kitchen." Rodrigo orders her out, unamused.

She sighs theatrically and leaves us in peace for fifteen minutes, allowing Rodrigo to share some family history. We're called to the table before he gets too far along, but we swap numbers and he encourages me to keep in touch.

Brunch begins with cutlery clinking in the strained silence. I might have found an ally in Rodrigo, but I am not in Gloria's good books, not by a long shot. By virtue of being thirty-two and not catholic, I am both cradle robber and heathen, and my Stanford graduate and best-selling author status don't warm her up either. While I politely stuff my face, she grills me on how I plan to coach her son and juggle a full-time career. When I say I'm taking a break from writing, she looks at Chavez, mortified, as if I have somehow pulled off the scam of the century and bamboozled her son in the process.

Thankfully every family has a resident diplomat, and Rodrigo saves the day by stepping in with the wine. With the coaching drama temporarily washed away in Napa Merlot, Carmen takes over as the afternoon entertainment. At UCLA studying urban planning, she brims with intelligence and opinions and is unafraid to crush you with either. She, unlike Gloria, is intrigued by my Stanford cache and accomplishment as a writer.

And, well, it seems she's intrigued by other things also.

Chavez keeps a watchful eye on the proceedings as his sister gets progressively drunker and more touchy-feely. The bathroom calls him away eventually, and Carmen pounces on the opportunity to exchange numbers.

"How my brother caught your attention is a book unto itself," she says, "but trust me, he can be hard to handle. If you need some one-on-one, call me. Anytime."

By the time Chavez and I leave, most of the flint has left Gloria's eyes, and I consider her formal handshake a win. Chavez is much more at ease on the drive home, keeping the speed reasonable with one hand holding mine and Luis Miguel crooning softly through the sound system. Dusk is creeping into nightfall and the Santa Monica mountains are shadowy bumps in the distance.

I'm buzzing from the wine Rodrigo poured with a heavy hand and the strange context of being thrown headfirst into a family theatre with many unfinished acts. At one point, Carmen mentioned some friends back in Fresno, and I didn't imagine the weirdly unbalanced energy in the glance between Chavez and his parents. Why I was able to pick up on that and not how protective my parents had been of me is unsettling. I should have put it together earlier, but if you can't trust your parents, who can you trust?

"How long has your mother been off work?" I ask Chavez.

He grips the steering wheel tighter. "Who told you about that?"

"Your father. He mentioned they moved to LA from Fresno after her accident."

"That's all he said?"

"If you don't want to talk about it, that's fine," I say, picking up on his tone. Rodrigo and I never finished the conversation because we were called to the table. He pointedly moved on to another topic, leaving me with the impression he didn't want Chavez involved in any follow-up discussion.

"I wanted them to move here," Chavez eventually says. "I bought them the house and got them set up. Not sure they're stoked but, whatever. Had to be done."

The strain showing around his mouth tells me to let it go, and we lapse into silence. When we funnel off the freeway onto Beverly

Boulevard at four p.m., the loosened knots in my stomach tighten up again. He is taking me home. But my house is now a radioactive wasteland that I have to avoid. And so, I find myself scouring every inch of my yard as Chavez pulls into the driveway. I feel his eyes on me, louder than the tick of his engine cooling off.

"Thank God that's over with," he says, and brings my hand to his lips. "And thank you for saying yes."

I raise a brow at the measly gesture. "That's it? I feel like you owe me more."

"So, my good looks and charm are still in play?"

"Charm might be pushing it."

He laughs, bringing my hand to his heart. "You are one fiery mamacita, Miss Flynn. I think we'll get along fine."

"Is that what fogosa means? Fiery? You called me that the other day."

He draws my face close, and his fingertips move up the side of my face so gently I barely feel them. For the first time, I notice flecks of gold around his irises.

"Let me know if that's okay," he says. "Because I'm not calling you anything that doesn't make you feel good inside."

Like in the movies, our mouths come together in slow motion. I have never been so ready for a kiss, but he takes his sweet time. Licks the seam of my mouth and explores the dark, wet corners. Relentlessly teases me until my body grows taut with arousal and our moans mingle with our breath.

"You taste so good," he mumbles.

I nip on his plump lower lip, the weight of my desire becoming unbearable. All I can smell is my own desperation. "Can you kiss me kind of dirty?"

He laughs, his warm breath tickling my skin. "Dirty, huh?"

I know it sounds bad, and I don't care.

If we're going for a Christmas Day orgasm, may as well start the night on the right foot.

He shifts in his seat and pulls me closer, as much as the confined, awkward space allows. His smile turns rogue, and I know something is coming to catch me off guard. I open for him and tell myself to be in the moment, to simply let all the sensations travel through me. But I one-hundred-percent do not expect it when he pushes his tongue deep inside and fucks me with it. Forget about sweet nothings and peaches and cream—this is getting plowed from behind in a dark alley. It's a free-for-all in a Ferrari, and I can barely keep up. His greedy fingers plunder across my arching breasts, tracing invisible geography lower and lower.

Yes, I think, down, down, down, to my wet, tender flesh.

And when his hand slams under my dress to go for the grope, heading right for the honey, I brace for it. Splay my thighs to help him along. Hand me the rock, I am ready to roll.

And then he's gone.

Collapsed back into his seat, panting like a dog, and laughing like a crazy man. I'm seeing stars, stripes, squares, and everything in between. Hanging on by a thread with my heart rate spooling out of control.

"Jesus, Chavez. What the hell?"

"Oh, Miss Flynn," he says, catching his breath as he rearranges himself. "I am so sorry. Denial is how I make sure you come along for the ride."

"But, but…" I sputter. "You already bought me the plane ticket." He told me this on the drive home.

"You can still be a no-show."

I bring both hands to my mouth, unsure if I'm trying to stop a smile or a sob. "I thought you were useless at self-control?"

"Gotta commit to change at some point, right?"

He winks, knowing there is no comeback. He's got me by the proverbial balls. A supernova of shitty timing.

"I admire your resolve."

He leans forward to find my eyes with a bratty smile. "You don't look like you're admiring it."

"Remember the other night when you asked if I'd murdered anyone?" I say.

He breaks into a fit of fresh laughter, and I could never cause bodily harm to anyone whose laugh buzzes through me like a great, numbing scotch. Damn him for grinning like the Cheshire Cat and being so absolute in his game plan.

"Why do I sense everything will be a challenge with you?" I ask.

He shrugs and says, "You've got no one but yourself to blame. You made me chase you. Can't complain now that I'm controlling the point."

"Maybe I'll need to ask Carmen for some advice. In person."

"Uh-uh," he says, shutting down the play. "I'm keeping her far away from you. The only person more determined than me is my sister."

A softness shines through in him that did not exist before, and I chalk it up to meeting his family and getting at least their partial approval. I still might strangle him in the near future for the stunt he pulled, and I am about to lay down that warning when my entire front yard lights up like Broadway. My scream echoes off his fine Italian leather, and Chavez jerks in his seat as if a bullet ripped through him. The shock of industrial-grade lighting smashing on from the army of security lights on the front of my house thrums through me like 220 volts. I clutch onto the sides of my seat, hyperventilating. When a raccoon family waddles across the lawn, I'm so stupidly relieved tears sting my eyes.

"Are you all right?" he asks. "It looks like you're about to puke."

"I'm fine," I say, finding my breath. It feels like my chest is about to explode. "I ... that scared me."

"Yeah, I can see that."

Chavez radiates supernatural awareness, and I try to squash down the vulnerability I know he's picking up on. The fact is, we're both rattled by the incident, if the heavy silence is any indication.

He eyes me a moment longer, and then, "Come on, I'll walk you to the door."

"It's okay. You don't have to."

"Yes, I do." His voice is firm, like why are we back to square one on this issue? "This is what it's like when you're with me. I look after you, all right?"

Something in me lightens. When did that happen, that I am with Chavez? Do I have Carmen to thank for scoping out my boobs? Nothing like being outmaneuvered to fire someone up. But beyond the wine and the clatter of anxiety thrumming through my veins is the reality that Chavez is no run-of-the-mill placeholder I am forever hooking up with. And he's played me, like he's played his parents, and knows exactly what it will take to make this scenario work to his advantage.

Now I have to put some thought into my own play.

Australia, here we come.

"ONE SUITCASE?" VANDANA FLIPS UP HER SUNGLASSES IN SHOCK. "How is that even possible?"

Even on a scratchy FaceTime video, she's flawless in a gold lamé bikini, lounging on a deck chair with the soaring cliffs of Capri behind her yacht. She's joined June and me in a virtual confab to discuss my Australia adventure—our tradition of shopping until we drop on Boxing Day reduced to one Rimowa roller bag that can't possibly fit any more of my doubts into it. Chavez, the clever fox, was right about the no-show potential.

Buyer's remorse is alive and well this morning.

"I've only committed to the first tournament," I remind her. She's waiting for Morgan to jet in from Monaco and not entirely paying attention after half a bottle of Pinot Grigio. "And Australia isn't the Congo. If I need to top up, I'll hit a mall."

"I can't believe the stunt he pulled," June muses, sipping tea on her mom's sofa. After two days of soggy peas with bangers and mash in dreary Vancouver, she's chomping at the bit to fly home. "Bringing you 'round to meet the parents on Christmas without saying anything beforehand? That sounds a bit dodgy."

"He said their approval was important to him. I respect that."

"I suppose if you can get him back on track, that's just another feather in your career cap," Vandana says, forever spinning everything into a public-relations positive. "But what's up with the sex denial thing? That's ten times dodgier."

"Not everyone fucks on the first date," I reply. Meaning, I am not you. And I shelved the Santa Clause shag mission last night after the raccoon incident because it's hard to feel sexy after I've figuratively pooped my pants.

"Lord knows why," she says, oblivious to my sarcasm. "It's a time-saver. Why fly halfway around the world only to find out he's got a two-inch penis?"

"We dry humped, if you recall, so I've felt the goods. He's more than half a ruler." That's Vandana's bare minimum. "And ... he said he wants the real thing to be special."

June's face crumples into utter cuteness. "Aww! He said that?"

Not exactly. And it isn't fair to pile outlandish expectations onto Chavez like he's my knight in shining Adidas, but how many twenty-five-year-olds would admit to liking a woman and then not bang her at the first available opportunity? He's telling me something over and above the power-play angle, even if he, and I, are unsure of what.

But I don't want to dissect it, because I've been on this call for almost forty minutes, and I still have a bunch of research to do before we leave tomorrow. Chavez and I have only played tennis once, and the struggle to stay on the board consumed all my energy. I didn't have the time or intention to analyze his game then. But with so many of his matches available online, I can get a feel for his favorite setups and shots. Understand where, when and how his game is breaking down. Mental and physical muscle memories are interconnected. Fixing one without the other is impossible.

So, I beg off from my besties, promising a worried June that I will come back and not leave her alone in LA. I sit cross-legged on the four-poster bed I haven't slept in since Friday and scan my surroundings. The room is the same. What's changed is everything else. On a different sort of day, when I didn't have to look over my shoulder, the idea of a fiery soul tugging me and my heartstrings across the Pacific and Indian Oceans on a wing-and-a-prayer mission was downright laughable. I'm still in disbelief that any of this is happening.

But didn't I feel the same way when my parents dragged me out of my bedroom to make friends through tennis? I sulked the entire drive to the courts with no idea how it would change my life. Instead of uncertainty, I found white lines that never lied. If I was ever at a loss for words, my serve said what I never could. For all the time I got picked last for sports teams, I proved Flynn Dryden had guts and could win.

I suppose the blond and sunny Hamilton Davis fell in love with that version of me. The future tennis star. A charming, uber athlete, his first love was baseball. But Hamilton could play every sport decently, including tennis. We met on the courts in our hometown of Santa Cruz, and back then, we held hands and smiled at each other like the silly teenagers we were. We still had our dreams. The major league baseball scouts started to swirl around his undeniable talent, and Hamilton always said I had the goods to go all the way. No small shakes coming from a guy destined for greatness … until he met me.

A ray of sunlight streams through the window, and the warmth is a reminder that spring is around the corner. The dormant part of my heart, all of it to be honest, is desperate to bloom again. But the parallels between Hamilton and Chavez sends my head spinning in ten different directions.

Don't overthink it.

A random card from a bingo game is just that, right?

Lightning never strikes twice.

Chapter Eleven

CHAVEZ

THIRTY-FIVE THOUSAND FEET ABOVE THE GROUND WITH NOTHING BUT endless blue out the window is what Smythe would call a perfect scenario for inner peace. Tell that to all the thoughts banging inside my skull like pinballs. Flynn lies beside me in her first-class seat, shrink-wrapped in a blanket and dead to the world. Never in a million years did I think she'd say yes to the Chavez circus, and I'm still wondering what her real deal is. After the familia Christmas Day shit show, I thought I cracked her code. Then the raccoons came to town, and things got weird. It left a strange taste in my mouth, enough that I circled back ten minutes after I left to check in on her.

What did I find?

Her climbing into an Uber.

Where was she going? And if she had other plans, why not mention them before? The last thing a woman wants is some guy grilling her, and she already plays dodgeball with half my questions, so I'm treading carefully. I like my women intricate—give me something to figure out—but Flynn is like a five-thousand-piece puzzle I'm putting together blind.

"Good morning, Mr. Delgado. Would you like some water?"

This flight attendant, Rose, has been on me since we left LA and is coming in hard for the flirt since Flynn is out cold. She fills out her uniform nicely, but blondes do nothing for me, and I get the sense she takes passengers down regularly.

"I'm good, thanks," I reply. "But I'll take one for my girlfriend."

She hands me a water bottle with her fake smile sliding away, and yeah, I'm pushing it with the girlfriend talk. Mama always said I was impatient. I might be pulling the trigger too quickly with Flynn, but I'm telling you straight up, I've never come with a woman at the same time. I would sure as hell remember something that monumental. Fuuuck. And the fact she can play? God put her in my path for a reason, and if she's the one who can turn this crazy train around, I'll be on my knees at Sunday service for the rest of my life.

Out of nowhere, the plane suddenly dips, and everyone sits up straighter in their seats. The captain's voice crackles over the speakers as the chop intensifies, assuring us we are not going down in flames, and the commotion stirs Flynn out of her snooze.

She wipes the sleep out of her eyes and yawns. "Morning. Or is it afternoon?"

"It's morning and time to rehydrate, beautiful." I crack open the water bottle and hand it to her. "We land soon."

"Did you sleep at all?" she asks.

"Nope. I watched some movies, did a few laps to keep the circulation going, and finished your book."

She sits up, suddenly very alert. "Oh. What did you think?"

Ain't that the million-dollar question? What I had thought was smashed sideways.

"My bad for assuming, but when you said your parents had passed, I figured it was later in life. I didn't realize you were adopted. Are your adoptive parents still around?"

"They are," she says slowly, like she has to think about it. "But we don't talk. Their decision."

Her eyes flicker off mine and here we are again. Me having to grab the crowbar to keep her talking. That's if her T-shirt flashing some boob doesn't distract me before I can try.

"Is that a forever thing?" I ask. Because if it is, that's two sets of parents down the drain. And who doesn't want their family around?

"For now," she says, putting a firm point on it.

Fair enough. Moving on. I have other questions.

"Your accident sounds gnarly," I say. "I noticed the scar on your knee at my house."

"The surgeon tried his best to minimize it," she explains, "but patella fractures are nasty business. My shattered elbow was the easier fix, surprisingly."

She lifts her right elbow and white scar lines radiate like a starburst from the point. And here I thought I had noticed everything about her when she was wearing that tiny bikini.

"I'm sorry to hear about your boyfriend," I say. "I can't imagine life stuck in a wheelchair." That chapter was brutal to grind through. But it put things into perspective. When I threw out the Christmas brunch invite, she had looked at me like I'd goose-stepped over the grave of a loved one. And seeing her now, all closed off and fighting not to show any emotion, I can't help feeling there is more to the story, something she left off the page. "This might sound like a dumb question," I continue, "but why would you go white-water rafting when you can't swim?"

Bingo. Bullseye. Knife in the heart. All of these reactions play out on her face, and I decipher the shift in her seat to mean, *How many more questions do you plan to fling at me?*

She takes a long pull of water before speaking. "It's one of those rash and wrong decisions you make as an eighteen-year-old. If I could go back in time, I'd do it differently."

"How come you didn't play after your injuries healed?"

"I thought about it," she admits. "But my recovery took longer than expected and, as I said in the book, the whole incident turned me upside down. By the time I sorted out my head, I was at Stanford, writing the book on the side, and tennis sort of slipped away."

"It's a shame you didn't continue. You've got the right mindset. And the body."

She follows my sightline and quickly rearranges her T-shirt with a mortified laugh. "Jesus! Was I flashing everyone the whole time?"

"Nope. You were wrapped up tight like a mummy."

"That happens a lot."

A sadness taints her smile, and I poke her arm, trying to lighten her up. "So, you're a bed hog? Stealing all the covers?"

"I guess that's not an immediate concern for you," she says, one of her eyebrows lifting in question.

I booked separate hotel rooms under the guise of chivalry, but yeah, it's also part of my strategy—a different take on the walkaway. Separation to make the heart grow fonder. And it would be sort of weird to shack up right away. Gotta ease into the big casual.

"Not yet," I say.

She laughs and clips her seatbelt together. If I'm reading her right, the past couple of days tells me she is dying to get a taste of me, and I have a plan in mind that she may or may not appreciate.

"At brunch, your father seemed miffed that you represent the US instead of Mexico," she says out of the blue. "Have you considered switching?"

We start to descend and my ears pop with the shifting pressure. If only I could shrug off Flynn's question as easily. She clocked my irritation when Papa, spouting off as he does after too much wine, poked at the same bruise. Every time he brings that topic up, I'm back at the Westar Poultry processing plant in Fresno, a ten-year-old boiling with fury in a room full of fat, jowly white men who laughed at me like I was no better than a doormat they wiped their feet on.

"I haven't considered it because I'm an American. Just like you. I'll play for the country I'm a bona fide citizen of."

"I'm not implying you aren't American," she says. "Or that—"

"You can't understand it," I interrupt. "All the complexity."

She leans back with a cool stare. "Try me."

I have no interest in an argument neither of us can win, but a good old-fashioned example never hurt to set things straight.

"Have you ever walked into one of those fancy furniture stores on Melrose and the sales guy looks you up and down like the two of you shouldn't even be breathing the same air? I get pulled over by cops all the time who say I'm speeding when they can't handle the fact that a brown boy is driving a nicer car than they ever will. Because that's how they see me. Brown. Not American. So, you know what? When I win a Grand Slam, I'm winning as an American."

The uptight businessman sitting across from me clears his throat. He and his white buddy pounded drinks in the airport lounge at LAX, throwing looks at me and Flynn. Guaranteed their gardeners and maids look like me and do nothing but smile and say, *Yes, sir.*

"I can see where your father is coming from," Flynn says, diplomatically. "You could be a role model and an ambassador for the sport. You might inspire more kids to pick up the game in Mexico."

She's trying to walk me off the ledge, but something about how rational she sounds only adds fuel to my fire.

"The only thing Mexico has given me is brown skin and an uphill battle to overcome that, all right? I don't need to return any favors. And most of the kids there are into pádel now. Paddle tennis," I clarify. "Like that's a real sport."

After a long silence, her eyes never leaving mine, she asks, "I guess it's not a good time to ask who Earl is?"

My right leg starts to shimmy out of control. Flynn witnessed my rage when Carmelita threw his name in my face, but I don't want to talk about him because that hijo de puta deserves free press. Seven months ago, Earl Anderson shat back into my life like the human skid mark he is, and I'm lucky not to be in jail. But I will never rest easy until he learns a lesson.

"Nope," I say. "It's not a good time."

Flynn, the smart cookie, puts two and two together and lets sleeping dogs lie. But I feel shitty as she swivels to look at nothing out the window. She didn't grow up brown in an America that pretends to be color-blind, so she can't truly understand. But I do appreciate that she's trying to figure me out. Before she went down for the count, we talked training and strategy for two hours. Because she played, she knows all about the mind fuck. How sometimes you want to cut your head off during a match and stuff it in the towel box just to shut it up. Stopping the eternal voice in my head is the hardest thing, and last year was the closest I got to overcoming it. But then I fell apart at Roland Garros with Earl's voice haunting me.

Best be keeping your dreams real or have none at all.

King Earl said those fateful words to me on the day Papa brought me to Westar Poultry to show me around. He and Mama worked at Earl's chicken-killing factory ever since they were eighteen, and they wanted me to follow in their footsteps. But I had heard from other kids that workers had to kiss Earl's pointy rodeo boots to thank him for the luxury of working in a sweatshop with temperatures hotter than a volcano to get a paycheck that never let them get ahead.

Don't get me wrong. I love my parents. They got dealt their hand in life, accepted it, and worked their asses off to help me in every way. But I knew one thing growing up—I didn't want their life.

After a super awkward meet and greet with Earl, Papa went to shoot the shit with his crew, and I'd gotten restless waiting for him in the cafeteria. I decided to snoop around and got lost, ending up in the cool of the offices, where the air smelled like a fake forest instead of ammonia. Curiosity got the better of me when I heard a rowdy bunch of cheers coming from down a hallway. I tiptoed to the boardroom and poked my head around the corner. Earl and his cronies lounged like lions after a kill around the biggest table I'd ever seen, and they were all fixated on the screen hanging from the ceiling. Papa only watched futbol, and I'd never seen tennis played live. I was mesmerized. So much that I forgot I was somewhere I wasn't supposed to be.

The fattest dude took a pull of his Michelob and caught sight of me. "Who's this punk?"

Heads swiveled, and a cryptic grin spread on the grizzled roadmap of Earl's face. "That's Delgado's kid. He brought his son in to witness his future."

They all laughed like it was the funniest thing they'd ever heard. My blood turned cold, and I felt sick to my stomach. I knew right then I would never give Earl the satisfaction of witnessing this Delgado punch his timecard. But he clocked my fascination with what unfolded on the TV screen with great interest. He stroked his bolo tie, belly bursting over his belt buckle and boots on the table like a gangster kingpin.

"You wanna know why there are no Mexican tennis players, Chavez?" he said, pronouncing my name *Shavez* instead of the right way.

I didn't know that he was full of shit, that there were Mexican tennis players. One Grand Slam winner, too—Rafael Osuna. But then, in a room full of fat old white men, watching white men play what I believed to be a white man's sport on TV, I didn't know any better. I just knew I had to put them in their place.

"I'm not Mexican," I said, standing taller. "I'm American."

"Woah," the bald guy said, his chair creaking as he rocked back and forth. "You gotta feisty one here, Earl."

A dude with a bushy red beard and pale, cold eyes, sized me up. "You ever look in the mirror, son?"

I sucked up their laughter with fists balled tight and my throat burning with all the words Mama would have smacked me for if I said them out loud. The strange light in Earl's eyes faded, and they became crafty and unforgiving, like they looked when I met him an hour earlier and he pretended to like Papa. Funny how I could see through people, even back then.

"There's no Mexican tennis players, kid," Earl said, "because they're all cutting up dead chickens. Best be keeping your dreams real, or have none at all." He popped open a fresh beer with his belt buckle and swilled deeply before belching. A real gentleman. "Now you go find your daddy and run on home. And shut the door while you're at it. We don't all live like savages."

His dissing me was one thing. Inferring my family were savages meant war. My emotions got the better of me, as they often do, and I told him to go fuck himself. They all stared at me like I was the Devil. I bolted out of there with the grim understanding that I had drawn an irreversible line in the sand.

After Papa drove us home, I biked like a hellcat to Walmart with the last of Abuela's Christmas money burning a hole in my pocket. I bought the cheapest tennis racket, pedaled to the public courts near our house, and fished out dead balls from the trash cans with determination in my soul. Month after month, I creamed a thousand balls against a concrete wall and played with anyone who had a pulse. I played every night until the sky darkened, and the court turned invisible. I played like my life depended on it because it did.

I've achieved more than I ever thought possible, but it is still not enough.

It will never be enough until I blast my way into the boardroom of that white-trash fuck named Earl with a Grand Slam trophy in my arms so he and all his executive goons can suck my savage dick.

Chapter Twelve

FLYNN

I HAD LOW EXPECTATIONS FOR THE CITY OF BENDIGO, AUSTRALIA. FOR the entire two-hour drive northwest from Melbourne, there was nothing to see other than barren land that made me yearn for the sight of a rebellious skyscraper. The quaintness of the town surprised me, however. Maverick gold-rush pioneers descended into this valley in the mid-1800s, and the ones who struck it rich left a legacy of elaborate Victorian buildings and cute street trams that trundle through the downtown grid.

We stayed up as late as possible to overcome jet lag, but with my body clock still out of whack, I got up early to people-watch with my morning coffee before practice. The cafe next to our hotel is no frills, just like our accommodations. The Challenger Tour started covering hotel costs to offset the money grind and give the lower-ranked players a fighting chance. We could have stayed someplace ritzier, but Chavez wanted to be with the people, as it were.

"Mornin'. Or should I say, G'day?"

In the hot, humid air of the hundred-degree morning, the guy who scoped us out yesterday when we were checking in sits down at the table next to mine with a hopeful smile. I peg him to be around forty— a good-looking forty, with no spare tire and a cropped Afro without a single grey hair. A lawyer on his way to an early tee time in a collared shirt and pressed shorts, clinging to his youth with a pair of scuffed Stan Smiths.

"Hi."

He clocks the tennis racket leaning against my chair, or he pretends to while checking out my legs. "You're with Chavez Delgado. I saw you two in the lobby yesterday."

"That's right," I say, immediately on guard, wondering who this man is. He's American for sure, with a Southern accent thicker than syrup. "I'm his coach."

"Oh," he says, with a look of surprise. "I thought his father coached him?"

"They wanted to mix things up."

"Interestin'. Female coaches are rare, let alone attractive ones."

Jeez. Is he really going there in under a minute? I pull my feet off the chair they have been lounging on and double down on any body language that could read as available. His brown eyes are warm and playful and make me think he is not a threat—no more than any other guy taking an interest in me—and a thin, gold band sits loosely on his wedding finger, although that means almost nothing anymore.

I decide to stick to neutral territory. "Who is your charge?"

He laughs like it's a question he's answered many times. "I tried coaching for half a minute. The travel didn't agree with me."

"What brings you here?"

"I run a Challenger tournament in North Carolina," he explains. "This is a business trip, unfortunately." He snaps open the iPhone case in his hand to fish out a business card. "Brandon Dixler. Pleasure to meet you."

Matching a spoken name to the name on the card is a new habit, but you can never be too safe—anyone can create a fake business card.

I'll verify his title of Tournament Director online later. Another new habit.

"I heard Chavez was coming back to play the Challengers," he says. "Surprising, when he could have been in the main draw at the Aussie Open."

I let my guard down now that I know he's in the tennis world. "He wanted to shake off the rust without all the attention."

He chuckles as a good ole boy buzzed on morning bourbon might. "Good luck with that. Chavez is a popular player, and tickets sold out in a heartbeat. It might be hard to fly under the radar."

"You must know all the players, being in the biz."

"Sometimes I wish I didn't." He takes a sip of coffee and eyes me over the rim. "How is his game coming along?"

"Hey. I've been trying to call you." Chavez appears out of nowhere, piss and vinegar in his voice.

"Oh, crap." I pick up my iPhone from the table, scroll to the focus settings and swipe left. "I put it on do not disturb last night and totally forgot. Sorry."

He glances at Brandon, his mouth twitching into a frown. "Who are you?"

"I'm the tournament director with the Atlantic Tire Championships in North Carolina. Glad to hear you found a new coach."

He offers a hand that Chavez reluctantly shakes. The fact I have shared details with this man does not sit well with him.

"We better get going," Chavez says to me.

"I'd like to finish my coffee first. Do you want one?"

"Next rounds on me," Brandon offers, rising from his chair. "What's your poison?"

"I'm good, pal," Chavez replies. "Thanks."

For all his charms, Chavez seems to share a trait commonly found in mafiosi: cold-blooded indifference if he's not feeling your vibe. The poor stewardess on our flight from LA tried every trick in the book on him and *boom*—shut down.

"Well then," Brandon says, reading the mood. "I'll leave you two to your morning. A pleasure to meet you, Chavez." He turns to me with another hopeful smile. "I do apologize, but I never caught your name?"

"Flynn."

A flicker of calculations passes over his face. "What a pretty name. Unusual."

"If you need anything, you talk to me, all right?"

Arms folded and fire in his eyes, Chavez steps between Brandon and me. Brandon holds his ground despite being a good foot shorter.

"Sure thing."

He collects his coffee cup with the gracious defeat of a man ousted from the cool-kid gathering and disappears into the morning crowds on the sidewalk.

Chavez immediately lays into me. "What did he want?"

"Nothing," I say with a shrug. "He just struck up a conversation."

Chavez drags a chair from the nearby table and plunks himself down next to me. "I heard him asking you about my game. You know the deal, right? You don't say anything to anyone. Spies are everywhere."

I look at him, confused. "Spies? What do you mean?"

"Tennis is one of the top sports for betting," he explains. "You never hear of it with the top ATP guys because they don't need the money, but a lot of shady stuff goes down in the Challengers. Match fixing is a serious problem at this level. Guys are barely making it, scraping by on nothing. Shitty people take advantage of that. Some guy approached me as a junior and guaranteed me ten grand if I lost the match. I told him no fucking way. I'm no cheater. Not then, not now."

I point at Brandon's card faceup on the table. "He works for one of the tournaments. I doubt he's a spy."

"Flynn," he says, serious and in my face. "Listen up. As a coach, people will talk to you off the court, in the stands, and pretend it's friendly conversation when they are really trying to squeeze intel out of you. Even if it seems like the most casual conversation, you can't say anything about my game or my health. Match fixing is illegal. I can be suspended for life if they prove me or my team took bribes or shared insider info that impacts betting odds."

Chavez and I talked on the plane about doping and how much of a pain it is, but we never spoke about betting. The rules and regulations surrounding it are unfamiliar to me.

"Thanks for the heads up," I say. "I'll be more careful."

His gaze cuts to my bare legs as if I've broken some code of conduct. "Next time you come down here, wear something more than a tennis skirt, all right?"

"What else should I wear for practice?"

"You don't have to be flashing yourself around, is all I'm saying."

"Have you seen yourself in the mirror?" I point at his fresh pair of Adidas shorts slash male bikini bottoms, custom made and yellow as the sun.

"Whatever," he says, snatching Brandon's card off the table to stuff in his pocket. "It's not the same."

"Feel free to keep that."

"I will, and can you make sure your phone is on all the time? Please," he adds, in the wake of my loaded look.

"I take it you're not a morning person," I say, dryly.

"I'm an all-day kind of guy if you treat me right." His head swivels toward the lone barista hustling hard with the morning rush. "I need a coffee. You want another one?"

"I thought you were good?"

He shrugs in an impressive display of studied nonchalance. "A guy can change his mind."

I drain my coffee and gather up my belongings. There will be many more storms between us at this rate, and today is only day one.

"A woman can too," I warn. "So you better watch your step."

Note to Brandon: not flying under the radar is a slight understatement. At the Bendigo Regional Tennis Centre, home to the upcoming tournament, a mob of fans crowd our assigned practice court with cell phones filming our every move. For a sliver of privacy, we set our bags on the far bench where one court butts onto another. Chavez immediately strips off his T-shirt and pretends to ignore the sexy-time whistles erupting from the crowd, followed by a chorus of, *Who's your daddy!*

During his junior days, Chavez started the trend of pounding a fist to his heart after a blistering display of athleticism won him a rally, adding the battle cry that would become his signature phrase.

"I guess the flashing around stuff doesn't apply to you, huh?" I ask.

Chavez grabs a racket from the bag, whacks his palm against the strings and says, "Nope."

As he struts to the baseline, the nuggets of wisdom Rodrigo shared with me on Christmas Day about what to expect with his son percolate back. Attitude, of course, coupled with a challenging personality that see-saws from angel to disaster and leaves you wondering which one will surface on any given day. He's prickly when it comes to input on his game, and from the match videos I watched, Chavez is unbeatable when he's on. His forehand is as powerful as a stick of dynamite and serve placement more lethal than a .38 snub. But then the easy put-away suddenly stops being so easy. Drop shots trickle onto his side of the net. The serve starts to go.

The sudden collapse of form at crucial moments is evidence of a head case. Tennis is a mental game as much as it is physical, and I imagine the grey matter between his ears might have something to do with his uneven results. I picked his brain last night over Cobb salads to pry out the underlying issues. My general policy is not to hate anyone I've never met, but Earl Anderson makes a good case for an exception. The story cracked my heart. That dirtbag deserves a pack of wolves unleashed on him for crushing a young boy like a cigarette under his boot heel with his horrible comments. No wonder Chavez is a walking wall of defiant edges. He's got everything to prove. But holding onto old trauma only cripples you in the end.

Says the expert.

"Who's your mama?"

The impressively audible male catcall comes when I strip my tank top off to slather sunscreen around my tiny sports bra. Chavez spins around to eye my almost-naked torso and I shrug innocently, *What do you want me to do about it?*

After an unimpressed silence, he says, "Cross-court forehands to start. And you better make me look good."

Chapter Thirteen

ADVANTAGE, CHAVEZ.

He puts me through the wringer during practice. The heat rising from the court is so intense I feel it seep through the soles of my shoes into my aching calves as I flail to keep up with him. By the end, I feel like I've just come in from the losing end of a street brawl. We towel off and the bleachers are now standing room only, packed with female fans equally mesmerized as me at how fucking riveting he is, shirtless and misted with sweat. Keeners looking for autographs crush their way to the front of the stands.

"You better go and work your magic," I say. "Or else there might be a riot."

He carefully stacks rackets and used towels into his bag. "You're coming along. Team D represents together."

Several attractive women (and men) touch up their appearance in anticipation of his arrival. Chavez has owned the It Factor from day one, and being a certified hottie helps, but his appeal is more than the cliché of women wanting to sleep with him and men wanting to be him. He proved, much like the Williams sisters did, country club pedigree or wealth were not prerequisites for success. And the diverse crowd—old, young, male and female, every skin color—is a testament to his universal appeal. He works the fans like a movie star on the red carpet, the smile rocking as he poses for selfies.

And it bears repeating that his appeal reaches far beyond tennis, as is evidenced by the busty redhead with hair curled into a feathered flip warily sizing me up.

She asks Chavez who I am, and he slings an arm around my shoulder.

"Flynn is my new coach. What do you think?"

"You hit pretty good for a girl," she reluctantly admits. Full pout.

"She's pretty in a whole lot of ways," he says, and surprises everyone, including me, with a kiss that leaves nothing to the imagination and my thighs quaking from imagining it all. I was in no shape last night for any memorable one-on-one, but the fact he didn't even make an overture, not even a hint, demoralized me. And then, this. In broad daylight, like it doesn't matter. The fans eat it up, hooting and hollering like a tailgate party gone sideways. Over their clatter and my racing heart, the sniper-like sound of rapid-fire photography cuts through the din.

I wrench my mouth from his, startled, and skim the stands to find the culprit. A pro, based on the paparazzi lens. The kind that hides out in Beverly Hills shrubbery to ambush celebrities out for a casual stroll and nose pick.

Chavez follows my gaze and steers us away from the fans for privacy. "What's up?" he asks.

"Is that guy working for the tournament?"

He scopes out the snapper with a shrug. "Photographers are always running around. You must be used to that, being in the public eye."

"Yes, but … I didn't plan on being front-page news. Here."

"With me or in general?"

"Uhm … in general."

I'm giving nothing away, my sunglasses helping, but the paranoid quality of my voice is not so easily hidden. Chavez stands very still, the air strange. Fuck. Halfway around the world from home and I find myself in the same frigging place—on high alert. The furrow on his forehead deepens, and his lips join the suspicion party, drawing together in a move reminiscent of Gloria and all her love for me.

"I hope for your buddy Brandon's sake we are front-page news."

He spins his ball cap around to shade his face, and it does nothing to hide the truth stamped all over it. Sensing the show is over, the fans begin to disperse quietly behind us.

"You're not jealous, are you?" I ask.

"Like I'm going to be jealous of a dude in a pink polo shirt," he scoffs. "With the collar turned up."

He slings his bag over one shoulder and marches across the court to the exit closest to the clubhouse. Once we got into the zone during practice, Chavez forgot about being irritated with me, but we ricocheted back to that status in a heartbeat. I jog to catch up with him, feeling guilty and wanting to right the perceived wrong in his mind.

"For what it's worth, I think you'd look great in pink."

I smile, lower my sunglasses, and attempt to catch his gaze. When he gives me the honor of eye contact, it's one-hundred-percent fearless.

"Dream on," he says. "I'll wear pink when hell freezes over."

My alarm goes off seemingly minutes after I lay down for a nap. I stumble into the bathroom to get ready for dinner, out of sorts from the heat, the jet lag, and how Chavez reacted to the photographer's nonsense. He texts me as I'm styling my hair and says to meet him in the lobby. Unsure if that's a good sign or bad, I find him smiling and milling by the front desk in deep conversation about video game tactics with a bellman he introduces as Charlie.

The ruddy-faced ginger stares in wonder at my hair. "Your curls are bonza, girl. Are they real?"

"Aren't they dope?" Chavez twirls his finger into one ringlet, his grin telling me he has moved on from the earlier moody sideshow. He's rolled the cuffs back on his pin-striped dress shirt exactly twice, and a gold cross, hanging on a thin chain and just visible on his bronzed pecs, makes all my unchristian thoughts hard to ignore. "Charlie's got us lined up at the best steak house in town," he explains. "I hope you're hungry."

In LA, a decent hunk of Wagyu beef in a restaurant comes with a month-long waiting list. And all for the privilege of paying stratospheric prices served with a side dish of waiter attitude and a wine list intent on bankrupting you. But instead of being filled to the rafters with poseurs, the Woodhouse in downtown Bendigo barely seats thirty and is as unpretentious as it gets. A waitress greets us like we are family, and I marvel at how Chavez has everyone effortlessly wrapped around his finger.

"I'm always tight with the bell guys," he says, once we're seated. "They steer me right. Concierge just dumps you into every tourist trap."

His sweet young face makes me forget he's spent the better part of a decade traveling the world. I forget a lot of things when he's in front of me.

We both order filet mignon, and I'm warm and fuzzy from the meal and the huge pour of Shiraz by the time our plates are cleared. Our waitress has recommended an ice cream shop for dessert, and we're waiting for the bill to arrive when a guy I noticed earlier sidles up to our table. He and his generically handsome buddies sat kitty-corner from us, and they kept eyeing our table with furtive whispers. This lucky one got egged into being the sacrificial lamb.

"Hey," he says. "I don't mean to interrupt, but are you Chavez Delgado?"

"Yeah," he replies, polite but not thrilled with the intrusion. "That's me."

"Uhm … we're, ah, playing each other in the first round. Peter Kingsley?"

Poor thing, fidgeting with his hands and an uneasy smile on his face. Meek as a mouse and tall and gangly in off-the-rack dress pants that don't quite fit, pimples streaked across his chin like white braille.

"Hey, man. Look forward to the match." Chavez holds up his fist for a bump and the gesture flatfoots Peter, who looks to his pals to make sure they are witnessing this before bumping back.

"I just wanted to say I'm glad you're back. Tennis needs more guys like you."

Chavez lifts his water glass as a toast. "Appreciate you saying that."

The kid obviously has more to say but is floundering big-time with a starstruck tongue. "This probably sounds totally dumb, but is there, like, any advice you can give me? My goal is to be top one hundred next year."

It's the kind of comment some players would cringe at, but Chavez plays it the right way. "Never give up and always believe in yourself." He looks at me and winks. "And find the right team."

"Oh, yeah, hi," Peter says as if he's just noticed me. "Uhm, okay. Thanks. Well, see you around."

He hurries back to his buddies who pepper him with hushed questions.

"That was kind of you," I say to Chavez. "You probably made his night."

"We're all warriors trying to make it happen," he says, as our bill arrives. "But let's get out of here before he asks for help improving his serve."

We join the strolling summer crowds and treat ourselves to artisanal scoops of fat-filled goodness. Dusk is two hours away, but the light is incredible, the city drenched in the gold of magic hour. We munch the last of our cones sitting on a bench in a small plaza, and Chavez slips his arm around my shoulder like it's the most natural thing.

He plays absently with my curls and then asks, "Everything all right in your world, Miss Flynn?"

"Why wouldn't it be?"

"Should I not kiss you in public?"

Oh, shit.

"Kissing me wasn't the problem."

"So there was a problem."

He glances at me, and I feel a wave of nausea, no desire to be picked apart. "No," I insist. "I mean, sorry, the wrong choice of words."

Jeez. The princess of lies conducting herself in high style, yet again. And as if it isn't obvious with all my limbs cranked tight like a pretzel. After a sticky silence, he caresses my bare kneecap with slow, lazy circles.

"I realize this all went down pretty quickly," he says. "You've mentioned a few times how you like to feel safe, and then you jump on a plane to fly halfway around the world with a stranger. That's very unsafe." The pools of his eyes are hypnotically blue as they intently search mine. "I just wanted to say, no matter what happens, I want you to feel safe with me. Around me. Let me know what you need to make that happen, all right?"

He reaches for my hand, interlaces our fingers together and, oh my God, how do I not cry right now? How do I not collapse into his arms and tell him that is hands down the sweetest thing a guy has ever said to me?

"Look at me Flynn," he murmurs, a fingertip on my far cheek steering me to his wish. His hair, normally black as boot polish, gleams like it's been washed with diamond dust.

"What?"

"You've got something on your lips."

Perfect. Here I am believing my world can somehow be right again and all he sees is the spinach clinging to my lip. I cuff my mouth and ask, "How long has it been there?"

"Not long enough."

His lips land open on mine, both our mouths cool from dessert but eager and hot to get on with it. I can't believe I fell for his trick, but I forgive him. The sweet chocolate on his tongue mingles with the salted caramel on mine, and I soar into the stratosphere, gravity leaving my body. He probes and teases and my brain screams, *yes, yes, yes*. Yes to him being handsy and me dissolving into nothing. Yes to the exotic world of his spicy cologne where we're in Marrakesh on a pile of satin pillows and not on a hard bench in an outpost plaza going to town on each other.

You never know enough about yourself until you lose control, and we're flat-out going in that direction when he suddenly breaks our kiss, leaving me blinded by the setting sun blazing nuclear gold.

"What … Why are you always stopping?" I ask.

I'm on system overload, practically shooting sparks, panting as if I sprinted around the block. Our drastic level of PDA has drawn a lovelorn look from a mother pushing noisy triplets in a stroller who looks ready to ditch them for a three-way with us if we say the word.

Chavez, also breathing hard, rearranges his mussed hair. "I have a proposition for you."

"A proposition?"

His eyes are open wide, shining with delight, but that doesn't sound encouraging.

"Your books got me thinking about goals and rewards. How important they are to achievement."

Crap. I'm pretty sure I know what's coming. "So…"

"So, after I win my first tournament, my reward will be you and me sleeping together."

My stomach sinks. I knew it. "I haven't agreed to anything beyond this tournament," I remind him.

"I know," he says, working the smile. "That's your motivation to make sure I win."

"But what if you don't win?"

He leans forward, chuckling, elbows coming to rest on his legs splayed wide to give me a bird's eye view of the bulge in his dark denim. "That's not very coach-like."

I cross my arms and slump against the bench. There was a single, obvious path here, and we didn't have to drive far to start making our way down it.

"That's not very fair," I say.

"You took advantage of me and then cut and run," he replies. "Was that fair?"

"You didn't exactly tell me to stop," I point out.

"Can't stop a tornado now, can I?"

I might have created the template for anything goes, but I had no intention of grooming a protégé with the audacity to walk his fingers up my leg, onto my pelvis, and drum lightly above the goods in bold, broad view of downtown Bendigo. Yet I do nothing to stop him. I don't even trust myself to touch him. Not when the finish line was so close and then moved by a country mile. Moved clear across the country is what it feels like.

"What if you're runner-up?" I counter, hating myself for sounding so desperate.

"You're obsessed with my mouth, aren't you?" he asks, annoyingly changing the subject. "You keep staring at it."

"You have a great mouth," I admit, powerless just looking at it. .

"You ever wonder what it would feel like, traveling all over your body?"

His lips land like a velvet cushion between the swell of my breasts. Heat funnels into all my pulsating places, and a sharp little cry of bliss slips out. I lick my lips, trying to control the uncontrollable.

"Are you trying to give me a heart attack?"

"Do you want to see me win?"

He tugs on a curl, willing an answer out of me, his infuriatingly impish smile that of someone in total control. Discipline shapes your destiny is Flynn Dryden's Truth #4, and if winning means my mouth muzzled by a pillow, and his *FEARLESS* fingers sinking deep into my flesh, and that glorious butt pumping deeply, I will spend two hundred hours on the court to make it happen. Maybe three hundred.

And it's written all over my face.

Why else would Chavez tap my knee with his hand like a father encouraging a daughter to chase her dreams?

"Get me over the finish line, Miss Flynn, and I'm all yours."

Chapter Fourteen

THE NEXT MORNING STARTS CURLED UP IN BED WITH A SENSE OF madness drifting in. Why did Chavez have to go and make things more complicated? If he wanted to dispense payback for Brandon and my little on-court stunt, fine. But this? Grind out the entire tournament with the possibility of nada? I chew on a nail and wonder for the tenth time if this is remotely healthy. It alarms me how badly I want him. He does all the right things and even better, all the wrong things. The only way to get through this test of mettle is to concentrate on the small things.

The big picture is too difficult to comprehend.

My phone starts to vibrate on the nightstand, the ringer off, and I groan under the covers. It's too early, Chavez. Let me sleep. But I am playing with fire if I ignore him. I grope blindly on the nightstand for the phone, lift my eye mask, and squint at the screen wondering what aggravation he will serve up today. When I see the number, it snuffs out any joy from the morning. Nathaniel, hot on my heels like ants at a picnic, needs an answer. What I know about screenwriting can fit on the head of a pin and writing a textbook on string theory is more appealing than watching my life story unspool on the screen.

Then tell him.

I plump a pillow behind my head and my aching muscles scream in protest. "Hi."

"Did you get my FedEx?" he asks.

"I'm doing fine thanks. How are you? And yes, I did get it."

The envelope arrived the morning we left for Australia. Within it was another envelope, red as blood, and I was too nervous to open it. Last year he sent me a diamond tennis bracelet, and I found out he'd never bought his wife jewelry when she admired the glittering band on my wrist at their Labor Day gala. I half-expected Nathaniel to go over the top again—a stock certificate for a thousand shares of Apple perhaps—but he stooped low instead. The digital redemption code for my very own copy of the Final Draft screenwriting software is still crumpled in a ball and collecting dust in the corner of my kitchen, unless the maid recycled it.

He takes a puff of his pipe. "Not even a thank you?"

"I've been busy, believe it or not."

"That's a good sign, right? Not curled up in a dark corner, crying and fighting demons?"

He found me bawling in his boardroom last December, when the pressure of Christmas and the stalker, round one, had broken me. He did the gentlemanly thing and offered me a Xanax with a vodka chaser and a shoulder to cry on, but I should have known better than to reveal everything. Nathaniel files weaknesses away to deploy them against you when you least expect it.

"I decided I needed some sun."

"You live in a desert. How much more sun do you need?"

Oh, God. Here we go. Just say it. It's your life, not his.

"I met someone, and he invited me to Australia. I'm Down Under for the next two weeks. It's nine in the morning and I have to run," I lie. "I'm late for breakfast."

The number of times I've gone off the rails and done something completely whack? Exactly never. But leave it to Nathaniel to motor on like a life-altering decision of mine doesn't require any follow-up.

"I need to get back to Amazon with a yes or a no, sugar. Come on, I can get you six figures. Maybe seven."

I shut my eyes. Feel the pressure build in my temples. This is where I crack. The bright-eyed twenty-one-year-old who queried the overlord of non-fiction, who's been yanking my chain ever since. It's time for all gas, no brakes.

"It's a no, Nathaniel."

Pin-drop silence. The kind you might hear in heaven during nap time. Or at my funeral, which I might be forecasting, the longer he says nothing.

"Who is this guy?" he finally demands, as if another male could ever measure up to his 5'10" white-flab supremacy. "Maybe he's only after you for your money."

"Maybe he likes me for who I am."

"*I* like you for who you are."

"Maybe you like me because I make *you* money."

I sit up, dragging the sheet higher to cover me. He's ten thousand miles away and still manages to make me feel exposed.

"Since when did you become an ungrateful bitch?" he snivels.

Wow. A little pushback and here come the dirty gloves. I've seen and heard this side of him, but only when we've been on the same side of the negotiation table. Mr. Ice-in-the-Veins steamrolling hapless publishers like a RAM TRX screaming down on a Smart car. I considered switching agents last year after the same Labor Day gala when his wife made a play for me and he laughed off my discomfort, shoving another glass of champagne in my hand and telling me to loosen up.

"Thanks for that vote of confidence. I don't care if the Amazon deal comes with a crown. My answer is still no, and I'm officially going off grid. Don't call me, I'll call you."

"Flin Flon," he says in that threatening tone he pulls out as a last resort. "You won't be in demand forever. Don't shoot yourself in the foot over a cock. You will regret it."

Says the man who met his wife by plucking a set of keys out of a bowl at a swinger party. Good grief. Has he no shame? I probably shouldn't have hung up on him without saying goodbye, but I did. Instead of the, W*hat the hell did I do,* scaries eating me alive, Nathaniel vanquished leaves me sitting in the dark with a smile forming. I am legendarily bad at sticking up for myself with him, but maybe Chavez and his attitude are rubbing off on me. And his ears must be burning because he is already up and texting me.

CD: Morning mamacita. Coffee?

He's got balls. Mr. Business as usual. Like I'm not dying here.

FD: Hi.

FD: Yes, please.

CD: Meet downstairs in twenty?

FD: Thirty. I just woke up.

CD: Don't be late.

By the time I've showered and thrown on some clothes, I have the ultimate revenge planned. Today we work on serve and return, and Chavez will eat a hundred short and wide ones until he is blue in the face. Ready, and with a spring in my step, Coach Flynn heads for the elevator with my nose buried in a raging Reddit debate over mothers who steal their daughters' boyfriends. When the car arrives, I step inside without looking up.

"Flynn. What a pleasure."

Oh, shit. I pocket my phone and fake a smile. "Hi, Brandon. How are you?"

"Lucky, considering I'm riding the elevator with the prettiest woman this side of Texas."

His accent strips some of the cheese from that stinker line, but he has the good senses to blush because it's still dreadful. "Gosh," he says. "My apologies. That is one of the worse lines ever."

"I've heard worse," I admit.

And I've seen worse—unless Brandon meant to impersonate a Boy Scout today. I can give the bandana knotted around his neck and belted khaki shorts a pass, but if Vandana were here to witness the sandals and socks combo, she'd be throwing up a little in her mouth. The overpowering scent of his Irish Spring soap makes my eyes water, and as the elevator car hums lower, he leans against the glass panel with both hands sliding into his pockets. His casual stance contrasts with how alert he is—focused on me like a laser beam.

"Are you Flynn Dryden, the author?"

Every tiny hair on the back of my neck stands at attention. I'm acutely aware he knows the answer to his question. "Yes."

"I thought so. My ex read all of your books. I'm more of a sci-fi guy, but you look just like your photo. Very beautiful."

The air is stagnant and hot, and I shuffle as far away from Brandon as the tiny space allows.

"It's the curls," I say. "Hard to miss."

He winks back. "Impossible to hide with that hair."

I try to pick apart his smile, wondering if there is more to it than meets the eye. In another world, I might have dated him. He's the clean-cut corporate type I swing to now and again when I'm out of favor with the rocker dudes that usually gravitate to me.

"I fly back to the States on Friday," he continues. "Call me if you want to grab that coffee or have a hankering for something stronger."

He flips open his phone case to hand me another card, and I pause, every bone in my body screaming, *don't*. Just as I do, the elevator stops, the doors open, and Chavez stands in the hall. The scorch of his eyes falls on me, and I feel stupid. My face glows with it. Chavez steps inside, rips the card out of my hand, and faces Brandon. The vibration in the air turns murderous.

"You again."

Brandon eyes him coolly. "We are staying in the same hotel."

"And some of us are staying in the same room."

Chavez snakes an arm around my waist, and Brandon looks at me with genuine surprise. Without a word, he asks me if this is true, and my silence is tacit confirmation, albeit another lie.

Brandon clears his throat. "Pardon me. I didn't know y'all are together, together."

"We are very together," Chavez says. "And I'd appreciate it if you respect that and keep your distance, all right?"

I feel an itch of sweat at the small of my spine. By now, Brandon must know Chavez is one of those slightly dangerous types. If he pushes his luck, I can't be held responsible.

"Public spaces are just that, Mr. Delgado," Brandon finally says. "You don't control them, and neither do I."

He squares himself to face the doors—the ultimate fuck-you gesture—and time seems to go backward, dragging on indefinitely as we descend. Brandon and his mocking tone were a little over the top, but Chavez and his posturing were too. Underneath his machismo, however, lies a protective tenderness. And that is what makes my throat gather. I wasn't sure if the desire in his eyes last night had more to do with winning than with me.

That being said, the lobby can't come fast enough.

I'm coiled like a spring and ready to bounce when the doors open, but Chavez keeps his arm locked around me and holds us back until Brandon has exited the car. He takes off without a word or a glance back, and I feel guilty for not saying something to smooth things over. After we exit, Chavez chucks the business card into a nearby trash can.

"That naco is an absolute creeper," he mutters. "You can't trust a dude who irons his socks."

"They were very white and smooth," I admit. "But in the future, you don't have to be such a hard-ass. Remember, I'm here because of you."

The look on his face tells me it doesn't work that way with him. He is all bite *and* bark. "Promise me you will not talk to him again. Even in a public space," he adds, mocking Brandon's drawl.

"You don't have to worry," I insist. "I have zero interest in him."

"I need you to promise me."

I side-step out of the way as guests pour out of the second elevator and stream past us, but Chavez remains where he is, unfazed by the bumps and jostles. His belief is just as steadfast that he can force this issue, but I am not comfortable agreeing to anything that might serve as a dangerous precedent.

"Does this mean I can't talk to any man?"

"No," he says, trying for casual when, in fact, he means just that. "Let's start with him, all right? You're testing me, analyzing my strokes, my mind, all in the name of becoming stronger and better. Maybe I'm doing the same."

"If you are so worried about my numbers going up this week, you can tell a certain someone that he might want to adjust his strategy."

"Nice try, Miss Flynn," he says. "My strategy will not change, so keep your eye on the prize."

His smile reinstates—blazing white and assured, charm cranked up at an eleven. If I'd hoped to find a chink in his armour, #spectacularfail.

Chapter Fifteen

I KNEW IT WOULD HAPPEN. I FELT IT IN MY BONES. AS SURE AS THE SUN rises in the east and scum floats to the surface, gossip finds a way to slither front and center. Had I discovered the picture of Chavez and me kissing on some random website instead of accompanying a text message, I would not be clutching the bathroom counter with my faint tan turning white.

Unknown number: Flynn! What are you doing with a brown boy in Australia??? Do I need to bring you home?

Fuck. What a fool to think I had bought time and space traveling here. Not when technology has shrunken us into trackable bits and bytes so easily found and shared. This loser has tracked me, and I can only imagine what's next. Is he going to show up at the tournament waving a gun? Not knowing his capabilities is like facing a firing squad full of itchy trigger fingers. I run the tap and splash cold water on my face, my mind racing. I cannot breathe a word of this to Chavez. If he can barely control the urge to punch Brandon in the face, the reaction over this would be nothing short of ominous.

He cannot be distracted.

Today is round one, his first match, and on paper, everything favors Chavez over Peter Kingsley. He is a more experienced and talented player. In reality, all that means nothing because no match is a give-away—especially with the pressure of being the comeback kid. Surprisingly, he didn't cop to any feelings of anxiousness last night.

Maybe I've finally beat the Tornado out of him.

As Rodrigo warned, he has not been easy. Yes, he's focused like a bird dog tracking its prey, but he resists every time I suggest a tweak or a different approach. We had it out yesterday after a discussion surrounding on-court coaching during his matches. A recent overhaul in the rules means I can talk to him when he is on my side of the court and give hand signals when he is on the far side. The only caveat: he is not allowed to talk or signal back. He never let Rodrigo coach him on-court and has no interest in starting now.

"I know what I need to do," he argued. "I know my mistakes."

"What if I notice something you are oblivious to?" I tossed back.

He laughed in my face. "The likelihood of me not noticing is slim to none."

"Why am I here if you're just going to do the same old, same old? Let me put it this way. If I think you are employing the wrong tactics, you will hear about it."

He stormed off the court, refusing to return. I chased him down and said being a baby about things wasn't helping him.

He yelled, "I'm not a baby!"

And I shouted back, "You want a second opinion on that?"

The atmosphere in the shuttle van back to the hotel felt as welcoming as Saturn's. And leave it to Chavez to know how to hit back.

Instead of being a grouch, he flirted shamelessly at dinner, and we ended up slammed against his hotel room door making out in the hall like the world was burning down and we owned the only hazmat suits in town. Bodies and hearts crashed together, my hands slid down the back of his jeans to squeeze his divine butt as hopeless lust jolted my nether regions into a twanging mess. I thought he would finally open his damn door and spread me wide. But instead, he yanked my blouse open like a savage. A button popped off, and neither of us was that interested to see where it landed because my nipple had to be taught a lesson for being too perky.

Or rather, I had to be taught a lesson.

He sent me on my way minutes later, his whip girl with her panties drenched and imagination flying out of control.

But if he thought that was all it would take to tip the scales in his favor, he's got another thing coming. He might be gifted in the fine art of seduction, but I plan to unwrap him with such ferocity that the poor boy won't know what hit him. He will submit to every indecency I demand. The only hiccup is he needs to win; ergo, no distractions.

And I need to be something other than a bundle of nerves to make that happen.

We leave for the tournament in an hour, and I can already tell the anxiety jangling through me will feed into everything I do. I jump into the shower, determined to solve the stalker riddle. The workaround finally comes to me in fits and spurts, and the longer I dwell on it, the more perfectly the idea forms. By the time my skin is scalded and soaped, I have it nailed.

Chavez and I have not talked about the upcoming European tournaments he will be playing (or if I will join him), but what a great way to throw this goon off the track. If there is such a thing as a stalker who can jump on a plane and make my life hell anywhere in the world, if he really wants to play a game, I'm throwing down Catch Me if You Can.

Flynn Dryden Truth #5: Stay one step ahead of your fears.

While we kill time in the lobby waiting for the tournament shuttle, Chavez apologizes for being curt at breakfast. His mother called earlier, and the conversation did not go well. She came across our infamous photo and was near apoplectic with distress. Chavez danced around the details like a henpecked son would, but I deduced the gist of her complaints could be absolved by him finding a good,

Catholic Mexican woman who understood marriage and childbearing instead of one who flies around the world in sporting sin.

Despite the strides I thought I'd made with Gloria, the real reason behind her call has everything to do with the conversation she and I had in her kitchen while I helped tidy up after brunch. She asked if I wanted kids. My clever reply of, *Not yet,* usually saves my bacon. Those two words are the ultimate non-answer. Mothers believe it is only a matter of time until I swaddle a babe in my arms and my single sisters are like, damn right, Flynn, we can have it all without having a family. My position on the matter is not in a million years will I ever have children, and her shyster radar screamed imposter as she handed me a platter to dry.

"I guess you were right about that photographer," Chavez admits with a sheepish look. "I'll be more discrete from now on."

"Please put it out of your mind. It is what it is, and there are a hundred other things you should be focusing on."

He shoots me a doubtful glance. "Of course I'm thinking about it. You didn't feel comfortable, and now we are front-page news."

While I appreciate him acknowledging the circumstances, my immediate concern is how he will cope with today. His leg has been shimmying all morning and pacing around the lobby hasn't helped. The buzz in the hotel is on the upswing, and I feel the electricity of competition crackling on my skin. I wish I had eaten more at breakfast, but we both pushed food around on our plates like day one of a hunger strike.

Finally, the shuttle arrives. It's one hundred degrees in the shade and getting hotter, and dampness spreads under my arms despite wearing the least amount of fabric possible while remaining decent. Vandana encouraged me to glam it up, but my silk mini dress might become see-through if I sweat much harder. I glance at Chavez—at the muscle twitching along his jaw, his leg still pumping, the dark shadows under both eyes. It's crunch time. I think I am more nervous than him (if that is humanly possible). But stalker, or no stalker, I signed up to ensure he makes it to the end of this week. And for my own selfish reasons, let me repeat—I cannot have him distracted.

So, when our driver pulls into the roundabout of the venue, Coach Flynn makes the game plan abundantly clear.

"Let's go kick some ass."

THE MORAL OF THE STORY IS: NEVER UNDERESTIMATE THE TALL AND pimply. I mistakenly assumed Peter Kingsley would be a wet noodle Chavez would flay the court with, but the kid has done his homework. Two unreturnable short and wide serves are his opening one-two shots, and Chavez, the bonehead, does not adjust his service position as we discussed. When they switch ends for the second service game, I might as well be talking to myself. That's how defiant his ignoring of me is. He refuses to catch my gaze during the changeover when he's down 3-0, and the murmurs from the boozy crowd are of the upset variety. No one here saw a future for Peter other than he'd be pushing forty at a cocktail party and telling anyone who would listen he once played Chavez Delgado.

By the time Chavez claws his way into a first-set tiebreak, I'm losing my mind. He's displayed flashes of brilliance but tightened up on rudimentary shots or gone hog wild with overcooked forehands. On set point for Peter, I clench the fencing in front of me so tightly all the blood drains from my fingers. Everyone and their uncle know what serve Peter will pull from his repertoire. Everyone save for Chavez, who is stubbornly six feet beyond the baseline and still pretending I don't exist.

We went over and over these scenarios during practice, especially how not to succumb to old sticky habits in the heat of the moment. I know he doesn't want to hear from me but screw it.

Loud enough so he can hear, I shout, "If you're going to stay there, be ready in case he mixes it up."

Peter, for all his talent, has not perfected the disguise toss. Instead of a straight-up ball toss for every serve, he, being a right-handed player, tosses it slightly to his left for the kick serve in the AD court. In the split second before Peter's racket makes contact with the ball, Chavez reads it and moves left. He rockets it back straight down the middle of the court, and Peter, still recovering from the service motion, is caught flatfooted, the ball skidding past him. Set point saved. I feel the thunderous applause like a physical thing vibrating on my skin. With a freshness that only confidence can instill, Chavez cracks two back-to-back aces, and the first set is in the can. He whips around to look me straight in the eye and bashes his hand against his heart.

"Who's your daddy?" he yells.

The capacity crowd goes berserk.

It's all one-way traffic after that. Chavez kicks into a higher gear, and to witness the arsenal of his shot-making is like watching Jackson Pollock splatter paint—beauty created on a different kind of canvas. He closes it out with a sublime shoelace volley that dies like a lump of coal on the other side of the net. The collective nail-biting explodes into cheering that would wake the dead, and the metal grandstand shudders under the weight of a thousand fans rising to their feet.

Chavez and Peter exchange a few words and embrace warmly at the net, and the sportsmanship at the end of the match is one of my favorite things about tennis. No matter how tense and furious it gets, when it's all over, win or lose, it's the person on the other side of the net who makes it memorable. The fans wait for Chavez to shake hands with the umpire and roll into his post-match victory lap—the raising of a fist to the four sides of the court—but he chucks his racket to his bench instead, points directly at me and lays a hand on his heart while mouthing, *Thank you.*

After ghosting me the entire match, the emotion on his face, directed at me, unleashes all the nervous energy swarming under my skin. Relief flows out of me like a river. I've been here before and know how it feels, the baby steps toward bigger and better. Fans who realize that I'm part of the Chavez entourage offer congratulations, and tears well in my eyes at how heartfelt their words are.

And if I'm being honest with myself, my tears are not only for Chavez. They are also for my tennis career, cut short in its prime. Who knows if I would have reached the pinnacle, and I feel my chest tighten thinking about what might have been. But I tamp down the memories and tell myself, *No, don't go there*. Chavez is different, I am different, and the situation is different.

There will be no trouble.

But after his on-court interview, Chavez walks off the court without a glance back, and the feathering starts deep in my throat. On the day Hamilton told me he never wanted to see me again, he rolled his wheelchair down the aisle at Safeway, retreating from me without a glance back.

And one week later, on Christmas Day, he rolled himself off a cliff.

Chapter Sixteen

After his first-round win, I notice subtle but positive changes in Chavez. He is less stubborn and more relaxed with himself on the court. He's agreed to on-court coaching in small doses. His doing well here is no indication of success on the main tour where the competition is one notch fiercer. But with his game starting to shine again, who am I to complain? As a coach, I can't ask for anything more.

As a woman with needs, I could ask for a whole lot more.

But his answer to my not-so-subtle soliciting is still *Nope*. I'm reduced to another lusting female fan alone in bed at night, adding to the emoji meltdowns on the shirtless photos he posts on social media. (Photos I take that he asks me to send him! #unfair.)

Since he always makes sure my coffee has the right amount of cream and holds every door open for me, I pick my battles. Momentum and confidence can turn around a slump faster than anything, and with both flying high, Chavez storms through the draw to book his spot in the final.

On the morning of, we slug it out on the practice court and the mood is totally off. I thought we made progress all week with the mantras and visualizations to help quell the nagging voice in his head, but he is twitchy and quick to anger with every botched shot. He starts serving and overcooks ten in a row. From his look of utter disgust, I sense the explosion coming. If you have never witnessed the destruction of a racket, the way it crumples is pretty impressive. After Chavez punts the mangled remains to the sidelines, I call a time-out.

He slumps onto the bench and hangs his head, refusing to look at me as I sit beside him. I rub the small of his back, keeping an eye on the crowds in the bleachers. The stalker has not sent anything since the photo incident, but I am always watching.

"You want to talk about it or just sulk in perpetuity?" I ask.

"Don't joke around, Miss Flynn," he warns. "Today is no laughing matter."

"Remember what I said the other day? I can't help if I don't know what's going on in your mind."

"Can I blow up my mind?"

"The day after you win, you can do whatever you want."

He glances up to catch my small smile. "You have a one-track mind."

"Win-win, right?"

Despite my joke, a storm swirls in his eyes. Something is going on. "Let's go get some breakfast, all right?"

INSTEAD OF EATING AT THE TENNIS CENTRE, WE CRAM OURSELVES INTO a booth at a nearby diner. The frazzled, young waitress juggles plates and customer demands and surprises us with steaming lattes turned around in record time. Chavez blows on his coffee, his face an unreadable mask. He wanted us to sit side by side, and his body, flush with mine in the tight space, radiates heat like a furnace.

"It's not your mother again is it?" I ask, careful to sound neutral. I can see the battle raging inside of him.

"Yes and no," he says, spinning his mug on the table. "I never told you about this because I hoped it would all be over, but she got injured on the job last May. It's been an endless battle with that asshole Earl ever since."

I draw back, my eyes widening. "That's awful. Is that why she has a limp?"

"Yeah. Her leg got crushed in a machine that needed repairing. She'll never walk properly again."

Chavez explains he found out about her accident the morning of the infamous ball-smashing incident at Roland Garros. He burned it home on the first flight he could get and left a trail of smoking rubber northbound on the 5 freeway to Fresno. He stormed his way into Westar and came this close to being arrested after spewing multiple threats into Earl's face. I have witnessed his bullying behavior, but it's still shocking to hear that he bulldozed his parents out of Fresno lock, stock, and barrel and planted them in Echo Park. Chavez threatened to take Earl out for good (as any sane and loving son would) if they ever double-crossed him, and I'm not surprised Gloria and Rodrigo took his word for it.

"I'm sorry to hear that." I touch his thigh to comfort him. "What is happening now?"

"Earl refuses to pay out," he continues, "so we hired a lawyer to fight back."

"Is it looking good?"

The waitress appears with our breakfast specials, and we move our phones and mugs to make space on the scuffed tabletop. Once she leaves, he picks up where we left off.

"We thought so, but the lawyer emailed me this morning and said Earl has railroaded several employees into corroborating his version of the story. That the accident was Mama's negligence. He's threatened wage cuts and narcing out families who have illegals living with them." The sharp edge in his voice turns steely. "What kind of a monster do you have to be to create this much fear?"

I reach for his fist, balled tightly on the table. He looks absolutely gutted.

"I don't know what to say. I wish there were something positive to channel from this."

"There is no positive with Earl," he scowls. "He's a fucking bitter soul, hell-bent on being a bitch just because he can. The settlement money means nothing because I will always look after my parents, but it's the principle. He needs to do the right thing and won't because of me."

He stabs at his eggs without eating them and then gives up on breakfast entirely, letting his fork clatter onto the table. This is the worst timing for bad news. The last thing he needs is Earl back in his head for the final.

"Do you want go back to the hotel and work through this?" I ask. "We have time."

He glances distractedly at an incoming message on his phone and slides a finger over it to make it disappear. "I have to deal with some-thing before the match. I'll be back in an hour."

I glance at him, dumbfounded. "What? Where are you going? What about your food?"

"It's all good," he insists, clocking the look of worry on my face. "Nothing weird. And I'm not really that hungry. But you finish up."

"Anything I can do to help?" Uncertainty bubbles deep in the pit of my stomach. What errand can't wait on the afternoon of the final?

He tucks a crumpled fifty-dollar bill under his mug. "This will help me clear my head. I promise."

"How do you feel about today, in general?"

He should be fresh after his relatively easy wins. But what I'm feeling is a whole other story as Chavez studies me with his turquoise pupils. I believe June gets credit for coining the term *whoretex*— a sensation where time has no meaning as you get sucked into the force field of a man you are crushing hard on. Chavez rolled out of bed this morning without shaving or combing his hair and is unfairly scrump-tious for making no effort. My nails are ratty gnawed nubs. Five pounds I can't afford to lose have been sweated away in the baking sun going toe-to-toe with him during practice. And the ripe smell tickling my nose is me, who forgot to put on deodorant this morning. But he still buries his fists in my hair and draws me in with a slow, controlled pull until our noses touch.

"I feel like I'm losing my mind," he whispers. "You are my only motivation. I don't know what I'm going to do if I don't win."

I swallow hard. Hear the thunder of my heart and feel the throbbing deep inside it. He's been rocking zen-level calm, resolute in keeping his commitment to waiting, to the point June likened me to a depreciable asset, losing value and interest every day. Now that he's voicing the same struggle that's keeping me awake at night, my fantasies take on a dangerous life of their own. All week I have dreamt of his nude cock and the sounds he might make when it slides into the dark wetness of my throat. I want him to whisper cheap and common dirty talk as I suck him off. Curse his mother in Spanish when his firm and flawless ass gets the life squeezed out of it. I want our sex to be like a dream, unreal and out of control.

And I want to kiss him forever, starting now.

Chavez obliges my fevered mouth as I annihilate any belief that tonight we do not share a date with destiny. My middle-class upbringing clearly states thou shalt not create an erotic disturbance in public but screw that noise and the horse it rode in on. A little Eggs Benny with a side order of smoking hot Latin love, and even Jesus might have changed his tune. He never felt the weight of a dark, spicy cologne sinking him into a black hole where time and reality blur. Never felt the weight of Chavez pushing him hard against a wall with an audible *smack*.

"Oh, shit," he says, our coffee breaths mingling together as he cradles my head. "Did I hurt you?"

My ability to feel anything over the dopamine crush is pretty much toast. This is the most physical contact we've had since his hotel room door escapade left me in tatters. His chest brushes the tender flesh of my breasts and I no longer care how desperate I sound.

"You need to win, Chavez. For both of us."

Behind the tall backing of our booth, the waitress has not noticed her customers down for the count and steaming up the windows. Chavez picks up his fork, his hand shaking ever so slightly, and spears one of the fat sausages on his plate, watching the grease erupt. He slices off a nub and brings it to my waiting parted lips, watching in fascination as my tongue curls around it to pop the salted knob of meat off the tines.

"Make a list of everything you want me to do to you," he says, "and I'll do my best to check off each one."

WORD IS OUT THAT THE TALENTED TORNADO IS BACK.

It is party central in the grandstands at two in the afternoon, and the rumble in the air is infectious. Everyone wants their brush with a big-name tennis star to be brag-worthy, and the fans are itching for a three-set slugfest, which they may very well get. Branko Silvo is a tricky opponent. I scouted the Argentine during the semis, and he reminds me of a slightly less imposing Juan Martin Del Potro with a well-rounded game of a top-fifty player, not an upstart ranked 182 in the world. He did not look pleased with the ear-splitting roar that greeted Chavez's appearance on the court—compared to the tinkle of polite applause for his own entrance. I am keeping a firm eye out. You never know what will inspire someone to play the match of their life.

But Chavez is ready. After his errand and a short nap, he says he is feeling it.

Here we go.

They start warming up, the usual ten minutes of getting limber and match ready. I try to channel my adrenaline and slow down my cranking heart. Compared to being a player, the nerves are far worse as a spectator, sitting inert on the edge of my seat. There is no outlet for me. Chavez gets to chop through his butterflies with every swing of his racket, and all I have is a fresh sparkle manicure that I hope is too pretty to gnaw on. The umpire quiets the rowdy crowd which reminds me to silence my phone so as not to be the idiot interrupting match point.

Chavez struts to the service line in his custom yellow Adidas ensemble and acknowledges me with a determined shake of his racket. It's a balmy ninety-five Fahrenheit, and tension radiates out of both players like the heat waves shimmering on Lake Weeroona in the distance. Chavez won the coin toss and elected to receive. The strategy behind receiving first instead of serving is the hope your opponent will nerve out and hand you the easy break. You never want to jinx or hex your opponent, even if you secretly hope they ate tainted shellfish the night before.

But there is no need to cast spells on Branko 182 because he crumbles all by himself. His four double faults to open the game carry the same foreboding tremor that a perky blonde creeping down the basement stairs in a slasher film does, and the bloodbath that follows makes D-day look like happy hour. One hour and three minutes later, the sea of shell-shocked faces in the bleachers silently admire Chavez as he muscles his fifteenth ace past his flailing opponent. The fans are nowhere close to being liquored up and Chavez is spreadeagled on the hard court in his most lopsided victory ever.

6-0, 6-0.

And that, folks, is what we call a double bagel.

The post-match ceremony, his heartfelt speech to an adoring crowd that will not stop cheering, the hand to his chest when he talks about me—it all speeds by like a bullet train. This is what we wanted, and I'll take my wee slice of the glory pie, but I'd be lying if I said my thoughts weren't elsewhere.

Good thing I made that list.

Chapter Seventeen

"HI, BEAUTIFUL. ARE YOU READY?"

Oh, Chavez. If you only knew how ready. "Any hints to drop?" I ask.

"Nope. I'll be there in five."

I slam what's left of my mini-bar vodka and take a deep breath to grit out the final few minutes. It's only seven p.m. with the sun is still in the sky, but it feels like I've been waiting all night. The post-match hullaballoo—interviews, doping tests, massage, and photo ops—took longer than the damn match, and Chavez has tested my patience again, taking his sweet time in his room. Of course, take a breather, shower, and bask in the glory of your win etc. But come on already! He has something planned, I know that much. But at this point, I don't care if he waltzes in here with a bottle of Fireball as a cheap seduction ploy.

Someone needs the nervous energy pounded out of her.

The emotional roller coaster of today whipped me one last time an hour ago when my stalker buddy decided to reappear.

Unknown number: You can do better than him, Flynn. You are better than the browns.

The police drilled the fear of God into me last year and said I should never reply, but I've had enough of the intrusion. The nerve of this idiot and his infiltration into my mind. And the fact he's also a racist loser.

Sometimes you have to bully the bully.

FD: Get a life and leave me alone!

Fortified with liquid courage, I hit send and blocked his number. Between conquering Nathaniel and blitzing the stalker fool, I felt a weight lift off my shoulders.

And no better moment for a reset.

Many questions need answering tonight, including what happens next. Chavez did not book us return trips to LA because of superstition. (No chance to win the tournament if you're mentally on a plane home, is how he put it.) But we're done in Oz, so the next step is a plane ride. Where we go and when we go requires discussion, but not before we violate each other. Only after he lays my body to waste will the agenda turn to talking.

Not a minute before.

Two sharp knocks sound on my door, and okay, my time has come. Deep breath. Final inventory.

Strapless dress with a convenient back zipper? Check. Curls hanging loose and wild? Oh yeah, just the way he likes them. Evening clutch jammed to the tits with condoms? (Vandana taught me well— always come prepared.)

Checkity check check check.

My confidence is rocking as I casually open the door.

Lord have mercy.

Vandana also said never to pounce on a guy like a mutt in heat, but all it takes to turn me into a rabid frothing mess is a simple black T-shirt, jeans, sneakers, and a smile so seductive Mona Lisa wants it back. Chavez inhabits another world beyond my understanding, not the hallway of a four-star hotel. His hair is damp and black as coal, the perfect dark frame to make his eyes shine a more brilliant blue. And those lips. Plump and succulent and soft. In one sordid flash, all the teasing kisses and tentative touches I imagined would start us off skid out into a gritty B-roll of Chavez peeling off my panties with his teeth.

"Don't you look amazing!" he says, crossing the threshold to kiss my cheek. He pauses and sniffs the sweet-sour alcohol fumes clinging to me. Lined up on the mini bar are the evening's dead soldiers. "Taking the edge off?" he teases.

He smells as I imagine a Roman orgy might—dirty musk, hot muscles, and debauchery. It goes straight to my head.

"Am I overdressed?" I ask, wobbling in my heels.

The way his eyes sweep over me is the official answer, but he reaches for my hand and says, "What we're wearing is the least important thing about tonight."

OUR UBER PASSES EVERY FANCY DOWNTOWN LOCATION I SUSPECTED might be our destination. Instead, we head south and rise out of the valley. Ten minutes later we are in a remote neighborhood where the land between mansions is five times larger than the houses themselves.

Chavez instructs the driver from the back seat. "It's the one on the right. With the gate."

A beautiful Victorian home painted a shade of deep plum sits at the rear of a grassy yard like a majestic king waiting for his supper. Tall, elegant windows bracket a colonnaded entrance kissed golden by the evening light. A hanging porch swing drifts in the breeze, and if I didn't know any better, I'd say we are in for an evening of weak tea and a fierce Scrabble battle with the local society matrons.

"What is this place?" I ask Chavez.

"It's Charlie's grandmother's house," he explains. "She runs it as an Airbnb but she's on vacation and left it empty. He said it would be perfect."

"Charlie the bellboy?"

"I told you, they never let me down. I said I was looking for a special place for a special night with a special woman." We exit the Uber, and once it reverses out of the drive, he wraps me in his arms. "This is where I went earlier. Had to put eyes on it to make sure it was worthy of you."

Embarrassment floods over me. This is where he went today? What a fool I was for thinking he had a hidden agenda. "Really? That's so romantic."

He laughs. "Don't sound so surprised. Come on." He eases out of our embrace to tug gently on my hand. "I'll show you around."

The house smells of antiques and furniture polish. Elaborate moldings trim the high ceiling and slow-spinning fans push hot air around. Up a creaky set of stairs curling to the second floor, and at the end of a narrow hallway, is the master suite. A massive brass canopy bed dominates the room, decorated in shades of mauve and glossy cream. French doors open onto a half-moon balcony, and we step outside to admire the eclectic mix of statues and aboriginal art in the formal backyard garden.

"Wow," I say. "This is incredible."

Chavez draws me close, cups my face in his hands, and devastates my mouth with his. I bloom under his touch, knees weakening with every coax of his tongue. When he breaks our kiss, it's with a special smile just for me.

"Charlie had some food delivered if you're hungry."

I giggle, giddy from the booze. "I should probably eat, but food isn't high on my list of priorities."

"Speaking of lists," he says, "that kiss was number one on mine. Thank you for everything."

"Will you listen to me on the court from now on?" I tease.

"Whatever you want to say tonight, I'm all ears."

I drape both arms across his shoulders and sway back and forth. He is so handsome, it's a joke. And the heady perfume of gardenias rising up from the garden mingles with his singular scent, creating havoc in my brain. "It starts with you getting very naked."

"Me?" He is not expecting that. "What about you?"

"How long do we have this place for?"

"How long is your list?"

"I'll have to unfurl it to count every item. Could take a while. Not sure I want to waste time when I already know what's number one on the list."

His hands slide down my arms and I relish the silky feeling of my skin coming to life. "Talk to me," he murmurs.

"I won't be able to talk."

He cocks a brow at my devious smile. "If that's where we're starting, round one is going to be over in five minutes."

A laugh slips out. "Five?"

"It's been a party of one in my room every night and I haven't made it past that mark yet."

"So you have been thinking of me."

My hands rake across the defined muscles of his upper back and slide lower until my palms cup the tight orbs of his ass. He returns the favor, grabbing my butt and tilting his hips to meet mine. A small breathless sound escapes my lips. Every inch of him feels so familiar, yet unfamiliar.

"Not a whole lot of thinking going on if you want the truth," he mumbles, his erection knocking impatiently on my Venus door. "How does the lady feel about a pre-show? A bump and grind to get her in the mood?"

I pull back to meet his eyes. "Are you offering me a strip tease?"

"This never leaves your lips, but a certain Fresno kid once daydreamed about being in a boy band."

"Shut up," I say, trying not to laugh. "Mini Backstreet Boy?"

"It's the truth," he says, not at all embarrassed. "I have some serious moves."

All week I've watched him dance on the court. Tease the crowds. He is a natural performer, and how perfect for him to offer a private show. I slip out of our embrace and sashay my way back inside.

"I'll be over there in the front row," I say, pointing at the bed. "I hope it's the splash zone."

I kick off my heels and sit on the end of the bed, letting my legs dangle. Chavez fiddles with his phone, scrolling for the tune of the hour. Behind him, the sky is a riot of colors against the ball of the sun dipping west. Satisfied with his musical selection, Chavez props the phone onto a chest of drawers and swings his arms around as if warming up to play. If he's nervous at all, he hides it well.

"This one's called 'Muy Tranquilo,'" he says. "Because you got me feeling anything but."

I'm putting money down that this room has hosted a fair share of hijinks over the centuries but has never born witness to something like this. A sexy Latin-inspired shuffle brought to life by a man who owns every move. Fuck me. Full bloom, no shame, he camps it up, gliding like a skater in his sports socks across the hardwood, slowly easing his T-shirt higher to flaunt washboard abs. Chavez makes a living from understanding contact points, and his hips flare right and left, hitting the beats in absolute smutty harmony. With every indecent figure eight of his hips, it's impossible not to imagine him as a nine-year-old, slim as spaghetti, working it to YouTube cranking in his bedroom.

I cheer him on with a wolf whistle and he pops his shirt off, swinging it overhead like a playoff towel. He lets it fly high and laughs at how eagerly I snatch it out of the air. His belt is next, the leather whipping off his slim waist with a loud *crack*. I've never joined the shrieking hordes at ladies' night—the appeal of gay men in firefighter uniforms is beyond me—and I never will with the Chavez show in nightly residence. Watching him peel off his clothes as if we have been together forever and not two weeks into knowing each other is a hundred times hotter.

And he is so into it.

Hands knitted behind his head, he boogies his way to the foot of the bed. I've dreamed in the darkness about my hungry hands and mouth free to wander over his skin, and having it all on display now, gyrating so fearlessly, is a singular pleasure so arousing, the indecency of my thoughts verge on crude.

"You have such a beautiful body," I mumble.

"I need some help here, señorita," he says. "These jeans won't unzip themselves."

He doesn't make it easy for me. A slave to the music, his hips slowly circle as I fumble with the zipper.

"There's something in the way," I point out, laughing.

He runs his hands over my curls with a, *You figure it out,* look. "It's only going to get bigger."

"Dammit. Hold still for *one* second."

He actually obeys me, and what I've only fantasized about gets released with one spirited yank. Cut by Donatello and bouncing hard off his balls, the full glory of him is the very definition of a masterpiece. I stare at the satin smoothness, my mind calibrating length, width, depth. Angles.

Some women think blowjobs are demeaning. (And for the dudes who like to slap their meat across our faces, news flash: that is not helping your cause.) I would never share my toothbrush with someone, and yet have no qualms swallowing the most private part of a man into my unhinged jaw. Perhaps it's about chasing intimacy that forever eludes me. By now, Dr. Bradford should have put it all together. Me in my mansion, my big car, surrounding my loneliness with space. But he can only work with what he's given, and I'm guilty of holding back. I never mention the string of one-night wonders and how the high they produce gives way to the inevitable low. The fear of rejection and loss is crippling and never facing those things is the only way I can survive.

The only way I have survived until now.

I look up at Chavez, backlit by the sinking sun. Hopeless desire overwhelms me, and I feel all the way open for the first time in years.

"Flynn, baby," he says, stroking himself in case I've forgotten what we came here for. "I'm all yours."

Chapter Eighteen

CHAVEZ

BEFORE TENNIS BECAME MY CALLING, I DID DREAM OF BOY BAND stardom and fine, judge me all you want. Everything is a stepping stone, and you gotta hop and jump from one to the next to figure out your path. According to Carmelita, a herd of yowling cats sounds better than my voice, but the lesson learned from dancing is that my body had to be in motion in whatever I pursued. Moving makes me feel alive.

And so does Flynn.

Now that my show is over, she is fingering my balls and driving me bananas with the wetness of her tongue. No one ever said Chavez hates control, and here I am trapped at the foot of the bed, jeans and briefs dropped halfway down my leg and praying to God for staying power.

She peeks up at me from under her sexy lashes and whispers, "This all right?"

"It's perfect," I grit out, five minutes a distant dream at this rate. "Just go."

Some guys might be all weird about a woman sleeping with more than fifty dudes, but there is something to be said for experience. Flynn knows the angles to make it happen just right and kneels to give herself the proper leverage. And my fucking Christ, when she deep throats me without warning, the master puts all the imitators to shame. The tip of my dick smashes against the soft palette of her throat, and I could be in any country, on any planet—the details are meaningless when I'm devolving into something less than human.

"Fuuuck!"

Usually, I have to take over, steer the ship, and mouth-fuck my way to the end. But Flynn is a bona fide natural with this job description. Right on the money with the desperate ass-clutching of a lady appreciating every inch of me. I got nothing else to do but shut my eyes and give in to the pleasure of her deep, dark, and greedy mouth. Let the ache of need fill my brain so I can forget the arithmetic nightmare of ranking points, and sets won or lost, and tournaments to play, and instead revel in the true miracle that a woman exists who has a blowjob as item number one on her list. Her dedication to finding the perfect rhythm is like me serving two hundred balls a day into the deuce court.

Dyson vacuums, you got some competition.

Not even clearing the one-minute mark, the countdown begins. The earth moves and the cosmos starts to shift. I'm breathless and dumbed down to the most guttural, base need. My nuts start to tighten with a load I'm not sure she's expecting.

And it's always good manners to ask.

"I'm almost there," I mutter. "You want me to—"

She wordlessly deep-sixes any more heresy flying out of my mouth by crushing my ass closer. And then ... Houston, we have a problem. Her fingers slide deep into my great divide, but we never established that anything in the rear is in the no-fly zone for me.

My cheeks jam up, and now what?

Shutting a woman down in the home stretch is like shooting yourself in the foot, and I can't even do that because I am frozen like a popsicle. She keeps working me over, pushing me to a place I have never been. The roar in my ears becomes deafening, and my lungs are on the verge of collapse. And then, if I needed any more proof that

Flynn has the power to propel me outside of my comfort zone, I let it happen.

Unclench, and say adios to my boundaries.

Fireworks lit and fizzing with frenzy, an unspeakable, unstoppable rip-snort of awakening blasts through me. The sensation is like nothing I've ever felt, and it blows my circuit breaker to hell.

And damn if she isn't there to take it all.

I WAKE UP TO A DARKENING SKY AND THE ETERNAL LIGHTNESS OF A naked Flynn spooning me. Her nipples kiss the skin on my back with every slow breath, and I remember how sweet those pink and creamy wonders tasted before we drifted off. She was a sneaky one, undressing to slip into bed when I showered and tried to make sense of the world. In need of a recharge after the physical day and her titanic takedown of my goods, I crawled under the covers to join her. Even though my eyelids felt like they had anvils hanging off them, it was inhumane to fall asleep without giving her a taste of my suckling powers. I promised her rounds two to infinity would be blockbusters, and we fell asleep on that pledge after I got rid of all the stupid frilly pillows cluttering up the bed.

Life isn't meant to be littered with useless or complicated shit.

Flynn is slowly becoming less complicated. She settled down after the weirdness with the photographer when we first arrived and there is no denying we make a good team. Her mental strength is right up there with her oral skills and who knew rekindling my inner mojo would be this off-the-charts amazing?

Flynn suddenly stirs to life behind me, as if my awakening telegraphed into her.

She circles a hot palm over one of my ass cheeks. "Hey, stranger. You awake?"

I logroll to face her and brush curls away to engulf her mouth with mine. Even her sleep breath tastes nice, not stale like Sofia's, who freaked out when I told her to rinse in the morning.

"How are you feeling?" I ask.

"Like a stick of melted butter."

Now you tell me, what beautiful creature says that when, last I recall, I was the spasming mess, and she was writing the book on how to breathe and swallow at the same time? She can't be real, and yet she is.

I slide my hand into the warm skin between her thighs. "Where do we go from here? Work you back up into a solid?"

"No," she says. "We work our way *down* the list."

"Was me making love to you in your top ten?"

She giggles and nibbles on my lower lip. "Number two."

We have the rest of the night to compare notes, but a few things on my list are guaranteed to match up with whatever remains on hers. What hadn't crossed my mind suddenly becomes clear when the curtains draped around the patio door billow out like a liquid ghost and the sweet, ripe scent of a summer night rides in with the breeze. I do some quick math. The width of the doors, the stupid size of this bed. And Charlie said the nearest neighbor is a deaf woman in bed at nine every night.

He was thinking ahead, that kid.

"How about this?" I ask. "I could push the bed onto the balcony and have you seeing stars in more ways than one."

Her eyes go wide. "Do it outside?"

"Or not. Your call."

She pushes up on both elbows to gaze out at the blue-black sky. The yard is desolation row with no moon and is smothered by a quietness that probably never goes away. As if she's stumbled onto the very reason that brought her here in the first place, she looks over with a smile that a less informed person might think unimportant but speaks volumes to me.

"I never imagined you were such a romantic," she says. "You are a gentleman *and* a gladiator."

The softest kiss brushes the tip of my nose and whatever is

holding me together right now disintegrates as she burrows closer. I should clutch her tightly and never let go, but genius me rolls onto his back because it's easier to lie in silence, shoulders touching, hands together under the covers, and listen to the call of some strange bird in the distance than fumble through my limited vocabulary only to find something that would fall short of what I really want to say.

When I do speak, the words stumble out after a hard swallow. "No one's ever called me a gentleman."

"It's a compliment," she says.

"I know."

Praise the Virgin for the dark, because I am too vulnerable right now for light and scrutiny. I stare up at the canopy, calculating what it will take to remove that dust-bunny party house without a million spiders crawling out of it.

"Have you given any thought to Europe?" she asks, out of the blue.

My heart skips a beat. All week I've wanted to ask, been too scared, and mentally started packing my bags alone. "You want to come along?"

"How would you feel if we flew from here to Italy?"

"Meaning, not go home?" I turn to face her because I am not trusting the cheap thrill rippling over my skin. Papa could never wait to jump on the first flight back.

"I don't need to if you don't."

In two weeks, Italy hosts the next Challenger event, and I plan to hit a couple more tournaments in France during February. If I post strong results and get some buzz going, the hope is Indian Wells or Miami (the two marquee ATP events in March) will offer me a wild-card entry. Then I'd crank it up during the spring clay court season for another shot at the Roland Garros crown. I would love her to be there with me, be with me every step of the way.

"And stay on the road until after France?" I ask. "A working vacation?"

She curls up like a snail and massages my leg under the covers. "I thought it would be great to keep the momentum going. With your game, and us. If we don't have to rush around, we can put a little more emphasis on the benefits part."

I'm so damn happy, swinging like an ape from the canopy might be my next move. When was the last time I had a real vacation with the warmth of a woman's body next to mine?

"And I can pay my own way," she adds. "I don't expect—"

"Hey," I interrupt. "Don't make this about money. Fair enough that you wanted to do this trial run pro bono, but if you're going to be my coach, you deserve to get paid. If only for putting up with me."

Ain't that the truth, is what her smile says. I am quick to cash this check before it bounces.

"I'm holding you to this, Miss Flynn. You can't change your mind."

Under the sheet, her warm fingers wrap around a vital piece of the puzzle. "I won't," she says. "My list is very, very long."

Ding-a-ling.

Round two is calling.

I can confirm those stories about people infused with superhuman strength in times of great emotional upheaval are more than an urban myth. Our Olympic-sized bed weighs more than a bus, and I move the sucker onto the balcony in under three minutes. I owe Charlie for the destroyed canopy, but Flynn seeing stars while I work her clit into triple overtime is my kind of priceless.

SOMEWHERE AROUND FOUR IN THE MORNING, WE CALL IT QUITS. POOR Flynn is the very definition of ridden hard and put to bed wet, and my ass muscles are screaming from the endless thrusting. God, she's fucking insatiable. I am in awe of how we read each other, the give and take. Guys aren't miracle workers; mastering the universe of how a woman works and what she wants is impossible without guidance. Even Galileo and Copernicus—the ancients who studied the sky—

they'd be like, stars and galaxies? No problem, we can tell you every-thing. Clit or pussy for the orgasm? Fuck if we know.

But Flynn is a true blessing. All I gotta do is slip her some tongue and away she goes. Hot little moans telling me how fast I'm getting her to ground zero, letting me work my skills. Not one of those pushy tour guides telling me to be here or there and taking all the fun out of it.

Let me rejoice in this magical moment—all my limbs electrified and body buzzing from sweet surrender.

The low industrial hum of the hotel's air conditioning kept me tossing and turning all week and it is surreally quiet out here with a dome of stars above us and the yard muffled in inky darkness. I cuddle into her softness, and she pulls the covers up and over our shoulders. She lays one hand on my head and keeps me secure like a babe against her breasts while her other weaves through my hair, massaging my scalp until I'm man down and moaning at how good it feels.

"You are my cielo. My sky," I whisper into her ear. "You make me feel limitless."

It's slight, but I feel it, how her body stiffens. And I'm thinking no, how could I be so stupid? Did I just Romeo and Juliet the situation with the sappy poetry of love-starved Shakespeare Chavez? The cardinal rule is that guys shouldn't talk for at least half an hour after sex because our brains are sloppy, sagging messes, like our dicks, and being in a pussy trance only leads to loose lips and babble, shit we regret. I might as well wrap this up with a red bow and ask her if she wants kids.

"I'm coming to Europe on one condition," she says.

I stop breathing and pray for absolution from my verbal diarrhea. "What's that?"

"None of this waiting around for you to win, okay?"

Aiy, Jesús! Thank you. My relieved smile spreads against her neck and she reads it the wrong way—puts just enough pressure on my head to say, careful cowboy.

"I'm serious. It's not happening any other way."

I have some witty remark about her not calling the shots, that we're on my time, all the usuals. But who am I fooling? Once in a blue moon, all the planets align perfectly, and you can't go wrong to save your soul. After tonight, there is no way I'm surviving, let alone hitting a single ball, without enjoying the daily wonders of Flynn's body. All I want to do is fall asleep and wake up in the morning sun to re-evaluate with a clear mind how I even got this far in life without her. Then I'm going to slowball her until she's liquified and the deaf lady calls the cops to report someone screaming down the block.

"Deal," I say, and we seal it with a sloppy and very tired kiss.

Chapter Nineteen

FLYNN

For the next thirty sex hours—oops, I mean thirty-six—Chavez and I live like debauched Romans on the loose. Naked on the kitchen counter, feeding each other scoops of ice cream and licking the spills from body parts. A chocolate blur of sucking and fucking. (Chavez looked adorable cleaning up the sticky mess naked, save for yellow dish gloves and wielding a sponge.) After I won our croquet wager, I scrubbed the grass stains off his knees in the shower. We sixty-nine each other under a sky thick with stars. (Number eight on my list, with bonus starlight.) In between it all, Chavez squeezes in a few media commitments, interviews and such, sprawled out in the downstairs parlor wearing a fluffy bathrobe and looking very much like the lord of the manor.

The next time we set foot back in the hotel, the dash is on to pack our bags and scramble for the airport. Chavez organized our entire trip in an hour, on his phone, and he bounces all over the Emirates airport lounge with excitement.

"I love Italy," he says. "Have you ever been?"

"Once. To Rome and Florence. I've always wanted to go back."

"Forli is near Bologna on the east coast. A smaller city and super chill. I'm sure you're going to like it."

Vandana, June, and I visited Italy for two weeks of cultural enlightenment only to find the fleshly sights of Italian men far more intriguing than the historical ones. We shagged our way through Rome and Florence and spent our mornings on cobblestones plazas, swapping out hangovers for espresso jitters and comparing the good, bad, and ugly of our escapades. I can safely say, amidst the man-drama, the pasta, and the copious amounts of wine, the town of Forli never once popped up on our radar.

There is not much to see when we land. Morning fog shrouds the countryside, and a bumpy landing on the small commuter flight out of Bologna is nothing like the first-class smoothness of our Emirates jumbo jet. After getting used to passing people on the left down in Australia, I bump into a few polished and polite Italians inside the terminal who smile and give me a wide berth. (Had I scuffed their designer shoes, it might have been a different story.) Unprepared for the seventy-degree swing, I shiver against Chavez as the porter loads our bags into the hired car.

"I need a hot bath and a sweater.'"

He wraps an arm around my shoulder and says, "Let's go shopping after a snooze."

The Grand Hotel Castrocaro is a ten-minute drive from Forli and is a dream-like destination nestled into the countryside, built exclusively for lovers who plan for nothing beyond room service and how many creative ways to incorporate a rooftop hot tub overlooking a medieval tower.

I stand at the railing of our room's balcony, drinking in the landscape of rolling hills and vineyards. The sun is trying to make an appearance and God beams cut through the low-hanging mist. It almost looks fake, it's so perfect.

"So pretty, right?" I whisper because it's that kind of moment.

He bearhugs me from behind, nuzzling my neck with kisses. "Kind of like you."

Our imperial suite, which, in Italian, translates roughly into enough square footage for a gymnast to execute a floor routine, comes with two bathrooms Chavez insisted we split. (There is something to be said for keeping a bit of mystery and privacy intact this early in the game.) After hot showers, we intend to rumple the crisp percale sheets into oblivion, but fall asleep in each other's arms, exhausted from the long journey.

The late afternoon sun is waning when we wake up. Bundled in several layers to keep warm, a taxi drops us at a trendy boutique near the town plaza. A willowy salesclerk sensing rich Americans plies us with gorgeous Brunello Cucinelli sweaters and Armani jackets made from felt as soft as fur. She declares everything we try on *bellissima!* and chatters mindlessly as she puts a major dent on Chavez's American Express card. Loaded down with shopping bags and caught in a sudden thin rain, we dash for the taverna our bellman suggested we try. It's early for dinner and the elegant tables are empty, votives in the process of being lit by yet another runway-ready Italian woman who tucks our retail haul into the coat room and seats us next to a wood-burning fireplace.

Chavez thanks her for our menus and moves his chair to my side of the table.

"I like this," he says. "Some downtime. Not rushing in to hit the ground running. Good call."

"Your mom can't be thrilled," I venture, deciding to test the waters. Chavez is none the wiser that Carmen has been texting with me since we left LA, but I know all about the hysterics, and how, to Gloria, our not coming back to LA is tantamount to me kidnapping her son.

"She's a work in progress," he says diplomatically. "We just have to wear her down."

Lost in his beauty and the earthy smell of mushrooms and rosemary simmered in butter, I lean against his warmth and finger the fine wool of his sweater. Two grand worth of baby alpaca looks good on him, but he could wear a garbage bag and still turn heads.

"For the next four days, I just want to forget everything."

"Everything except the separate rooms?" he asks.

We have four days at our heavenly resort and then move to the tournament hotel, and yes, I was surprised to find out we would not be sharing a room. But when Chavez explained that he has never had someone in his space during 'work' and would have to adjust, I understood. The concept of space to feel safe requires no explanation. And tennis players are known for their superstitions. Andre Agassi needed his girlfriend to sit in the same place in the stands at every tournament. Other players line up water bottles with military precision in front of their benches. A career full of endless travel and time and language changes demands that anything within your control gets controlled.

"We have all year to adjust, right?" I glance up and feel my heart twist. A mischevious spark glints in his eyes.

"All year?" he asks. "Did I just hear that right?"

Maybe it was a slip. Or maybe it wasn't.

Maybe there is something in the air tonight.

For another three hours, it does not cross my mind.

The wherewithal to think about anything continues to be lost on me when Chavez devours what he calls dessert back in our bed. He suckles my clit until I lose my mind with the unholy rapture. Chavez has pulled the lever of my orgasm jackpot, and they pour out of me like hard, copper pennies in an old-school Vegas slot. He holds me tightly through the shudders, and I barely register the slickness of his face and how genuinely interested he is in making it slicker.

"Flynn, baby," he whispers, "you are coming like rain. Tell me what's next."

In Bendigo, he proved he could spend all night creating havoc between my legs with nothing more than his tongue, but we still have a way to go on the list, and Chavez is happy to oblige. Whispering the filthiest gutter talk into my ear, he fingers me until I'm spiralling into madness, into the great beyond. Then he yanks my ass higher into the air to plunge balls deep with a single crushing thrust.

"Fuuuck!" he growls. "You are molten."

Mighty and merciless, he becomes a man on a marauding mission. Like he's cracking down aces, he thrusts harder, faster, the *smack* of each blow driving my face deeper into the pillow. An exquisite pain channels through me, sharp-edged and searing.

Unstoppable.

"Slower," I beg. "Please."

His breathing is short and clipped, but he is fully in control. "Tell me when you're ready so we can go off together, all right?"

His fingers dig deep until the soft flesh of my hips burn from the sensation. I absorb his thunder until I can't.

"Yes, now," I mutter through gritted teeth.

We climax together and he's with me, riding the waves of pleasure crashing through me in an endless sequence until he softens. With a *pop,* he slides out of me, rolling both of us on our sides so we can spoon. His chest heaves against the contours of my back, and the only sound is our ragged breathing and the stillness after a rainfall.

"You okay?" he whispers, the words hot in my ear. "I lost it there at the end."

I bite back an exhausted laugh. Okay? I hope the Italians don't mind teeth marks on their pillows.

"I'm good. Decimated but good."

Chavez drops kisses along the damp nape of my neck until my breathing steadies. The frequency and intensity of my orgasms have left me utterly spent. A heavy, dreamless sleep beckons and, just before I drift off, I remember.

They say memory becomes what we need it to be.

We create truths from lies and spin failures into successes.

The filing cabinet of our brains is not always accurate, but what I will recall with dreamlike clarity from tonight was me speaking the truth. It wasn't a slip. Because Chavez is the real deal, the actual unmistakable thing worth risking it all for.

It will only be a slip if I somehow screw this up.

Chapter Twenty

Somebody please, pinch me. Am I living in a dream world? Chavez left an hour ago to hit with a local at the tournament tennis center and left me tangled in the sheets that smell like us wearing nothing but a smile. The fog has lifted, a pale sun slowly warms the bedroom, and I'm content to loll like a hippo at the watering hole after being hand-fed buttery croissants. My newly mended shirt drapes over the back of a chair, and the long list of Chavez skills now has tailor added to it. After his shower this morning, he hopped back into bed with a sewing kit and the shiny black coin of my missing button.

"I found it in the hallway in Oz before we left for the airport," he said, sitting cross-legged and drawing the sheet over his lap as a makeshift workspace. "Bring me your shirt, and I'll get you fixed up."

His fine-boned fingers threaded the needle as he talked about his Abuela, the grandmother who taught him how to sew. She died peacefully in her sleep last year, and he got choked up talking about her.

"She was the only one who understood I could not see myself growing old with Sofia," he said, pulling the needle up through the back of the placket like a pro. "She told me to break it off. If it wasn't for her, I'd be trapped and miserable."

"How did you and Sofia get together?" I was genuinely curious.

"The usual," he said. "Pushy Mexican mothers."

"You don't strike me as someone who would do arranged."

"This is true," he admitted. "And it's not entirely Mama's fault either. As I said, it's hard to make relationships work doing what I do. I was traveling around, making decent money, and taking advantage of all the perks, if you know what I mean. My parents weren't thrilled, and looking back, neither was I. After a while, you want to crawl into bed at night with someone you love, right? Sofia and I knew each other, and my parents sacrificed a lot for me. I thought us getting together might make them happy." He plunged the needle back down through the button, pulling tight on the thread.

"Look," he said. "I liked her, and maybe I even loved her for a bit. But I made the wrong decision. Trading in my heart and soul to satisfy the dreams of another is no way to live." He shook his head as if remembering many fights similar to the one I witnessed. "She drove me crazy more than I drove her crazy, and that's saying something. We are better off not together, and she will realize I am right one day and stop crucifying me for walking away."

I recognized the defeat in his eyes before he looked away. Decisions we feel right about at the time can often be wrong. When I stood in front of Hamilton's parents and tried to explain the unexplainable, they looked past me with a similar expression, not wanting to register the woman responsible for their new life of misery. It's hard to face the things you cannot change.

I stroked my thumb along the letters inked on his hand. Fearless, even while assessing his faults.

"Your candor is impressive," I said.

"What does that word mean?"

"That you can be open and honest about things."

After a thoughtful silence, he said, "I like that I can talk to you about stuff like this and you are okay with it."

Then he searched my face as if to say, *Your turn to tell me something*. But I said nothing and felt a lick of remorse for side-stepping the deeper, more primary lesson— that honesty, not sex, creates real intimacy. I could have opened up, but I didn't trust the moment. If he did not embrace me for all my flaws and fears, then what?

"Anyway," he eventually said. "That's what you are up against with Mama. A wrong I can never right."

"Great. No pressure, then."

We both laughed and the heaviness lifted. He finished with the button much faster than I could ever attempt, and handed off my shirt with a proud smile.

"Time for you to try this on and admire my mad sewing skills."

Me, bottomless while parading around in my shirt, is what got me into trouble. But I will continue to court trouble daily if it means his version of discipline—the kind that leaves my core pulsing and my brain unable to compute the basics. He called my body a culinary wonderland, and he should know because fine dining is his thing. The burrata last night slid down my throat like silk, and I'll be gaining back all my lost weight if he keeps feeding me creamy carbonara. I could squeeze in a workout this morning but, Nah. Our afternoon sightseeing trip to Bologna will burn a few calories, and I need to tackle a few things before then. My virtual assistant asked for more social media content ideas, and after seven texts between them, I better give up some details of our Aussie tryst or else Vandana and June might implode.

I pad into the bathroom to find my phone and the perfect morning fizzles hard with the shock of seeing Brandon's name on the screen.

BD: Dear Flynn. I hope you are doing well. This is Brandon Dixler. We met in Australia.

I skim the next bubble of text with a frisson of unease.

BD: This message is coming out of the blue, but I reached out to your agent Nathaniel to see if I could send in one of your books to get autographed. He suggested I reach out to you directly and gave me your number.

A hot ball of outrage claws up my throat. What an asshole! Any knucklehead agent knows the drill about author privacy, and I have been crystal clear with Nathaniel on this matter. But this is his juvenile way of getting back at me. I ignored all his calls since I hung up on him in Bendigo, but he is about to get an earful.

Right after I finish reading the final message from Brandon.

BD: I also wanted to apologize if I created any ruffles between you and Chavez. I'm a newly divorced guy who needs more time before I'm let loose on the dating scene. Smiley face emoji. Congratulations to both of you on his recent win and good luck with the rest of the season. Best, Brandon. PS If you don't sign the book, that's okay. Not surprising if my first celebrity crush falls flat.

Jeez. Pitiful and self-deprecating but also endearing. We've all been there with crushes and letdowns, but I don't want to feel any fluffy emotions as they relate to Brandon. Chavez had asked me out of blue during a practice session in Oz if I had run into Brandon after the elevator showdown. He'd watched me, almost suspiciously, but took my no at face value. But no amount of explaining will ever convince him I didn't encourage this chat.

I'll delete Brandon's messages, but first things first.

Nathaniel, keeping his usual vampire hours, answers right away.

"Sugar," he says, all charm and smarm. "Peace pipe time? I knew you'd come to your senses."

"You're fired, effective immediately. And if I find out you have given my phone number to *anyone* else, my lawyer will sue you for breach of contract. Remember the privacy clause?"

In the silence right after, my heart flutters with survival instinct. This is it. Kill or be killed.

"I needed to get your attention," he whines as if that somehow rights the wrong. "Seeing as how you're all distracted with your new boyfriend."

Of course, he's seen the photo. Everyone has. But that does not justify his behavior.

"My love life is none of your concern. If anything, you should be happy for me."

"Happy doesn't make you money, Flin Flon."

"That makes sense, seeing how miserable you are. I cannot believe you would do this," I say, hating myself because I should be strong and not show the hurt. "After everything I've been through."

"We both know you can't dump me, Flynn. I know more about you than anyone else."

After a long beat, I ask, "Is that a threat?"

After a much longer beat, he asks, "Are you recording this?"

I feel the hairs on the back of my neck rise. He knows damn well he's overstepped the boundaries. "Go ahead and write a tell-all. My lawyer will make sure it's the last book you ever publish."

Me saying lawyer twice is an irrevocable laying down of the gauntlet. The phone clicks to speaker, and he's out of his chair, pacing around the desk that I once sat on the other side of while he played footsie with a twenty-one-year-old too unsure of herself to stop him.

"Can we rewind, in case you've forgotten how this works?" he yells. "*I* turned your piece-of-shit manuscript into a bestseller. *I* got you everything you have. *You* clearly have no clue what you're doing because if you really wanted to tap into the Latino market, there are better ways than fucking a Mexican."

I sit down hard on the toilet seat, my stomach roiling. "How can you even say that? You're disgusting."

"Says the lady diddling a fifteen-year-old."

"He's twenty-five!"

"Tell that to the fly-over states who will see you next to him and truss you up as everything wrong with immigration and the morals in this country." He laughs morosely. "Forget about *my* book blowing up your world. You are sprinting down the road of career suicide all by yourself. And if you think anyone will represent you after I kick your ass to the curb, guess again. Good luck out there, Miss Mystery."

Five seconds pass before I realize he's hung up. And just like that, the second-longest male relationship in my life is over. Despite the dizzying wave of uncertainty, I know I did the right thing. In public, Nathaniel virtue signaled out the yin-yang, but behind closed doors, in his safe circle, he spewed that kind of garbage on an alarmingly regular basis. He is no better than Earl Anderson. I should have recorded our conversation, although none of it would be admissible in court. And I know we will end up there. Nathaniel will not go down without a fight.

But he has never gone up against a Flynn Dryden who is channeling Truth #5 like there is no tomorrow.

Change is power.

Get ready to rumble, you stone-aged clown.

Chapter Twenty-One

"Earth to Flynn."

I flash Chavez a guilty smile across the bistro table. He was talking about how well he played and that I should hit with him tomorrow, and I briefly lost my train of thought again. My mind was winding all afternoon, like the famous staircases we climbed, and it continued to wander as we strolled through the porticos that define the bustling university town of Bologna. With every minute that passes, the barely contained mess from this morning keeps ballooning in scope. The repercussions with Nathaniel. That I replied to Brandon, and he texted back immediately.

And maybe, I texted back.

"I'd love to come tomorrow," I say, gushing a bit too hard.

Chavez fills up our water glasses with a furrowed brow. "You seem a little out of it. And you can't blame wine because you haven't had any. Talk to me."

He is nothing but observant, always watching me. But unlike the interested gazes of my fans, his penetrates beyond my skin and fake smile. I'm conscious of being careful. Nathaniel's cheap blackmail shot will not incite a riot, but if I tell him about Brandon reaching out, our

154

Italian paradise will go up in flames faster than the 498 wooden stairs we climbed in the Asinelli Tower.

But I have to tell him something.

"I fired my agent today."

"What?" He sits back, stunned. "Why didn't you say anything?"

"It's all good," I assure him, brushing it off. "It was high time."

Chavez shifts his chair to allow a group of chattering Japanese tourists to squeeze past. It's packed in here, far livelier than my mood.

"You have to tell me these things," he says, the bottle of San Pellegrino wobbling as he leans onto the table with a stung expression. "Here I am, wondering if you're having a good time or if I've said anything wrong. You've been with that guy your entire career, right? That's pretty big news. You mind me asking what the issue was?"

"Oh…" I can't help the nervous flit of my gaze. "Just this and that. A bunch of things."

He gives me a long look. "Whenever I ask you for details, you never give them. You ever notice that?"

"What details am I not giving you?"

"*A bunch of things* can mean anything."

I open my mouth, only to close it again. I'm not sure why I feel so raw telling him.

"He's not the right guy to represent me for fiction, and that is what I want to do next. Write mysteries."

There. I said it. In public.

"So you're giving up the motivational stuff?" he asks.

"Yes. I mean, I'm still helping you," I'm quick to add. "As far as the writing goes, I've decided it's time to stretch my wings."

"Hey," he says, leaning in to kiss my cheek and then cupping it with his hand. "Team D is all about you and me helping each other. And if you want to do something else, or if something is weighing on your mind, I want to know about it. I think it's cool that you want to write mysteries. I like them. It's probably why I like you."

"I'm a mystery?" I feign surprise at the noun even my besties use to describe me.

"In a good way," he clarifies. "What I mean is…" He pauses, as if pulling on conversational kid gloves, and lowers his voice. "When I'm kissing you or we're making love, I feel like I'm getting the real you. You're in the moment. The rest of the time, you have this protective layer on. One step removed. I don't know if anyone's ever told you this, but you are the master of spinning the conversation away from you."

"Mi scusi, il dolce." The cheery waiter in suspenders arrives with our tiramisu, a fluffy square so giant we're forced to move our dinner plates to accommodate it.

"You better get in there before I do," I joke and turn my attention to the waiter for a coffee order.

Chavez frowns, fully aware I have done it again—pivoted the spotlight elsewhere. He lets it slide, maybe in the interest of keeping things copasetic. Or perhaps he caught wind of the couple at the table next to us—far more interested in our conversation than their own.

So, we prattle on like tourists about the sites we saw and what impressed us the most. Bologna, like all of Italy, has endless cute nooks and crannies that, after a while, you don't bother taking pictures of because if you did, you would end up never putting your phone down. Dusk has faded into a moonless night when we walk hand in hand to the sedan parked under a cone of acidic streetlight. The driver Chavez hired speaks only broken English and seems relieved his customers are content to crash against each other in the back seat and not engage. Chavez keeps his arm tight around my shoulders the entire drive back to Forli and absently fingers one of my curls as he gazes silently out the window.

One morning, soon, with the warmth of his body against mine like it is now, I will open my heart. Fear is stifling, the worst kind of spiritual poison, and in the end, you feel swallowed up by nothing. But Chavez needs to get through this tournament and maybe the next one before I take that step. The clock, however, has started to tick.

I'M BLOATED, GRUMPY, AND IN NO MOOD FOR TENNIS ON THE DAY WE move hotels. But today is a practice day, and I promised to come along. Nestled amongst sun-dappled vineyards, the Carpena Tennis Club is quintessential Italian with sharp-dressed staff and questionable efficiency. Chavez, sensing my irritation that our court isn't available yet, leaves me in the bleachers to talk shop with the other players. Four days of bliss ended abruptly this morning with Mother Nature roaring in. After all my bluster about Chavez not making me wait for a win, I'm off limits for a week. He doesn't wade through the crimson tide (how he politely put it), and had he not turned me into a budding nymphomaniac, I might be okay with this. But now we're back at square one, alone in separate hotel rooms in the dumpy tour hotel, me without the joy of his talents to look forward to.

Fuck.

Slouched in my seat, I scan the courts on the hunt for familiar faces from Australia. Like the ATP tour, players pick and choose which Challenger tournaments they want to play. Given the lower prize money, most players don't jet from Oz to Italy, which explains the sea of new European faces. New voices, too, braying loudly like donkeys from behind me.

"Who's that hottie?"

"His new coach."

"I wonder if she'll do a private. Off the court."

"You jonesing for a little MILF action?"

God, the uncouth laughter of idiot boys. If they'd been entirely unoriginal and tossed out the word *cougar*, I might have overlooked their stupidity, but I draw the line at *MILF*.

I glance over my shoulder. "Are you two looking for a coach or a black eye?"

They elbow one another with a chorus of *Ooos*. Americans, of course, and ranked somewhere in the mid 100's, I imagine.

The one with shaggy brown hair trying to grow a goatee asks, "What are *you* looking for, baby?"

I roll my eyes and turn back to the court. They remind me of the Santa Cruz boys who never liked me back. The arrogant, entitled rich kids who thought they were all that. The ones who labeled me different, and not good different, like I was a genius outlier going places, or really bad different, like I should lay off the heroin. I was middle-of-the-road different—not severe enough for sympathy and not cool enough to be put on a pedestal.

But here comes one of them, plunking himself down in the seat next to me, all limbs and arms with a baller smile. He introduces himself as Nathan.

"What's the dealio, Babes R Us? Can you give us a two for one?"

"I don't do cheap, sorry."

"It's all good," he says, unaffected by my rudeness. "We're just looking to score a little intel, that's all."

I side-eye him. "What does that mean?"

He nods his chin at Chavez shooting the breeze with a group of players on the court. "What's the story with him? Why's he playing the Challengers?"

"There is no story. He's playing tennis, like everyone else here."

"C'mon," he says, elbowing me like we're old friends. "Everyone's talking about it. Eight months off the tour. Making no money. You think he's going to make it through the first round?"

"I don't know. Are you?" I gaze at him coolly and he shrugs.

"We might play each other in the first round. Depends on the draw. I'm just sayin', if that happens, we can make a quick buck. Seventy-thirty on the odds. Seventy for you two."

I fight to keep it under control, but I am deeply offended. And pissed. "You realize what you're asking me?"

"What am I asking?" he says, brazenly holding my stare.

"You're asking for trouble."

"From what I see, you're pretty okay with trouble. Isn't there like, some code of ethics coaches have to follow? You know, not fuck their players."

My fists ball in my lap. Cruel was always their default with my kind of different. It still makes me feel unworthy.

"You can leave now. Thank you."

"What else are you coaching him on?" he asks, an endless,

annoying bag of hot air. "Not to mack on the girlfriends of other players?"

It's a trap. I know he wants me to take the bait and I do. I blame my emotional state. "Like who?"

He calls out to his friend. "Georgie! Who was Arlo's girlfriend? The Russian skank?"

"Vanya the Velvet Vagina."

Nathan chuckles like he made up the classy name himself. "You didn't see those two on Insta last year? You can still find the pics online. Check 'em out. Why do you think Arlo hates him so much?"

Arlo. Arlo. Arlo. Python mentioned the name when he and Chavez were hitting together in LA. It has to be Arlo Märklin. The current number five player, and a 6'4" slab of Hungarian meat who has no business being a tennis player when he's built like a linebacker. He's a heavy favorite to win the Australian Open, a topic Chavez and I haven't talked about. I get the sense he doesn't want to be reminded that he should be there instead of here.

"Just wanted to give you fair warning," Nathan says, nonchalantly. "I'm sure I'll see you around in the next few days, so if you change your mind…" He rubs his thumb against his fingers, indicating money. "Doesn't have to be the whole match. One set."

What a dipshit. He has no clue about Chavez's financial situation and assumed I'd be desperate enough to entertain his crackpot, and illegal, idea.

"One more word out of you and I'm talking to the officials."

His features darken at my unexpected pluck and he stands up, muttering, "You don't have to be a bitch about it." He motions to his friend to head out but not before he makes a V in front of his mouth with his index and middle finger, waggling his tongue through it. "And if your uptight cunt wants some real action, call me."

I wait until they and their sniggers are gone before I slide out my phone. My cheeks are aflame, and my thumping heart screams I should not be doing this, but what choice do I have?

I can't get past Vanya the Velvet Vagina.

If only for the alliteration.

The photos are buried, frozen in time on page twenty of a trash celebrity site. Grainy but clear enough to gut me. Aside from Sofia, his eighty-three conquests have been nameless and faceless. Abstracts. But these images are chunks of hard concrete landing on my baby toes and cannot be ignored. A gorgeous Russian ice princess pushed up against a wall with one half of Team D groping her double D's. Their mouths fused. A mini skirt so short it's like, why did she even bother?

I set the phone down with an awful taste in my mouth. This morning he'd suckled me and said, *Your boobs are perfect.* I know my emotions are running amok, and that time of the month is muddying my ability to not be affected by this, but how can he love mine when they are tiny bumps compared to hers? I glance again at the obscene amounts of flesh oozing through his fingers and feel hollowed out. I tell myself the guy who sewed on my button while sitting naked on the bed and got engaged to a woman to make his parents happy is not this guy.

But it is.

Seconds away from spinning down the oh-so-familiar path of self-destruction, a text message suddenly appears with an attached photo. I might not have opened it had the image of Vanya and Chavez not been on my screen, haunting me.

BD: Good luck in Italy! I'm rooting for you.

The POV is of his sandalled feet crossed on the footrest of an Adirondack deck chair, a beautiful hush of twilight on the horizon just visible beyond the can of Old Milwaukee held up as a toast. Whether it's the beer or the USA Today newspaper folded beside him, another bout of homesickness lands hard. The first hit me out of nowhere the other day while listening to a conversation in a coffee shop; the kind of light banter we all engage in when going about our errands. But when your grasp of a language is limited, these little moments are lost. It made me yearn for home and, in a weird way, stability. Thanks to Vanya, what rolls through my mind now is whether Chavez and I have any real future together. Yes, things seem to be working out, but I am older, and no competition for the next generation of big-boobed sluts.

And if having a family is a priority for him, my expiration date seems inevitable.

Without thinking, I prop my feet up on the bench in front of me, snap a photo, and send it.

FD: Thank you. Just about to hit the courts.

BD: Courts? All I see are some mighty fine legs.

In retrospect, it is stupid of me not to think about the semantics.

I'm rooting for you.

Stupid not to consider that he is tracking our movement.

Stupid to continue texting with him and justifying it based on a cold wash of jealousy and wanting a warm boost of my spirits.

And I continue texting until Chavez calls my name, and I tuck the phone away.

Chapter Twenty-Two

OVERNIGHT, THE NOVELTY OF BEING A COACH WITH BENEFITS MORPHS into a job suddenly stripped of any benefits. Breakfast, practice, match. Post-match forensics followed by a pre-match analysis of his next opponent. After an early dinner, I get one abbreviated make-out session and off he goes to bed. Alone. I give him space because he wants to be in the zone, but the Italy tournament feels like it drags on forever.

And something flips with Chavez early on in the week.

He shuts down a bit, forcing me to push him harder. Then he starts winning ugly, and my frustration settles more deeply. The patchy play concerns me, especially after his strong start in Australia, and even Rodrigo admits this is what drove him nuts. The inconsistency. I was worried something like this might happen. To jump in and make sweeping changes with a player without the benefit of time and familiarity is hard. The fact that I played and have coached or motivated millions means nothing.

In the end, it boils down to my belief that I can help him.

My belief in us.

And that is one hundred percent my screwed-up brain at play.

The hours I have spent scouring Vanya's social media and self-sabotaging is unhealthy, especially since the fling with Chavez appears to be limited to that one night in a club where a bystander caught them on camera. But last night we were kissing, and *boom*, all I could think about was the two of them, and how my body was not hers.

It's so stupid, my inability to get past it.

On top of it all, Brandon and I have started to banter. A photo here, a *How is the tour going* there. Nothing damaging, but still. If Chavez and I were in the same hotel room, this would not be happening. Instead, I'm bored at night, and filling up my time with internet stupidity.

But our nightly separation has given me time to start putting together my fiction career. The agents I've reached out to have expressed interest in representing me once my contract with Nathaniel is null and void. Then it gets tricky. Technically, I owe him another book. My lawyer, Jax, reviewed the fine print of our contract and said we could wiggle out of it based on my next book being fiction, but go figure, that area in the agreement is every shade of grey. We've decided to go for it though, and next week the official termination letter ships out. Here and there, I've been finding pockets of time to write, but I'm missing the daily commitment of planting my ass down for two to three hours at a time. To the point that I plan to ask Chavez how he feels about returning to LA after this tournament. There is a two-week break before the next event starts in Cherbourg, France, and that's enough time to warrant a trip home.

The truth is, I also miss my friends. June, bless her, has been looking after my house, sorting out the mail and other odds and ends while putting on a brave face during FaceTime. With both her besties gone, she is struggling too. Meanwhile, Vandana and I are in constant communication, in the same time zone and all, and she invited Chavez and me to Monaco for my birthday, which falls right after the Cherbourg tournament. I have not mentioned this to Chavez, nor does he know Carmen and I have been leaving each other long WhatsApp voice messages since Australia. (She asked to keep it on the down low.)

It started with her asking for career advice, but it's gotten more personal. She wants to come out and is scared shitless about how her parents will react. My fans ask for advice on myriad issues, including coming out, but that is a charged decision with varying degrees of fall-out. With no direct experience, all I can offer Carmen are suggestions on the best way to approach it. Like Chavez, she has a tough outer shell that gradually softens when she realizes I am here for her and invested in the outcome. And she is lovely. Smart and scathing, with a penchant for sarcasm and a deep love for her brother. She left the door open for me to talk should anything come up, and if my emotions were not so fucked up this week, I might have.

Balancing the roles of coach and lover with Chavez, confidante with his father and sister, and trying to steer my career while not obsessing over a Velvet Vagina is driving me crazy.

I hate to say it, but when Chavez prevails and lifts his second tournament trophy, I'm glad it's over. He wasn't a brilliant tactician during a tight three-set final, but he overcomes spotty play and a spirited opponent to maintain his cool in a nervy tiebreak that could have gone either way. After all the post-match commitments, we meet in his room before heading out for dinner.

Freshly showered, he gives me a peck on the cheek and asks me to sit with him on the bed. His body language is subdued and the hum in the air says, *A talk is coming.*

"You look so serious," I say, trying for lighthearted and failing.

He nods, validating my comment. "I made a mistake. Things are going to change."

My skin prickles. "What do you mean?"

"What do I mean?" He laughs for what feels like the first time in days. "This," he says, indicating the hotel room. "Stupidest idea ever, separate hotel rooms. I don't play well without you in my bed, in case you hadn't noticed."

A wave of relief washes over me. "I might have noticed." I also notice that his room is far tidier than mine.

"I've been a dick all week, and I know it. No excuses. I'm just..." He pauses, and I can tell he's searching for the right words. "It's been hard trying to find my groove after Oz," he continues. "You've been super helpful—"

"But?" I interrupt because it is there, on the tip of his tongue.

"It's not a *but*. I'm confused. How I interacted with Papa does not work with you, and you're not just my coach. It's been messing me up all week. And I've been getting this vibe from you like maybe you're not happy and I want to ask you how I—we—can make it better. Or easier. Or … I don't know." His attention rivets onto me. "The bottom line is, I don't want to lose you."

The adult thing to do is come clean and tell him about my obsessive spiral with Vanya, but I don't want to see his face when I say her name. And if I mention the real reason why I watched Nathan play it will blow up this heartfelt moment. Best not to bring it up at all.

"In fairness, I have been a little off this week," I admit.

"I know," he says. "You've been lost in your phone, or earlier in the tournament I saw you watching some other guy play, and you seemed so invested, and I thought, fuck, maybe she wants to coach someone else."

I have zero interest in coaching smart-mouthed Nathan, although I did sneak off to watch that idiot get creamed in a 6-1, 6-1 double breadstick. The sucker kept his head hanging as he walked past me on the way to the locker room and so he should. But I had no idea Chavez was watching me.

"I don't want to coach anyone else. Let me be clear on that."

"Okay. Cool. I just want to bring it up because that's part of what I've been struggling with." His gaze cuts to the floor, and he takes a heavy breath. It rings mournfully in the quiet room, and I brace myself as his eyes lift shyly to meet mine. "Being jealous."

He holds steady on my eyes but swallows hard. His vulnerability lances like an arrow into my heart.

"What would help me is not being relegated to the sidelines one week a month," I confess.

He traces a finger along my upper thigh oblivious to the shudder coursing through me. "Anything more than a quick kiss would kill me," he says. "Once I get into with you … I'm not a halfway kind of guy."

"There are other options," I remind him.

"You need to get off, too. Only me feels unfair."

Says no man ever.

What planet did he come from?

"Flynn baby," he continues, his voice tender. "You are always front and center. If my shit behaviour gave you reasons to think otherwise, I promise to make it up to you."

He smothers my mouth with a blistering kiss, and I close my eyes, drifting in his spicy scent, the heat of his body. Need springs like hope eternal between my thighs because the red flag is over, and as much as I love tennis and seeing him win, I have missed the game of us. I dig my nails into his back, but he responds to my desperate clawing by pulling away.

"Not that again," I say, flustered, my libido raging.

He tucks a curl behind my ear and laughs. "Here's what I was thinking. If you're cool, I'd like to stay in Europe until the end of February. I've been looking at some house rentals in Cherbourg. Legit houses, with an office for you. You always seem happier after you've been writing. Take all the time you need. We can stay there for the next two weeks and during the tournament. Fuck the tour hotel," he says. "That shit is done."

I was one step away from bringing our adventure to a close and he throws a wrench in the plans by offering up a near-perfect compromise.

"That sounds … really nice."

"And after Cherbourg," he adds. "I thought we could go to Paris for your birthday."

My breath catches.

Number one, I forgot he knew when my birthday was. I'm a Pisces, obviously, and he brought it up one night in Australia that he's a Cancer, a July-first birthday boy. He told me sheepishly that he looked online at some astrology site that said our signs were a good fit for one another.

And number two, Paris?

"Paris?" I ask, just to be sure.

"Yeah. The Ritz Hotel. I booked us the Ernest Hemingway Suite. I thought it might inspire you."

Oh my God. Not even Vandana has stayed at the Ritz! And more importantly, "You're an Ernest fan?" I ask. Chavez enjoys reading—the to-be-read list on his iPad is longer than mine—but he never mentioned he likes classics.

"It's way better to read about history in a story instead of a textbook and I just finished *For Whom the Bell Tolls*. My mom's grandfather fought in the Spanish Civil War. That side of my family is Catalan, from Barcelona," he explains. "And your writing reminds me of Hemingway. Simple and clean."

I laugh, feeling the glow of that compliment from my head to my toes. "No one has ever compared me to him."

"Maybe after your mystery comes out, more people will."

He kisses me again, his breath bitter from coffee, and I think, how crazy is this? Here we both are, unsure and stumbling the entire week, and neither of us courageous enough to admit it has to do with the other. The day is suddenly one I can repeat indefinitely.

"Paris sounds incredible. And if you want, my friend who is dating the yacht designer invited us to Monaco. We can go before Paris. Or not at all."

"Let's do both," he says without missing a beat. "But after Cherbourg, all right? I want you all to myself for the next little while."

THE ONLY THING I AM CONSCIOUS OF IN THE FOLLOWING DAYS IS ravenous desire. I forget about time and how blankly I used to fill it. Nothing matters except us. We christen every drafty room in our rambling seaside château, and Cherbourg sightseeing adventures turn into location scouting for the perfect outdoor boudoir. Why not take advantage of the empty gardens of Ravalet Castle, find a patch of bulrushes by the lake and try not to laugh as swans glide past us with curious black eyes?

During a miserable Monday rainstorm, we duck into the cover of a doorway, a padlocked entrance to a long, unused passage on the side of a magnificent church. It smells of dampness and alchemy. He drapes an arm around my shoulder, shielding me from the gusting gloom. The only thing better than Chavez is wet Chavez and my heart stutters at his sooty lashes sparkling with raindrops.

"Looks like we have a storm to ride out," he says, a twinkle in his eye.

After, I jokingly blamed him because he just had to go and kiss me.

The wind howls, rain hammers sideways, and not even five novenas can save our corrupt souls. His fingers deliver a sermon of seismic shudders until twelfth-century grout scrapes along my spine as I slide down the wall onto my haunches, weak with spiritual ecstasy and, most certainly, one step closer to hell. There is nothing else to do but sell my soul to the Devil. I unbuckle and unzip, his head falls back with a gasp, and his voice cranks an octave higher as he whispers, "*Please forgive me.*"

 But I am an unforgiving bitch.

And the French soils that had seen strife and bloody warfare can now witness the joy of depravity.

C'est parfait, as the locals say.

And everything does hum along perfectly.

Every morning Chavez works out at a nearby gym or hits at the local tennis center, leaving me with time to write. The story spills out of me faster than I can type, and it's been in my head for so long it feels like I'm plagiarizing my own memory. Most nights we stay in. Chavez whips up feasts worthy of kings with instinct and feel, never once cracking open his phone to troubleshoot a recipe. His command of a kitchen is remarkable and I watch it all unfold, perched at the kitchen island and getting drunk on cheap wine. (Five Euros for half-decent stuff!) Life as I remember it becomes this—waking up to him beside me, the waters of the English Channel lapping softly outside the bedroom window, and tennis and writing the topics of the day.

Two weeks pass far too quickly, and suddenly it's the night before his first-round match. We're bundled in blankets and watching the sunset from the covered porch. My breath leaves misty plumes in the cool night air, and all the scents are clear and sharp, ocean and earth layered against each other.

I lean against his shoulder, tipsy again, introduced to the wonders of mulled wine from a very enthusiastic merchant.

Warm and fuzzy, it just slips out. "Carmen says hi."

In the silence, I sense he's debating how to answer. Finally, "I knew it. I told you she was determined." He glances over with a brow raised in what might be worry. "She send you any nudes?"

"Not yet."

"Have you sent her any?"

"Not yet."

We both laugh and he snuggles into my shoulder. "So, what's the deal? You both talk shit about me?"

"We hardly talk about you at all. I think she views me like a sister. And she loves you, mierda and all."

His jaw squares and I wonder if it came out the wrong way. In the murky light, I can just make out his eyes settling on the horizon but not charting anything.

"I love her too," he eventually says, his voice gruff. "More than she will ever know. She got the short end of the stick growing up. Papa on the road with me, and Mama at work or at home worrying about me and Papa." He burrows his nose in my hair and breathes deeply. "I don't know how you can be any more of a goddess but thank you." When he pulls back a minute later, his eyes are softly sweeping over me.

"What?" I ask.

"I re-read part of your memoir yesterday. The chapter about you and your boyfriend. The fight, and what happened after."

My skin prickles with foreboding. "Why that section?"

"Because I didn't think it through the first time. How it must have felt for you to be eighteen and fighting with your boyfriend for the first time, then waking up the next morning feeling like shit only to over-hear your parents spill the beans that you're adopted. It must have destroyed you."

The world indeed collapsed around me that summer morning, a star's death resulting in a black hole of unescapable lies and betrayal. The urge to run away from a life that no longer made sense burned through me like wildfire. I ran out of the house and never stopped until I reached Hamilton, packing up for a white-water rafting trip in his parent's driveway. I begged him to forgive me for our fight. I begged him to take me rafting with him.

And when he asked why, I lied. My fine legacy of lies started right there.

"Is it okay to talk about this?" Chavez asks, finding my eyes and seeing the wildness within them.

Oh, God.

I swallow away the rawness in my throat.

In my dreams, the ones where my elbow and kneecap did not shatter on rocks in the rushing rapids, my hand found a safety harness and my fellow rafters pulled me back inside the boat. And Hamilton saved me instead of becoming paralyzed when a rogue log charging down the river broke his back.

The clash of memory and the sensations surrounding me, warp the here and now. I swear I can see Hamilton floating away in the drifting tide of the English Channel, his arm no longer reaching for me.

"You're brave Flynn," Chavez whispers in the dark. "Strong and smart and inspiring. If you can do it, so can I. Fight the battles in front of me instead of the battles behind me."

An emotional tidal wave washes over me and I duck for the cover of his lap, hugging his legs somewhat awkwardly. I can feel the muscles beneath his jeans. Hear my heart thudding out of control.

"Watcha doing?" he asks.

"Nothing," I whisper. "Just … being."

I am surfing the edge of things again, but with my mind in turmoil, it is all I can do to remain still. Chavez rubs slow circles on my back, both of us content to let the sound of crickets starting their evening calls fill the space instead of words. His body heat radiates through the coarse wool blankets wrapped around us, both barely enough to stave off the damp seaside chill.

I'm about to suggest we head inside when he asks, "You ever thought of having kids?"

A bitter taste fills my mouth. Someone once said the more something threatens your identity, the more you avoid it, and with frightening efficiency, I have sealed myself off from the concept of motherhood. I never believed myself to be worthy, that I would somehow screw it up, and screw up my child in the process.

Or worse, wish I had never had them.

But yesterday, as we binge-watched a thriller series while spooning together on the couch, his hand absently rubbed my belly and I thought, what if I was wrong? What if there was nothing to be scared of but my own happiness?

What if I stopped fighting the battles behind me?

I stare into the black night and feel myself slowly dissolve into it. My voice finally comes, small as it might be. "With the right person, I'd consider it."

"That's how I feel," he says, and we drift into a companionable silence.

It's funny how the most powerful moments in a relationship are never splashy, blowout events like New Year's Eve or birthdays. Or even the smutty events with hips straddling your face as you sit in a dark corner sucking the very Catholicism out of your man. Sometimes it's overlooking the waves in a coastal French town, draped on someone's lap and thinking for once, I am not the woman getting a man into trouble.

I am the woman changing his life.

Flynn Dryden Truth #6. Pick your success team wisely.

Chapter Twenty-Three

CHAVEZ FALLS IN THE SEMI-FINALS AT CHERBOURG, DESPITE SHOWING grit and flair. Although I sense a darker undercurrent troubling him from the tough loss, he talks candidly about where he needs to tighten up his game. All I cared about was his second-round match against Georgie, the foul-mouthed buddy of Nathan. They both signed up for Cherbourg, and my sick sense of glee when they got handed walking papers early on was immature, but I felt it, nonetheless.

Sue me.

I'm on a creative roll and nothing, especially tennis man drama, can stop me. I grind out an insane daily word count with my mind free and body on fire after my boyfriend takes creative liberties with me. And it is true—we are official as of last week. A group of autograph seekers approached us on the street, and Chavez introduced me as his girlfriend instead of coach for the first time. He fumbled after, embarrassed, and asked, sweetly, if it was okay to call me that. Of course, I said yes. Everything shifted one level higher after our seaside bench moment, and this was a natural extension.

Packing up the chateau is more emotional than I expected. Three weeks slipped by like nothing, and even the questionable plumbing did not dim our first experience at playing house together. Our time there was magical, almost like being in a dream.

And the surreal world continues as we haul ass across the Mediterranean in a helicopter owned by Morgan. We'll have two days of fun before our romantic weekend in Paris and then the final tournament in Pau, France. If anyone had told me back in December this is what my life would be like come February, I would have laughed non-stop. Hard to believe I was one phone call away from leaving Chavez to figure his shit out in an Echo Park driveway.

He glances over his shoulder with a beaming smile and talks loudly to overcome the rotor noise. "This is pretty dope."

I give him a thumbs up from the back seat in hearty agreement. The luxury life takes no time at all to embrace. A driver greeted us at the Nice airport, took care of all our bags, and Morgan insisted on spoiling us with a suite at the iconic Hotel de Paris in Monaco. It sure beats being stuck in traffic on the 405 while eating an egg salad sandwich from Circle K.

Vandana and Morgan are waiting for us when we land in Fontvielle, the far-west neighborhood of Monaco. My first impression of my bestie's Bae? Morgan is less real human and more like a hologram of computer-generated male perfection. Slick-backed hair, none of it out of place. Ten grand worth of suit cut to fit him within an inch of his life. The color of his Bentley matches the sunglasses that frame his lightly bearded face, and a warm smile shines through the blond and copper stubble.

Paired with the always dazzling Vandana, I'm not surprised when Chavez whispers under his breath, "Jesus. Real-life Ken and Barbie."

"Behave," I say, keeping my smile bright as she rushes toward us.

"Oh my God!" Vandana cries, throwing her arms around me. "It's so good to see you."

After our bear hug, she introduces herself to Chavez and Morgan to us. June had the opportunity to meet Morgan in person when he visited LA in November and had nothing but rave reviews. What I know about him from Vandana is that he has a cock the size of a fire log and likes to stick it in all sorts of places. Something I try not to think about during his full-contact hug.

"Bonjour, Flynn." He kisses both my cheeks, and his salted, fresh scent is what detergents always promise but never deliver on. "Very nice to meet you."

"You too. Thanks for the helicopter ride."

"Anytime," he says, his attention scarcely alighting on me before extending a hand to Chavez. "Welcome to Monaco. We are honoured to have such an accomplished sportsman join us."

"Appreciate the love," Chavez says, graciously allowing Morgan to pump his arm well beyond the normal limits. "Doing my best to live up to the accomplished part."

Vandana pulls me aside to whisper, "Morgan is a total tennis fanboy. I had *no* idea."

In those few words, she reveals the actual truth. Our being here has as much to do with Vandana and me connecting as it does with benefitting Morgan. She mentioned once, offhandedly, that he doesn't have a lot of male friends. And this is what many people miss behind the glamazon facade of Vandana. She cares. And will go to the ends of the earth for you.

"Shall we?" Morgan gestures at his car and then loads our luggage, refusing any help from Chavez. Vandana eyes our small roll-ons with concern.

"We packed light," I explain. "Is there a dress code?"

As soon as the question leaves my mouth, I realize the stupidity of it. Life with Vandana is an endless runway, evidenced by her tweed Chanel suit, making her look like a royal-in-training, complete with a scarf tied loosely around her hair. My Veronica Beard dress feels like a rag in comparison.

"Not to worry," Morgan says. "We arranged a car service to take you around to the shops this afternoon."

"For what?" Chavez asks, gently herded to the front seat by Vandana so she and I can talk in the back.

"Flynn's birthday," she says, with a chiding tone. "We're going to start with a tour of Monaco, lunch at the yacht club, and then drop you two at the hotel to freshen up. The car service will pick you up at three, and dinner is at eight. The restaurant is down the block from the hotel, so you'll have plenty of time to enjoy the suite."

She grabs my hand with a wicked smile while Chavez sits shell-shocked in the front passenger seat. I never mentioned to him that a day with Vandana is like a state visit, with every minute planned and accounted for, and veering off schedule is a giant no-no.

Thankfully, he shrugs and allows it all to happen. "Okay."

And we're off to the races.

FOR SOME REASON, I IMAGINED MONACO TO HAVE A EUROPEAN JERSEY Shore vibe—hairy-chested men sporting gold chains and linked arm in arm with trashy blonde babes. But no, it is all very civilized, and the poorly dressed people are tourists. And, oh my God, the yachts. Morgan tours us around the docks of Port Hercules after lunch, and Vandana drops names and bits of gossip as we pass each mega vessel. She's always been a socialite, buzzing from charity breakfast to client luncheon to black tie galas—rinse, repeat—but I marvel at how at ease she is here. The queen has finally found her homeland.

With lunch and the tour stretching longer, Chavez and I barely have half an hour to prepare for our afternoon of shopping.

"Wasn't this supposed to be a relaxing trip?" he asks, scrubbing his teeth while I reapply eyeliner.

But even he has to admit being chauffeured around in a Rolls Royce and having staff in glamorous boutiques wait on us hand and foot do not warrant complaining. Chavez chooses a suit in under fifteen minutes but is happy to dote on me in the Dior dressing room, holding beads out of the way to zip me up or adjusting the cap sleeves on dresses so beautiful that making a decision is impossible.

I twirl in front of the mirror, assessing gown number eight, a butter-soft column of black silk that feels like nothing on my skin "Which one do you like the best?"

"You look good in everything," he says, no help at all. "But I do like that one. It looks nice with your hair."

When we stroll arm and arm into La Môme, I know I made the right choice. We turn every head in a restaurant full of beautiful people, and the gossip train starts once we are seated with Morgan and Vandana. Lots of looks and whispers. Morgan is oblivious to it all with his new buddy beside him. He and Chavez are instant soul mates, discussing sports and yachts and planning what to do when, or if, we are back here for the April tournament. Morgan wants to introduce us to Prince Albert and Vandana brushes it off like it's no big deal, because *everyone* knows the prince.

While the men gossip, we catch up on our news—all the tennis, their recent client trip to Russia, the new design company she incorporated here, and dinner comes and goes in a heartbeat. We're all poised with our spoons ready to crack the burnt-sugar tops of our creme brûlées when the unkind stare of none other than Arlo Märklin appears at our table. Blond and dirty-hot, he is a my-shit-don't-stink blueblood with a dead-fish personality and skilled, but unspectacular, game. For some reason now it crosses my mind that he lives in Monaco, as many tennis players do.

His eyes bounce from Morgan to Vandana and then to me before he smirks at Chavez. "Slumming it at the big kids' table?"

"If you want to join in," Chavez replies, "I think they have a highchair."

I want to cheer, *Yes! Excellent comeback.* We had a long conversation about Arlo in Cherbourg (minus the topic of Vanya, who Chavez is unaware I know about) because he'd just won the Australian Open. Chavez can't stand him, and the feeling is mutual. Unfortunately, their matches have always swung in Arlo's favor— five-zip, all of them straight-set victories played either on grass or hard courts. But they have never played each other on clay, which is the surface Chavez loves the most. He is itching for a showdown with Arlo on his turf.

"No thanks," Arlo replies. "I better get back to my table and my trophy. Do you want to see it?"

"Congratulations," Chavez says, his leg shimmying hard under the table.

Arlo fixes his gaze on me with the comfort of someone who regularly towers over everyone else. "You're the infamous coach, I take it? What's it been like bottom-feeding with him on the Challengers?"

Chavez stands so abruptly that his chair screeches across the parquet with a sharp wail. He dumps his napkin on the table and gets right into Arlo's face.

"You want to take this outside?"

Arlo's head falls back with a laugh. "Sure, my friend. Make it six-zero?"

Across the table, panic swells in Vandana's eyes. The sun has barely set on her scandal with Morgan and the last thing she needs is to be associated with another.

"Chavez," I whisper urgently, but it falls on deaf ears.

It all happens so fast after that.

Chavez slams his palms against the wall of Arlo who stumbles back, knocking hard into a passing waiter. The man's tray of steaks upends, and the charred airborne beef filets float in the damning silence of a situation about to go from bad to worse. The waiter and Arlo tumble onto their asses, and a busboy rushes in to help but skids out, the heel of his shoe squished into a steak. He crashes onto the two men already on the floor and in the unglamorous tangle of limbs, I can't make out who is who. Our fellow dinner guests turn to ogle the brewing commotion as the notes from the piano player on the deck a few yards away tinkle into nothing.

Under her breath, Vandana mutters, "Shitty, shit, shit."

Face blotchy with rage, Arlo scrambles to his feet as gracefully as a giant can. Chavez shrugs out of his blazer and chucks it onto his chair, the street fighter ready to go. Vandana, Morgan, and I all stand at the same time. I rest a hand lightly on his sleeve, urging him, "Don't, please."

He shakes off my gesture with virtual steam coming out his nose as a small army of dispatched staff swarm to clean up the mess. Morgan uses the distraction to swoop in and save the day, inserting himself between the two bruisers and pushing them apart with surprising authority. What I glean from his patient and modulated French is that he gently encourages Arlo to get the fuck out of here.

Arlo straightens his tie and floppy hairdo and can't resist one last jab. "See you around. If you climb out of the trough."

I grab onto Chavez, this time holding firm as he mutters, "Asshole."

His head swivels to stare down everyone staring at us, challenging them until they look away. The manager who joked and blew smoke up our asses earlier hovers close by with a tight smile that is no longer accommodating. Morgan assures him that yes, we are leaving.

Tragedy averted, Vandana touches her diamond choker and whispers, "Thank God."

She clocks the tattoos on Chavez, his hands fisted and ready, and without saying anything, I know she has reassessed him. The ripple of tension in the room slowly dissipates, and the guests go back to enjoying foie gras and their one-percent life.

Morgan, bless him, remains in good spirits and jokes, "Never a dull moment in fair Monaco."

"Thank you," I say and squeeze his forearm. "We appreciate you stepping in."

He leans in with a conspiratorial whisper. "No one likes him anyway. I was hoping your man might take him out."

He winks at Chavez, who feels compelled to smile while privately seething. His temper has been in check, more or less, all month, but to have Arlo show him up in front of me, my friends, and Monaco society is going to result in the kind of blowout that sells tickets.

"Don't worry," I say, trying to soothe him. "You'll get your revenge on the court."

But a black cloud hangs over his head, so I gather my wrap and evening bag, mentally preparing for the worst back at the hotel. Nothing says we can't end the evening on a lower note.

Chapter Twenty-Four

"You okay to walk in those shoes?" Chavez asks me.

"I'll make it."

Morgan has gone to fetch his car from valet, and Vandana hugs me under the covered entrance at La Môme.

"Any thoughts on tomorrow?" she asks. "We'd love to take you out on the yacht before you leave."

"I think—"

"We'll get back to you on that," Chavez says, cutting me off.

Vandana blinks and finds a smile. "Of course." Her careful look intones, *I don't know about him,* and the wind in my sails from earlier, when she said he was cute, blows out as fast as it came in. She whispers, "Good luck," in my ear and glances sideways at Chavez who taps his foot impatiently.

"I'll text you later," I say. "Thanks for the great day."

The Hotel de Paris is a short walk up a steeply graded street, and Chavez reaches for my hand as I try to find my footing. I did partake in several glasses of expensive champagne, making it hard to discern whether it's the bubbles or the residue of what just happened that is fizzing in my brain. His mood swings concerned me from the get-go, and everyone warned me he would be a handful. All the emotional management tactics I suggested he try have been intermittently successful and tonight leaves me questioning how solid we can ever be if he chooses not to tackle his behaviour.

The words I want to say are just out of reach, and Chavez remains tight-lipped, his features like granite. The night is warm, and despite the late hour, tourists crowd the wide boulevard to snap selfies with the yachts lit up in the harbor like billionaire glowsticks. A cruise on the water tomorrow would be fun if I could overcome my fear of not being able to swim.

But we are a long way away from that decision.

When we're inside our hotel suite, he kicks off his dress shoes and promptly spread-eagles onto the bed, covering his eyes with the back of his hand. I turn on the chandelier and dim it for ambience. The maid folded our jeans and left the neatly folded squares on a velvet divan overlooking the Mediterranean. This room is so over the top. What a shame to end our only night here with a question mark looming over us. I sit on the edge of the bed and pick at my nail polish, buying time. Chavez is motionless, blocking me out, and the longer he says nothing, the harder it is to know what to say.

How do I express my feelings without hurting him?

"Next time," I start, "can you—"

"Don't worry," he interrupts. "There won't be a next time."

My heart does a strange flip-flop. "What are you saying?"

"I'm saying, what's the point? I've wasted so much time and mental energy trying to prove myself, and for what? I got nothing to show for it." He curls up and over to one side, facing away from me. I can hear the deep frustration in his labored breathing. "I hate it that he won a Grand Slam before me," he continues. "I fucking hate it. And I want it so bad, but I'm a giant waste of space out there. Never even made it to a semi-final."

There's a desperate edge to his voice that's painful to hear. I fall silent, collecting my thoughts.

"Don't downplay what you have already achieved or get impatient about moving forward," I finally say. "One step at a time." I touch his leg in an effort to console him, but he shrugs it off, refusing me.

"You can't fix the unfixable, Flynn."

"You're not unfixable," I insist. "Things will not change overnight."

"Nothing is going to change," he says bitterly. "I didn't say anything, but I lost in Cherbourg because I couldn't stop his voice. I lied to you. I'm sorry. Earl is always there, and I don't know how I'll ever make him go away."

Huh, I was right. There was more to his loss than he copped to. I stare at the carpet as if it holds a clue as to what I should say next. All the 'right' things, meaningless platitudes. The truth is, nothing ever goes away. Our pasts haunt us unless we change how to perceive them and choose to not give them the power to impact us moving forward.

God, I'm full of great insight. One day I might follow it.

"What if you spoke to Earl?" I ask. "Cleansed your soul?"

His breathing slows to the point of stopping. "How would that help?"

I weigh my words carefully considering his delicate state. We have talked extensively about Flynn Dryden Truth #7—What you believe is your potential—and I don't need to hammer it home.

"He has power over you because you give it to him. If you speak the truth, all the reasons why he's messing with your mind, it might help. It might be the first step to breaking free."

He snorts a laugh. "After my last visit, he probably has security guards at every door."

I cup his heels and let the warmth of my skin sink into his. He likes it when I touch his feet. "Think about it, okay? Sometimes the most obvious solution is the hardest."

Eventually, he rolls over to face me. A little muscle works around his jaw. How his eyes rake over me is different, and a small part of me gets ready to be thanked for righting this ship.

"I really wish you hadn't thanked Morgan a hundred times for saving the night," he says.

Ah, the other reason for his mood. But he wasn't the only one impacted tonight.

"First of all, you need to own your behavior. It could have ended far uglier." Off my look of reproach, his lips mash together. "And yes, I did go overboard, but in my defense, it was mostly for Vandana's bene-fit. She is trying to make a name for herself here, and the blow-up I told you about is still a thing she needs to overcome." Miraculously, Chavez was the only person on the planet oblivious to their international scandal. The good news is he could sit across from Vandana without visualizing her naked body split in half by Morgan and his fire log. "The fact he handled the situation with grace goes a long way toward making sure they maintain a positive reputation in Monaco," I add. "Effusive thanking was my way of showing support. I always support my friends."

He digests this, can't fault me for it, and comments, "It's funny you two are friends. You're so naturally beautiful, so legit, but nothing feels real with her. Those two are like a magazine picture."

"She has a heart of gold. And I think Morgan is borderline obsessed with you."

He cracks a half-smile. "I got that vibe too. And look, Vandana's nice, all right. They both are. But take away all her paid-for bullshit—boobs, eyebrows, eyelashes—and what's left?"

"She's pretty stunning even without all the extras," I admit, because I will always defend my best friends, and well, it is true. But his observation, while flattering to me, lands wrong for other reasons.

"How do you know she has fake boobs?"

"Guys know," he says with a shrug. "You were braless the day we met, right?"

Was I? It seems like a lifetime ago since we crossed paths in Beverly Hills. Struggle and vulnerability have softened him, but he is still a formidable and infuriating force. I am endlessly conflicted.

"My other BFF, June, would have called you a cheeky bastard and promptly slapped you had you commented on her chest."

He smiles, pushes up to sit, and undoes his tie, flinging it across the room. "My parents named me after Cesar Chavez. I come prepackaged with attitude."

"Cesar the activist? I thought his MO was like Gandhi—no violence, no anger." Hint, hint.

He rolls off his socks next, wiping away tufts of black lint clinging to his toes. He has nice toes for a tennis player—straight and unmangled. "You are a smart cookie, Miss Flynn, and it's one of the many reasons why I like you. My point is, Cesar challenged the status quo. He had rebellion baked into his soul, and that is me in a nutshell. I live, play, and fuck the same way, with purpose and intensity."

I raise an eyebrow. "If the expectation is for me to argue that, it's not happening."

"That's exactly why I'm bringing this up," he stresses. "You accept me for me. And I know there are things I need to change, and the only person who can do that is me. But it's easier to change with someone championing you. So, thank you." He crawls on his knees to take a seat beside me. He smells woodsy and dangerous, like the Big Bad Wolf, and as he strokes my thigh, I forget to be mad at him. "None of my pity party tonight changes how I feel about you, all right? When we get to Paris, I want to spend our first day in bed. Kiss and cuddle and talk about *your* hopes and dreams. All we ever talk about is me."

"Speaking of you, I think we should go on the yacht tomorrow. Morgan would like to hang out with you."

"You sure?" he asks, searching my face. "Don't push beyond your comfort zone for a couple of dudes to rip around on jet skis."

"If it gets intense, I'll sit inside." And maybe this will be my first step on the long road to opening up. Overcome one fear and the path gets easier.

"Morgan is pretty cool," he admits. "What do you think about him?"

"He's very nice."

"Nice? C'mon." He knocks me with his elbow. "Every woman fantasizes about a guy like him."

My cheeks redden. "What do you want me to say? He's not hard to look at."

"Just so we're clear, I'm never going to wax my balls."

"You think he waxes his balls?"

"Of course, he does," Chavez scoffs. "Look at him."

I crack a smile. "I'd rather look at your balls."

He playfully grabs at my hand coming in for the grope, and we faux wrestle until he draws me close. He feels hot, even through the fabric of his suit, and when he strokes my arms with the lightest touch, the sensation leaves a trail of tiny electric shocks.

"I'm sorry for screwing up tonight," he whispers and runs a finger across my lower lip before capturing my mouth with his. His skillful tongue parts my lips, searches for mine in the wetness, and finds it warm and willing. We fall back onto the satin bedspread and his hard chest presses down on me like a sublime burden. He frustrates me, fascinates me, and leaves me breathless and wanting in equal doses. I can't say no to him. Not now, not ever.

He is my kryptonite.

He presses hot, open-mouth kisses to the soft skin of my neck, moving higher to skim my lips. "Flynn," he murmurs, the sound so soft I barely hear it. "Can you take your panties off and lie on top of me?"

I swallow hard. His boldness never ceases to give me a thrill. "Leave my dress on?"

"For now."

"What about you?"

He cups my breast, squeezing it. "This is all about the birthday girl. Don't think I forgot."

I bite my lip and smile. "Then you should take them off."

"You got a deal. But I need you to stand."

He sits up and helps me to my feet, positioning me between his splayed legs. The sateen of his Dior shirt shimmers softly in the low light, and his eyes glow like he's lit from within. His hands slide up my thighs, disappearing under the black silk of my dress. He presses his thumb pad against my clit, and a shuddering groan escapes my lips. My panties are drenched.

"I can smell you from here," he whispers and slowly pulls my Hanky Pankys down the length of my legs. I slip out of my heels and kick them and the scrap of red silk to one side. He scoots higher onto the bed, his feet propelling him. I hike my dress to climb up and on top of his reclined body.

"No, no," he says, stopping me before I straddle him. "Your back on my chest."

"But ... how are we going to kiss?"

"We got lots of time for kissing."

Chavez steadies me as I turn around, laughing softly at how uncoordinated I am in my drunken state. Positioned on top of him, but facing forward, I fall back until I can feel the beat of his heart against my spine.

"Lift your butt, beautiful," he says and tugs the dress up to my belly button. His hands skim over my soft inner thighs, gently pressing them wider. My sensitive parts are slick as a spilled can of paint, and his finger wastes no time zeroing in.

"I love how responsive you are," he says, his voice like deep-amber honey. "It makes me crazy."

My body feels wildly new every time he touches me—a pliable mess of clay ready for shaping. A slow hum builds in my clit and even though I can't see him, I see him in my mind. He looked so handsome tonight in his suit and tie, and I forget about how exposed I am, forget almost to breathe.

"I respond to you," I whisper back.

And he to me—hard and pulsing against my butt. His blatant joy in pleasuring me and how fevered he goes about it turns my arms into wet dishrags, flopping uselessly at my side. The muscles in my thighs melt and give out, splaying wider. Chavez buries his finger to the last knuckle into my wet welcome and fucks me hard and deep, curling two fingers and then three into a single pulsing demon. I feel the jolt of each stroke in my belly, hard questions demanding answers. His rhythm edges me close to the breaking point, and my fingers dig deep into his thighs with an aching cry.

"Fuck, Chavez. I'm going to come."

He bites my neck hard, like a feeding vampire. "I want to eat you," he says, his voice wavering and a little desperate. "Just to have you inside me."

An unbearable tension funnels lower and heat brands the soles of my feet, curling them into tight half-moons. Dimly aware of the moonlight spilling through the window and a building crescendo of violins somewhere in the distance, I remember a thousand things I thought I had forgotten and then forget everything. Crests of violent rapture take over, and it feels like I'm hitting speed bumps at two hundred miles an hour. Flying and crashing, careening out of control.

He arches into me, moaning, and tangled in the agony of his release is the sound of my name and something else.

Something that sounds like love.

Chapter Twenty-Five

CHAVEZ

I RALLIED IN MONACO. OR SHOULD I SAY, FLYNN SMACKED SOME sense into my wallowing, pathetic self. I could be a ponce in a designer suit and wailing about the injustice of it all, or I could man up and make my dreams a reality. Fearlessness and victimhood do not go hand in hand. And she walked her talk—took the plunge, conquered her fears, and waltzed onto Morgan's yacht, owning whatever came next. I sat inside with her while we cruised to our anchor point, and I made sure the pallor of her skin returned to normal before we dudes raced around on jet skis, leaving the ladies to the tan-and-talk scene. I'm digging Morgan, and yeah, there's a bit of a bromance going on.

Vandana?

She will take a bit more work.

She reminds me of those stuck-up North Fresno girls who would never be caught dead with the likes of me. The look she gave Flynn last night before we left the restaurant had a hundred messages in it, all of them variations of, *You can do better than this hot mess.* I was like, thanks. Nothing better than kicking a man when he's down.

On the walk back to our hotel, I had no clue where to even begin a sentence, I was so angry and pissed at myself for letting my temper run away again. For letting Flynn down. My failures hurt so badly, I literally shriveled up on the bed. But instead of taking my pussy behavior as a personal rejection, Flynn kept a calm head and made me consider an alternative that spiked fear in my heart. To rummage through the basement storage area of things too scary to think about.

All of this going down on her birthday weekend, when it should have been about her.

I believe I made it to up her. I only hope I didn't scare her away.

With her going off on top of me, I lost my mind, possessed with the need to possess her. It flew out of my mouth. If she heard, she chose not to say anything about it. The long and short of it is I can no longer comprehend a future without her in it.

I turn the shower off and shake like a dog after swimming. Last night, we hopped on Morgan's jet and flew to Paris. Flynn wandered through the Ritz, wonderstruck to be in the same space Hemingway once inhabited. She couldn't believe we were staying here, and I have all sorts of things planned, including a sweet-smelling, squeaky-clean wake-up call for my snoozing baby.

I will be gentler than I was in Monaco. Try to be. I've been told I'm intense during sex, and I don't deny it. You are who you are in the most extreme moments, good and bad. Passion and fury are cut from the same cloth, just draped differently. Flynn isn't bothered by it. If anything, it turns her on. And there's nothing sexier than a woman who appreciates who you are in the heat of the moment.

All I have to do now is get Mama on board. She thinks our age difference amounts to blasphemy. But years on this earth mean nothing when gauging chemistry between two people. Relationships work with respect and love. And they also require not turning into a crazy woman like Sofia did, snooping on my phone and laptop and generally being a cold bitch when I wanted some action after time on the road. How was I supposed to marry her when she viewed sex as some twisted form of control? In the end, it only bit her in the ass. I stayed loyal until the writing was on the wall and then took advantage of the ladies prowling hard around the tournaments looking for some tennis-stud love. I dabbled where I shouldn't have dabbled, but I knew it was only temporary.

I know what I want.

Starting my own family is a given, and any woman I kneel in front of with a ring needs to be on board with that game plan. I'm not entirely sure Flynn was telling the truth about wanting kids, but she was hugging my legs like I was her bedrock in a storm when I brought it up in Cherbourg, and that has to amount to something. I know I have to take it slowly. Smythe has been telling me that since day one. But when I see my future, and it's everything I want it to be, it kills me not to move things into 'official' territory.

I'm a bag of nerves because today is the day I will ask. Not the M word, or even the E word, but feel her out about moving in the general direction of commitment and maybe bring up the kid thing again in a roundabout way. I would love a daughter with hair like hers. My two curlicue chicas.

I run a comb through my hair and rinse with mouthwash. Satisfied I look and smell like a guy worthy of devotion, I reach for a condom from my toiletry bag. Flynn is on the pill but will not let me in bare. I suppose I can't blame her. Eighty-three is a big number to swallow and truth be told, not all of those times did I use a rubber sock. When we get back to LA, I'll get tested to give her peace of mind.

The muffled sound of incoming messages on a phone rises out from under the face towel I left crumpled on the counter. Flynn charges her phone in the bathroom because she likes to sleep without being bothered. I shouldn't look, I never have, but lift the towel anyway.

It's like God wanted me to see the texts, both of them coming in a few seconds apart.

Cori: Dear Flynn. It's mom. I know you don't want to hear from us, but I wanted to let you know your dad is in the hospital. He had a stroke and asked me to reach out to you. Please call. Love you. Xo

I blink, not sure I'm reading that right. But in the space of three seconds, the Flynn I know, the Flynn I thought I knew, doesn't exist.

And then the second text lands, and my heart does this funny thing I never want to feel again. It squeezes into an excruciating ball and explodes at the same time.

BD: I hope you enjoyed Monaco. Any yacht photos?

I back away from the counter as if a pile of black mambas are hissing at me. A sick sense of betrayal twists my intestines into a balloon animal. Brandon? No way. She promised me. She looked me straight in the eye and said she had zero interest in him. But this is a buddy message—comfortable, with many exchanges happening before this one. A muscle under my eye starts to twitch uncontrollably. What else has she been lying about? I float like a ghost into the bedroom and stand motionless on her side of the bed. That angelic face. Those sweet curls. Goosebumps cover my entire naked body. The only thing keeping me from smashing her phone into smithereens is a far-flung belief that I am wrong.

Maybe she smells the Confixor in my hair or the splash of cologne. Her nose does this cute little wrinkly thing before those thunderous lashes peel open.

"Morning," she says. But as her eyes focus on my stony-faced mug, the smile sputters.

No time to dance around. Not when my life is flashing before my eyes. "You got a text from your mom. And Brandon."

Just like that, her eyes shut down, darkening into a place I recognize. The same murky territory that was on display after the photographer snapped a photo of us in OZ. That's when I know.

She sits up and sounds flat, like a robot. "I have never looked at your phone. Not once."

"Don't accuse me of snooping, because I wasn't."

"Give me my phone please."

"Not yet. I'm going to read you what I just read and then you have some explaining to do."

I will never be a public speaker, not like her, but I get it all out without breaking down. Nothing changes in her face. She's dead fucking calm.

"I told you I had adoptive parents," she says.

"What you told me is that they haven't spoken to you in years. Call me loco, but that text didn't read angry and bitter. It sounds like someone on the opposite end of the bitter stick."

She wraps the sheet tight across the nipples I had planned to decimate. "Is this an interrogation?"

"It's about being honest with me, which you haven't been. How long have you and Brandon been phone buddies?"

Her eyes slip off mine. Since Australia, is what I'm guessing.

"He got my number from my agent," she says. "It's a long story, and it's one of the reasons why I fired him."

I sit down hard on the bed, my universe falling apart. That day in Bologna she was so out of it, claiming agent woes while snapping photos to send to Douchebag Dixler. Fuck! How could she do this to me?

"Did you two…" I can't even say it.

Seeing my alarm, she makes a calming gesture. "Nothing has happened like that, I swear."

"Then unlock your phone and prove it."

I hand her the phone and surprise, she doesn't take it. "There is a thing called privacy, Chavez."

"Privacy?" Is she for real? "How about secrecy? I've been trying to figure you out from day one. Can we talk about a motivational guru begging for anti-depressants?"

She pales, and yeah, that was a low blow. "That's confidential information," she says.

"Seriously? That's your concern? I'm asking you to be up-front with me."

"I'm not depressed. I have anxiety."

"No shit! You think leading a double life might have something to do with that? 'Cos that would sure as hell keep me up at night."

She inches to the other side of the bed. "Don't yell at me."

"I'm going to shout at the top of my lungs until you come clean."

"What do you want to know?" she shouts back.

"Everything! Starting from the top. You got this big-time career, out in the public, you musta been photographed a hundred times a day on the road. And yet, one photo with me and you're jumping like a scared rabbit. After dinner with my parents, I dropped you off but then circled back. All I wanted was one more kiss, but you were jumping into an Uber. And what is the deal with your family? Because if someone who loves you is in the hospital and you don't give a shit, then you might as well walk out that door."

Her eyes widen at my litany of accusations. Weeks of lies I'm calling her on. Her jaw grinds back and forth.

"I don't talk to them," she finally admits, "because they lied to me. You read that in my memoir. They never told me I was adopted. And when I found out, they also told me my mother was a train wreck who didn't want anything to do with me. But I'll never know the truth because she died two months before I found my adoption records." Her voice turns cold and bitter, something I've never heard before. "You want to know what it feels like to have your entire world as you know it flushed down the toilet? I don't think you do. Because it's a pain you never forget."

It craters my soul to see how lost she looks. I reach for her, to show her she is not alone in her battles. "Flynn, you're shaking like a leaf. You have an avalanche of issues barrelling down, and—"

"Don't tell me you sympathize or understand," she snaps. "I was so messed up I made a decision I've regretted my entire life. I am responsible for someone else ending their life. And I can *never* talk to my real mom, even if I wanted to. You have the option, but you'd rather be at war with your family and yourself and the tennis world, fucking the Vanyas and God knows who else, like your reputation doesn't even matter. No wonder Arlo wanted to punch you out."

It's like she's kicked me in the balls. Vanya? Where is that cold shit coming from? And making it sound like Arlo's in the right? I am shaking so hard my teeth hurt. "Is that why you're sexting Brandon? Because of some one-night stand that I wish never happened?"

"Everyone knows it happened."

"They call it history for a reason, Flynn. And if you remember, I cleared the decks on day one, date one. If you had an issue with my numbers, you should've said something then. Digging in my past to throw it in my face months later is bullshit."

Rain starts to spit against the window, a wild wind whipping the drops around. Her face sets in an expression somewhere between anger and mistrust, and I momentarily lose my bearings.

"Do you even understand what's going on here?" I ask, the pitch of my voice rising. "For someone who went to Stanford, you're pretty fucking stupid if you can't figure out that I am falling in love with you."

For five long seconds, I think finally, I've touched her. We can start on the rocky road to repair. Then she peels out of bed, drags the sheet around her, and her eyes narrow into slits. "So now I'm fucking stupid?"

I throw up my hands in frustration. Why do women do this all the time?

"Did you even hear the other part? The part where I am in love with you? Jesus Christ, Flynn. I'm trying to think of what my life would be like without you in it and I can't. I am struggling to make sense of how you make me feel. And I've said nothing because I don't want to scare you off, but I always have this feeling you're not with me one-hundred-percent. And this just proves it."

"You just proved spying is fine in a relationship," she fires back. "Looking at my phone or telling me who I can or cannot speak with is unacceptable. If this is how it's going down, I'm out."

My God. Where has this harsh woman come from? She is shutting down, blocking me like a stone gate covered with padlocks. I don't believe it. I throw down my last hand, hoping it's enough to beat this ugly situation.

"If you want to be with me, I need honesty. I need commitment." I corner her up against the wall and jab my finger into her chest. "I need to own your soul."

She swats my hand away, eyes flashing fire. "You can't own me, Chavez. I'm not a trinket."

And there it is. Despair rolls off me in waves. It is time for all the understanding in the world and not ultimatums, but I can't have my heart stomped on. I storm to the door and practically wrench it off its hinges.

"Fine. Then I guess we're done. Here's the goddamn door."

My voice is a quivering shell of itself and I can barely focus, let alone see as my eyes glaze over. So, I do not register his presence. Not until Flynn takes a startled step back with a look on her face like she's about to puke all over Paris.

And that's how life as I know it ends: with a cop the size of a bloated gorilla in the doorway, twirling his moustache and doing his best not to stare at my dick flapping in the breeze.

Chapter Twenty Six

FLYNN

THE COP CLEARS HIS THROAT AND FINDS SOMETHING ON THE FLOOR TO observe. "Monsieur Delgado?"

"Yeah," Chavez says, puffing out his chest despite his nakedness. "Who wants to know?"

"My name is Armand Moreau," he says. "I am part of the unit that specializes in betting and match-fixing investigations. There were reports of suspicious betting on three of the matches you played in Cherbourg. I need to confiscate your laptop and mobile phone as evidence. You are provisionally suspended from playing professional tennis until further notice."

A complete look of bewilderment washes over Chavez's face. "What are you talking about? I've never bet on any match in my life." He looks over at me, hoping. "Is this a joke?"

Police don't show up at the Ritz on Sunday morning as a joke, I know that much. I'm still reeling from our argument, but there is something to be said for maintaining a shred of dignity. I slink to the bathroom and return with a robe that Chavez shrugs on. Mine got left at the pool last night, so the bedsheet will have to do.

Chavez knots the belt and slides my phone into one of the robe pockets. "I'm telling you, I am not a cheater," he insists. "Someone has made a mistake."

"Why does he have to give you his laptop and phone?" I ask. Armand gives me a careful once-over. "I'm his coach," I add, my professional tone somewhat pointless given my toga party attire.

"They're allowed to ask," Chavez interjects. "But only when the evidence is suspicious. What matches did the betting happen on?"

"Please, Monsieur Delgado, the electronics." Moreau stands firm, and from his tone, the wedding band on his finger, and his general air of tiredness, I deduce he has young children requiring a constant hand to control their shenanigans. He doesn't strike me as overly vain, but his slack and pouchy skin is an odd shade of orangey brown that speaks to a spray-tan addiction. "The Tennis Integrity Unit oversees all corruption investigations. Please contact them for the details."

I blink, dumbfounded. Corruption? No one tosses that word around flagrantly. Outside, the rain starts up again, turning torrential.

"How am I supposed to contact them if I don't have a phone?" Chavez demands.

"Perhaps..." Moreau's eyes shift ever so slightly toward me. He has the nerve to smile. "Your coach may assist you?"

He's unmovable; a solid mass of French 'no.' I feel a brief flutter of suspense, of something beyond my control. First it was Nathan peppering me with questions in Italy. Then he and Georgie were in France. And now that I think about it, Brandon also knew Chavez was playing in Cherbourg. Everything suddenly complicates. Timelines. Motives.

"This is fucking unbelievable," Chavez says, expressing my thoughts to a T. He stomps to the bedside table, unplugs his phone, and digs through his carry-on bag for the laptop. "Here," he says, handing both over to Moreau. "All I can say is they better have some cause for this."

"De rien, Monsieur Delgado, for your cooperation." He hands Chavez a business card with a caveat. "We are not responsible for the final decision, so please do not contact me for information. Once the investigation is over, you can call that number to claim your electronics. Please be aware that match-fixing is a criminal offense in France," he continues, adding a whole other sparkling dimension to the morning.

"Who do I contact at the ITIA?" Chavez asks, accepting his fate with a bald look of fear.

"They will assign someone to your case. Call them tomorrow morning. They are based in London."

"Is he—are we," I quickly change, "allowed to leave France?"

Moreau nods. "For now, yes. If a hearing takes place, it will be online, through an independent court in Switzerland." He tips his hat as if saying adieu to friends at the market. "Pardon for the interruption. I'll let you get back to your day."

He lets himself out without a further word, brushing past a hotel employee standing guard outside the door. A higher-up of some sort, judging from her smart business attire. She clasps her hands together tightly, tighter than her smile, if that is possible, and introduces herself as Madeline.

"Bonjour," she says. "Is everything okay?"

She does a sweep of our room and our faces. I really should not be draped in a sheet.

"Yeah, we're fine," Chavez says.

Madeline nods slowly. She'll double check with Moreau on the fine part. "If we can be of assistance, please don't hesitate to contact the front desk."

Chavez lets the door slam shut and stares at me as if seeing nothing and everything. Something doesn't fit, not quite.

"How much have you been blabbing to Dixler?" he asks.

"Nothing. We..."

"We?" He interrupts, a cold bite in his voice.

I run my hands through my hair, unsure what to say without creating a shit storm.

"Flynn," he says. "Tell me what is going on. I can see it in your face. You know something about this."

I cross my arms, wondering where to start and worrying how this will all end. "In Italy, this guy approached me. Two guys. You played one of them in Cherbourg. Nathan Abbott."

His brow furrows in recall. "You were watching his match in Italy."

"I was, but only to watch him lose," I clarify. "He was an idiot. They both were. They saw you kiss me in the bleachers, that first day I came to practice, and came over to harass me."

He moves to the gas fireplace, flips the switch, and a flame jumps across the grill. It is chilly in here, or maybe it's that all my blood has left my extremities.

"I told you never to talk to anyone about this shit," he says.

"I know," I say, distress rattling my voice higher. "It wasn't like that. Honestly. He brought up odds or splits and I threatened to talk to the officials—"

"He specifically mentioned betting? When did you plan on telling me this? Oh let me guess, never." Chavez laughs, but it's a dead laugh, one with no humor. "Do you realize my career might be over?"

"But I didn't say anything!"

How can I make him believe me when I don't know the truth? I would do anything to go back in time, but as it turns out, I will have to go way back, all the way to the beginning. As sure as the Parisian weather can turn on a dime, so too can this day plunge off a cliff.

My phone buzzes in his robe pocket, and he reaches for it with his eyes never leaving mine. From the moment he skims the message I know something very bad is about to happen.

His voice is barren when he asks, "How many dudes are you stringing along besides me?"

"I'm not stringing you along."

He leans against the mantle and observes me with a stark look. "It's great to know you and your boyfriend refer to me as a brown boy. That's the cherry on top of everything. And I can't believe *you've* been betting on my matches."

All the air disappears from the room. I lick my lips, trying to kick-start my lungs. My heart. My brain.

Brown boy.

I blocked the stalker's number last month. How many phones does this idiot own?

"Give me the phone, Chavez. Now."

Maybe it's my tone, the rise of panic. The sound of guilt. His attention pricks. I need to see the message so I lunge at him, but he steps back, holding the phone high above his head.

"You don't understand!" I yell. "Give it to me!"

"Oh, I understand," he says, the cut in his voice sharper than a blade. "I have been an absolute idiot to trust you. Flynn Dryden and her truths are the biggest joke of all. You are nothing but a liar."

"I would never throw you under the bus. You know that."

"Just like you promised me you'd never talk to Brandon. Or that you would never talk about my game to strangers?"

He tosses me the phone. My hands shake so violently I can barely see the screen.

Unknown number: Flynn, I told you, you can do better than a brown boy. I bet against him and won. Now I can bring you home.

My heart trips and stumbles. A gloom that might not ever dissipate buries my soul.

"This is not a boyfriend," I say. "This guy has been stalking me for the past year. He went away but then showed up again in December. That's why I freaked out about the photographer in Oz. I didn't want this guy to know where I was. He found out where I lived in LA and—"

"Hold on." Chavez stops my babbling with a raise of his hand. Utter bafflement erases any trace of anger on his face. "So, you have a stalker and you don't tell me about it?" He shakes his head in disbelief. "Jesus, Flynn. I want us to build a life together. How do we do that when you lie to me and keep all this shit inside you?"

Wind pelts debris against the windows, and the angry sky is every shade of grey. My throat constricts, and I feel a surge of panic. As soon as I saw El Corazon hanging in his Ferrari, it was my ticket to run as far away as possible. That card is a curse, a prophecy of trouble. Reality sinks in, hitting me like surreal waves. I stumble to my side of the bed and start frantically yanking on clothes lying crumpled on the floor.

"What are you doing?" he asks.

I stuff my phone into my purse, my laptop next. Pull on my boots. I need to get out of here.

"Flynn!" Chavez approaches me like I am not quite right in the head. "Look at me. We need to talk about this. All of it. Who is this guy? Are you in danger?"

"There is nothing to talk about," I say, shouldering past him. "I am trouble. And you need to stay far away from me."

I dash for the door with Chavez right on my heels. "Talk to me," he pleads. "What is going on?"

It's actually worse that I can tell how hard he's trying. I yank on my pea coat, feeling dirty and covered in scum. Chavez might not be in a wheelchair because of my stupidity, but he might as well be if he can't play tennis again.

"Flynn, please," he begs. "Don't leave. Let me help you."

Chavez stands so still and for someone forever in motion, it feels wrong and unnatural. Pinned by his weighted gaze, I want to tell him how wrongheaded I have been. But even saying sorry is impossible because I have no more breath. In a secret place, beneath flesh and bone and my pumping heart, lies an appalling silence.

I slip out the door and stumble like a drunk down the hallway, blinded by tears.

Flynn Dryden is on the run again.

Chapter Twenty-Seven

THIS CAN'T BE HAPPENING.

But it is.

I stagger across Place Vendôme with the wind shrieking around me. Pellets of rain sleet hard in the cold grey morning, and I huddle into the shell of my pea coat. Any rational human is tucked away in bed on this miserable Sunday morning, but when it comes to sensibility, I have lost the plot. Hamilton's mother once called me a lying bitch, and she certainly had the first part right. Her son would never have taken me on his white-water rafting trip had he been privy to my emotional state.

And now, history is repeating itself with more lies and more trouble.

I am cursed, just like that damn card.

If only...

The sudden blare of a horn snaps me out of my thoughts. I've wandered out of the plaza, onto a street, and a Peugeot roaring past kicks up a monster spray of water. I scurry back onto the sidewalk, drenched and shivering.

Fuck!

Hot tears streak down both cheeks, cutting through the street grime splattered on my face. Before my toes turn blue with cold, I need to plant my ass and gather myself. Figure out how to untangle this diabolical mess. Up ahead is a hotel, and I suffer through the scrutiny of a front desk clerk unimpressed with a dirty, wet American clueless as to how many nights she plans to stay.

"There is nothing available right now," he informs me with what I think might be understated glee. "We were sold out last night. If you leave your number, I will call with an update. You are welcome to wait in the restaurant. Complimentary wifi."

He says this like I'm a street urchin whose mission in life is free internet access. Note to self: if I ever move to Europe, I'm bypassing France and heading straight for Italy.

I cross the lobby, my boot heels ringing on the marble floor. The hotel is eerily quiet for nine a.m. Not even remotely hungry, I detour from the cavernous restaurant into the cozy confines of an empty cocktail bar. The clubby room has a low ceiling and wainscoted panels. A privileged and pricey space where bankers would tip back martinis and bitch about interest rates. The perfect setting for me to dwell on how bankrupt my life has become.

Next to the bar, a server with chubby cheeks and brunette hair flowing to her shoulders in soft waves stacks glass racks on a trolley. She looks up when I enter and assesses me head to toe. "Good morning. The bar isn't open until eleven."

"Is it okay if I sit in here? I'm waiting for a room and could use a quiet space."

Maybe it's my hairdo from hell. Or that we are similar in age. Or the quiet desperation oozing from my every pore. Something resonates with her.

"Go ahead," she says with a shrug.

I set my purse down on the polished marble slab running the length of the bar and hike myself onto a leather stool. With a grunt, the woman lifts another rack of glassware onto the trolley, positioning it until it clicks securely into the one beneath it. I can sense the muscles beneath her black dress shirt. She watches me wipe my face with a paper cocktail napkin.

"If you want," she says. "You can order something from the restaurant and eat here."

"How about a bottle of Jack Daniel's? And a straw."

She slants her head to one side. "Guy trouble?"

I think about that and how much I want to reveal. But isn't that my overall problem? Not revealing anything? "General, all-around crisis."

She wipes her hands on the white apron tied tight around her waist and offers a hand. A tattoo of a thorny rose stem circles one of her thick wrists. She could probably bench-press me. "My name is Annie. How about you start with a latte?"

I shake her hand and introduce myself. I've only been in her company for a minute or two and already feel calmed. "You're probably right. Coffee first."

The espresso machine at the end of the bar is one of those high-end jobbies with too many levers and buttons for my one-pod Nespresso mind. But Annie is one of those efficient, can-do types you want in your back pocket for a camping trip. She whips up a coffee in no time and slides the steaming cup across the bar.

"Enjoy."

I nibble on the cinnamon-flavored cookie she provided, and my stomach grumbles. I am hungrier than I thought.

"I can't figure out your accent," I say.

Annie wipes down the foaming wand on the espresso machine with a knowing grin. She's been asked this before. "Paris by way of Quebec City, Canada."

"Is Quebec near Flin Flon?"

She cackles at the lunacy coming from the mouth of the drowned rat sitting at her bar. "Not even close. You must be American."

"I take it that's not a compliment?" Her forwardness is refreshing, actually. I am not offended, and neither is she. She sees through my sarcasm and it feels like she sees right through me, too.

"You don't strike me as the type of person to be in a crisis, Flynn. What am I missing?"

I dip the cookie into the foam and watch it dissolve. "Are you saying that because I look so put together?"

She smiles, the tiniest bit amused. "You are in dire need of a dry cleaner, but yeah, you come across as someone who knows what they're doing."

I laugh wryly. Story of my life, right there. Nathaniel takes full credit for transforming me into the persona of Flynn Dryden, but like a woman transformed through plastic surgery, I was new, shiny, and pretty only on the outside. I am forever unsure on the inside. I bring the latte to my lips and take a sip before setting the cup back down. "Sometimes I don't know who I am anymore."

Annie leans onto the bar counter. There's an understanding between us I can't pinpoint, but it comes from a shared experience. Maybe she knows what it feels like to be broken.

"So, your crisis is existential?"

"I found out at eighteen I was adopted." I take a deep hit of coffee before saying aloud words I have never spoken to anyone. "I've struggled with a permanent identity crisis ever since."

Annie whistles under her breath. "Damn. Why didn't your parents say anything earlier?"

My gaze drifts to the wall of booze bottles behind her. "I was super shy and socially awkward. They felt I would become more self-conscious if I knew I was adopted. In retrospect, they were probably right."

"And you never suspected anything?"

"Once or twice."

I had wondered several times over the years. No real reason for it, other than a vibration of something being off. But Cori had curls similar to mine, my height and slim build matched Edgar's, and I could patch my features together by analyzing their faces. Based on pure genetics, there was never a question mark.

But I never posed the question.

"Did you ever find your birth parents?" she asks. "I've heard that can go one of two ways."

I shake my head. "My mother died a few months before I started my search for her. I never knew who my father was."

"That's harsh. Sorry to hear that." In the long pause, she buffs the bar with her rag. Then, "Where does the guy fit into all of this?"

Oh, God. Chavez.

I rub my temples, attempting to squash all the horrible memories arising.

That long-ago night on the Santa Cruz boardwalk, waiting for Hamilton to arrive for our date. A cute taco vendor came over to chat me up, and we flirted back and forth—harmless fun—until Hamilton showed up just as the vendor palmed me El Corazon with a sweet smile. We fought bitterly afterward, and he ditched me for his friends, leaving me to walk home alone in the dark. Terrified I had screwed things up, I tossed and turned all night and then wandered like a zombie into the kitchen far earlier than my usual ten a.m. Cori and Edgar sat on the back porch with their morning coffees and spoke freely, believing they were alone.

"We have no idea how she will react if we tell her after all this time that she is adopted," Edgar said. "If it ain't broke…"

"Maybe you're right," Cori replied. "Maybe we wait until after Stanford."

I'll never forget the sensation of being frozen in time, floating in the kitchen like I was no longer part of the world. Cori came inside to top up her coffee, saw me in my pajamas and froze. She knew I'd heard. She tried to explain. Edgar too, when he came rushing in, but how do you explain obliterating the very foundation of me? You don't just blow past something like that. I ran upstairs, threw on some clothes and bolted.

After the rafting accident, my heart permanently closed. I became terrified of relationships and screwing them up. I moved to Palo Alto with nothing but a suitcase and answered an ad for a third roommate. Vandana and June became my Stanford family, and I told Cori and Edgar never to contact me again.

"Mademoiselle!"

A stern-faced woman in a grey pantsuit frowns disapprovingly at Annie and me as if we were swilling directly from a bottle of vodka. She says something in French to Annie that sounds like, *Get a move on, miss,* and stands there long enough to let us know she is offended before swishing back into the lobby.

"My boss," Annie explains with a grim look. "I have to get brunch set up in the restaurant, but you can stay here. Don't worry about the coffee. It's on the house."

"Thanks. And thanks for listening."

She smiles again. A different smile. "Do you know what your guy values the most?"

Funny she should ask that. The one thing missing from my life is what he values more than anything. My hands tremble, as does my voice, in case I need a reminder. "His family."

"Are you close to anyone?"

"His sister and I are friends."

"My ex was tight with his brother. He ran interference in a lot of our fights. Just saying." She squeezes my arm, and yes, she could bench-press me with no problem. "I hope things work out for you."

Left alone with my thoughts, numbness crawls into me. Chavez looked devastated when I left, but he might come to his senses and kick my ass to the curb. The thought of facing him paralyzes me. I finish the latte and spin the cup on its saucer, debating every scenario.

I have to try, or else I might as well have drowned in the river.

But before I say anything to Chavez, I need an impartial person to hear me out and convince me I am worthy of forgiveness. With a heavy sigh, I rummage through my purse for the phone.

It's one in the morning in California, but Carmen picks up.

"Hey, sister," she says, a fly-through of caution in her groggy voice. No one calls at this time with good news. "I'm guessing he's being an idiot."

I shut my eyes and force myself to breathe. On a wretched Sunday in Paris, it's time to re-open my heart.

"It's not him, Carmen. It's me."

Chapter Twenty-Eight

Come Monday afternoon, the knot in my heart refuses to unbundle. My chest aches. Both lungs are shredded from bouts of crying. I have tried to sleep and to have something more substantial than gum gnashing between my teeth. Aside from the bottles ransacked from the minibar, my Westin hotel room looks unlived in. Chavez has left multiple messages, and I'm still too scared to call him back. Carmen said she talked to him yesterday and tried to summarize my hour of gut-wrenching babble into something coherent.

I'm in no mood to talk to anyone right now, and the grand irony is yet another text lands from Brandon. He's been sending me messages all day. He wants to talk in person but does not indicate why. How stupid of me to lead him on in the first place. I am about to delete our entire text thread when the number from the Ritz scrolls across my screen. A feeling of vertigo washes over me. Chavez deserves some kind of actual, thoughtful girlfriend and not a woman too frightened to tell him the truth.

Just answer.

"Hi."

"Hey," he says.

Oh, God. Two words and dead silence, other than the sound of his breathing, which is more than what I can offer at this point.

"Where are you?" he finally asks.

"Down the street."

"You wanna come over?"

The muscles around my mouth twitch out of control. The moment feels immense and, at the same time, tiny as a pinhead. "Sure."

The Westin is sprinting distance from the Ritz, but in the dark and wild Parisian night, walking is all I can muster. Chavez spoke kindly on the phone, but there is the possibility of a harsh diatribe. How far apart we actually are. The hallway to his room makes me feel like I am walking the green mile.

You can do this. Whatever this is.

I knock on the door and leave it to him to throw all my spazzing emotions into the blender and hit *CRUSH*. He is improbably beautiful in flannel lounge pants while I'm in yesterday's wrinkled clothes with mascara clumped in my lashes from a sleepless night. He stares hard at me, his eyes swollen and red-rimmed like mine. Fear, exploding like shrapnel, lodges in my throat.

What have I done? And can I repair it? His gaze strips whatever leftover confidence I have in me.

"Hi," I say, braving my fear.

He steps aside, allowing me to enter without acknowledging my hello. The door slams shut, and he flicks on the light in the foyer. The bright burst is too much, and I shield my face. I realize he finally has what he wants. Me in the spotlight, unable to squirm away.

"Here's what's going to happen," he says. "I sit on the couch, and you get the hot seat. You answer all my questions *honestly*, and you don't get to ask me anything. After, you and I will decide what to do. Yes or no?"

He's not doing anything to make this less painful, and why should he? No one ever said life was fair.

I bow my head, my face burning with shame. "Yes."

I TELL HIM EVERYTHING. THE UGLIEST PARTS OF ME. HOW BEING discarded like an unwanted toy by my own flesh and blood mother festers in my heart like a tapeworm. My inability to form relationships with men for fear of rejection. He listens without interrupting, arms crossed tight and never allowing a hint of give until I voice my most private confession.

"Is that a lie too, Flynn?" he asks, tiredly. "Because I just have to look at you and you come."

"It's the truth. I swear. I don't know why it's different with you."

He knocks down what's left of his water. A flicker of emotion passes over his eyes. "Is that why you cut and run out of the cabana?"

I clench and unclench my hands. After a long hour and my throat stripped bare, I feel like one of those prisoners stretched out onto a medieval torture rack. I have nothing left to hide.

"I did have an appointment, but yes. I was overwhelmed."

Chavez looks beyond me, his eyes charting nothing. "You weren't upfront with me from day one. I know it was you in the parking lot scoping out my car. The security guy described you to a T. How do I know I can trust you?"

"Because you know everything now," I say.

His gaze fixes on mine. "Do I?"

I sigh. Finally, I see light at the end of the tunnel, only to get called out on another lie. This shit ends here, once and for all.

"If you expect a running tally of every one of my thoughts 24/7, I can't do that. Nor would I ask it of you. But I promise I will never lie to you again."

He leans forward, elbows landing on his knees as he hangs his head. The lightbulb in the floor lamp sputters and dies, leaving us in darkness. I can hear him breathing but have no idea what he's thinking. And I am sick of talking about myself.

"Can I ask how things are going?" I venture. All the main sports sites blared the news of his suspension today, and I could barely choke booze down, let alone food, my stomach was so curdled with despair.

"Not good," he says. "I spent all day on the phone."

He brings me up to speed on the conversations with the Tennis Integrity Unit, executives from the Cherbourg event, and officials with the Challenger and ATP tours. His round of sixteen, quarterfinal, and semi-final matches had unusual bets placed on their outcomes. Large bets favoring a Chavez loss, large enough to alert the IBIA, the organization that monitors global sports betting activity. The payout on his lost semi-final alone was high five figures. The money remains in safe-keeping pending the investigation outcome. None of the matches involved Nathan or Georgie, although Chavez dropped their names and passed on the details I'd shared.

When I ask if they will face any disciplinary action, he says, "If they're clean, they're clean. But hopefully, this smartens them up. Cheating destroys sportsmanship. And there is no way my name will be associated with it."

I pick at the nubby fabric of the armrest, and for the first time, it doesn't feel like I'm sitting in an electric chair. "Did you mention the stalker to them?"

"I brought it up. But it's so far removed for them, like a fucking movie. I didn't push it. And how do we prove anything?"

We. My heart feels like it might burst. "For sure he is part of this, and I'm going to do everything in my power to figure it out. You are not going down. I will never let that happen."

"You can't chase this guy, Flynn. He could be dangerous."

The caring in his voice makes my eyes brim with tears again. "What do I have to lose?"

"Don't talk like that," he says, quietly. "Carmen would be bummed if anything happened to you."

I chew on my lip. "What about you?"

His eyes flicker to the floor, and he breathes hard out his nose as if he's trying to hold back what he wants to say. Ten seconds passing feels like an hour.

"I love you, Flynn," he says. "I am not falling in love. I am neck-deep in love quicksand. You are the song on my playlist that I can't stop listening to. I need you on heavy rotation, every day, for eternity." He looks up, pain etched on his face. "But if you don't love me, I can't do this."

I wandered around the Westin like a zombie last night while debating what limb I could live without if it was the price of getting another chance with him. I've been lied to, told too many lies, and held too much back. Lives have been lost and shattered. To stand here and be allowed to turn things around, to make peace with all the wrong, becomes a physical thing vibrating deep in my throat.

"Can we hug?" I ask.

He crosses the distance between us, approaching me cautiously like a wounded animal. When his arms engulf me in a net of forgiveness, relief briefly topples me, coming out as thick, strangled sounds that he soothes away with every stroke on my back.

For several long minutes, we do nothing but hold each other. I feel the quivering deep in his chest.

Eventually, he mumbles into my hair. "Flynn, baby. It's going to be all right."

"Is it?"

The words burn like acid in my throat. Chavez pulls back to free my hair from the elastic and fluff it out. He scoops my face into his hands and the tenderness in his eyes is too good to be true. Did he misremember the facts?

"We'll figure this out, all of it," he says. "And if we go down, we go down together, all right?"

"I didn't realize I loved you," I whisper. "I forgot what it felt like. But I almost walked into the Seine yesterday to stop the hurt, that's how bad it was."

He's silent for a long moment, searching my face. Every sweeping glance feels like a lash of fire on my skin. Rougher than sixty grit sandpaper, his voice is barely audible when he says, "Love is worth fighting for when it hurts, Flynn. That's when you know it's the real thing."

His kiss melts away the numbness gathered inside me. We start slow and careful, our defenses gradually slipping away, like my clothes. Chavez strips me bare and forces me to stand naked with my legs splayed, silhouetted by cold moonlight. With the ghost of Hemingway watching, he lowers to his knees and writes his own salacious masterpiece, tongue as his tool and me his blank paper. The rush begins between my thighs, rousing and lewd, and I shudder in the darkness, fisting his hair to steady myself. He owns my soul and my mind, my ability to calculate two plus two. I beg for mercy and then for more until he demolishes me so completely that all that keeps me from collapsing is his arm circling my waist.

And his manhood has bloomed into its own poetic display, but he denies my covetous hand with a gentle slap. Instead, he lifts me into his arms like I weigh nothing, walks us into the bedroom, and lowers me onto the bed like an offering to the gods.

"Don't move," he whispers.

Time slows down waiting for him in the darkness. The moment stretches longer than the actual minute it is, and the lifetime of space threatens to swallow me whole. I was so careless with his heart. And with us.

When he returns from the bathroom and sees me trembling, he snuggles into the contour of my body. I can feel his erection, wrapped tight in a condom, throbbing against my thigh.

"If this is too much for you right now," he says, "we stop."

"No," I tell him, staring into the dark pools of his eyes. "This is exactly what I want."

And without another word, he rolls over and pushes into me. We give in to each other, Chavez crushing me in a deep-space assault of desperate possession. Tender turns into a torrent of primal, ass-grabbing fucking. He rides me hard, every deep, delicious stroke creating chaos like only Chavez can. It's an invasion, a merging of souls. I am boneless. Weightless. Nerve endings scraped raw and screaming for release. Punished and pushed to the brink.

And finally, the surge.

Pounded and nailed, my coming apart is a pinnacle of his tormenting design. If I am his sky, he is a shooting comet ripping across my darkness, and we leave the known for the unknown, promising each other in frantic hot whispers to always be truthful even if it hurts.

After, we lie panting in each other's arms. Ragged, smoldering embers, flushed and speechless. An aftermath where commitment needs no words when our mingled heartbeats say it all. We hold onto each other fiercely until the sweat misted on our skin evaporates, and Chavez crawls out of bed to run the bath.

Flynn Dryden's Truth #8 states that the path to greatness starts with forgiveness, and to be forgiven and entwined with Chavez in a soaker tub brimming with bubbles is far more than I could ever ask.

He pulls my foot out from underneath the foam and drops kisses on the tips of every toe. I shiver, my body still sensitive from our nasty session of salvation.

"Let's order room service," he says. "I don't want to go out."

If we stare silently at Big Macs and fries delivered by Uber, that is fine by me. I am not leaving this hotel room until we have a game plan. How to approach my parents after fourteen years is a daunting question, and his difficult task is to get the Earl monkey off his back. But the most vital piece of all of it is how we go about clearing his name. It means flushing out the stalker because I know this all circles back to him. Chavez insists I get the police involved and live with him in LA until there is a resolution. The problem is time. Who knows how long it will be before the police can make any dents in finding this idiot? And the betting case can drag on for weeks, Chavez tells me. We don't have weeks. He wants to play Roland Garros.

I am determined to find a way to get him there.

The question is how.

But for now, I have answered enough questions.

And later, after we've devoured a rack of lamb before moving on to each other, we lie in the dark, holding hands under the covers, listening to the rainfall in Paris.

Before our fight, I'd read how much Ernest Hemingway loved this city. But when his wife was pregnant and duty called, he moved back to the US.

And now we follow in the footsteps of Hemingway.

After two long months on the road, duty calls.

It is time to go home.

Chapter Twenty-Nine

There are two kinds of people in this world. The ones who wake up early and hustle everyone to join them, and then there is me, who could sleep until noon every day. If I have to get up early, breakfast coming in hot and served by Chavez in tighty-whities is the way to go.

"Hola, beautiful."

He sets the tray down on his bedside table and the aroma of fresh coffee and huevos rancheros wafts in the air like a sinful drug. We arrived in LA three days ago, and he has welcomed me into his home with open arms. Other than the five minutes it took to find the cutlery drawer and needing to step up my closet game to compete with his color-coded organizational system, I'm feeling okay. More settled.

I sit up and wipe the sleep out of my eyes. "Thank you. It looks delicious. And so does breakfast."

He laughs at my hungry eyes falling on a different kind of feast. Bless him and his morning wood that goes on forever. "We had some fun this morning, or were you still asleep?"

"I think you took advantage of my jet lag."

He smiles back. "I think you liked it just fine."

"I think you like me being captive in your house."

I mean it as a joke, but the words land awkwardly for all the obvious reasons. He escorted me to my house on the day we landed to collect what I needed and hasn't let me leave on my own since.

Today, that all changes.

Chavez perches on the side of the bed and studies me. "How do you feel about the trip?"

"Nervous," I admit.

"I wish I were going with you, but I understand you need time alone with them."

I fly to San Francisco in the afternoon, and Cori will pick me up for the drive back to Santa Cruz. Edgar has stabilized and is regaining mobility, but the road to recovery is long. I could hear it in her voice. And my anxiety is running at max. What will it be like to see them both after all this time?

"Next visit you'll come along, okay?" I kiss his cheek. Me traveling alone bothers him more than he's letting on.

"I have things to do here anyway," he says, shrugging it off. "I'm seeing my parents tonight. After Fresno."

Our eyes lock. This is news to me, but I know what it means.

"Is it safe for you to go alone?" I ask.

"I'm good," he insists. "And this is my battle to fight."

Yes, but.

"Do you want to go through anything?"

He reflects on that before answering. "Nope. I have it all in my head."

"You better call me right after," I warn.

"You might be my one phone call from jail, so you better pick up."

I swat his thigh. "Don't say that!"

He kisses me on the tip of my nose. "I do have some good news, Mamacita."

Sensing something big, my heart rate picks up. There has been nothing from the ITIA since we got home. "Are you cleared?"

"Not a hundred-percent, but they emailed me and said they found nothing suspicious on my phone or laptop."

"Why aren't they calling it a day?" I ask. "You need to tell them about the stalker. Make them understand what's going on."

"I did," he stresses. "And I asked for the name of the person who made the bets, but they wouldn't tell me. Confidential. They still have to sort through everything."

I run a hand through my hair, agitated. Bureaucracy can turn the most patient person into a raging lunatic. I reopened the case with the police the day after we arrived home, but it's too early for any momentum. If there was some way to connect the dots, we could end this betting debacle and put the stalker behind bars in one fell swoop.

To distract me, Chavez swings the breakfast tray onto my lap. "Eat up, Miss Flynn, and don't worry. You and I are going to be fine." He lifts the folded napkin off the tray, and my eyes widen at what he slides out from under it. "This is for you," he says. "A good luck charm."

I swallow past the knot in my throat. A yellow ribbon hangs through the punched hole at the top of El Corazon. During his Paris interrogation, I explained my checkered past with this card. If this is his idea of a joke, it's a grand stinker.

"Is this yours?" I ask.

"No, I made it for you. Mine's in the car. I never told you this, but I kept the card in here for the longest time. You know, thinking it might bring me some luck." He chuckles at his lame strategy. "The day I put it in my car is the day we met. Best damn move, ever. So from now on, this card is good, all right? It brought us together. Abuela is looking out for us."

He wraps me in his arms, and I dissolve into the shelter of his body. Chavez has always been specific about his desires, right from the first time. He loves kissing, and he is so fucking good at it. The electric thrill leaves me breathless, how he undoes me with his tongue. And the only thing he loves more than kissing, is leaving me in a permanent state of wanting.

He untangles himself from my embrace despite my clingy protests and says, "Time to hit the shower so I can drive you to the airport. Be back soon." On his way to the bathroom, he pauses, and with a coy look over his shoulder, wiggles his ass. "If you're lucky maybe I'll give you another dance."

My eyes roam over his body framed in sunlight, and damn that sweet curve of his butt. He is a living statue of physical perfection. "Just stand like that for a minute, please."

When my admiring goes on and on, he throws up his hands in mock defeat. "How much longer are you gonna stare? There is not much mystery left on this body. You've been everywhere, including places you shouldn't have access to."

I smile at his accusing finger with wide-eyed innocence. "Once."

"And only once," he warns.

After that first night at the Airbnb in Bendigo, I received a pleasant but firm lecture about where my fingers could and could not roam on his body. I apologized, heat of the moment and all, but to be honest…

"I think you liked it just fine," I say.

"Oh yeah?" He wags his finger at me a second time. "That smirk better be gone when I come out of the shower."

Chavez struts into the bathroom, and I reach for my coffee with the sensation of contented wonder swelling my heart. I shared the worst of me, and he's standing by my side. If our stars never aligned in Beverly Hills, where would I be? Not safely tucked away in his bedroom, stupidly in love and awash in sunbeams. I lean against the headboard and relish the quiet for as long as it lasts. The gentle patter of a rain shower filters in, and, sure enough, the Chavez show begins. I take a sip of coffee, cringing a little. I overheard him singing once in our suite in Italy, although I use the term *singing* lightly. Tin cans dangling from a truck on a gravel road sound better than his voice, but he gives it his all.

Bless him.

The boy band world is safe for now.

MY flight to San Francisco is less than ninety minutes, which is plenty of time for multiple sessions of second-guessing. The arrivals area is thick with tourists and muggy heat, and I can feel dampness under both arms and in the small of my back. Cori got held up in traffic but will be here soon. My heart stutters after reading her text. I'd be lying if I said this wasn't shaping up to be one of the most nerve-wracking moments of my life. My first talk in New York when I was twenty-two created similar anxiety, and I pulled that off, but there is no comparison. I worry that the three of us will be overly polite and dance around each other as if we are untouchable museum pieces.

Can there be a happy ending after all this time?

My phone buzzes in my hand and shit, it's Brandon again. How many more times does he plan to call? I wheel my roller bag to a quiet corner and decide now is as good a time as any to cut him loose.

"Hi, this is Flynn."

"Flynn," he says, shocked I have answered. "Brandon Dixler."

"Sorry I haven't gotten back to you. It's been busy."

"Understood. I've seen the news. That's why I wanted to talk."

The tone of his voice unsettles me more than I already am. "I don't have a lot of time. I'm at the airport."

"I'll be quick," he says. The phone muffles as if he's moving it from one ear to the other. "This is between you, me, and the fencepost, but I have a good friend who works for the IBIA. They—"

"I know who they are," I interrupt. "What about your friend?"

"I know this fellow quite well," he explains. "And I know how the back end works when they adjudicate a case. I don't know where you are with the investigation, but my friend might be able to provide information on who made the bets. Name, address, and so forth."

A spidey-sense tingle crawls up the back of my neck. Holy Toledo. This could be the piece we need. "Would either of you get in trouble for doing this?"

"As I said, it's off the record. But I am willing to risk it … for a friend."

Ah, here we go. If Brandon believes this is a you-scratch-my-back-

and-I-scratch-yours scenario, he is sadly mistaken. "I want to be clear, Brandon. Very clear. I am with Chavez, in every way."

"Oh, I know," he says quickly. "I'm not offering this up with any ulterior motive."

"Then why?" I ask, gently but firmly. Even if he thinks he has convinced himself, I need to ensure he understands reality.

"Well, let's just say, if I didn't like you, we wouldn't be on the phone right now. But I am offering it because I believe it's the right thing to do." After a beat, he adds, "I don't know Chavez like you do, but he's won the sportsman award multiple times and his fellow players cast those votes. He often overrules the ump to award his opponent the point if he feels the call isn't right, and very few players do that. The water cooler talk is that he plays by the book."

"It's true," I say, because I witnessed Chavez do that very thing in Italy—overrule a call to award his opponent the point. "He would never cheat or bring shame to the sport."

"He *could* use a stint in finishing school," Brandon muses. "But at the end of the day, I appreciate a fella who shoots from the hip."

I bite my lip to stop the laugh. That spot-on assessment will remain between us. "Let me run this past Chavez first, just to be sure he is on side with it, okay?"

I am sure Chavez will not say no to this offer, but when he finds out that Brandon and I have spoken, he might have a few other choice things to say.

"Just so you both know," Brandon warns, "this call never happened. And no guarantees. All I can do is ask."

"Fair enough, and thank you," I add, meaning it from the bottom of my heart. He is going out on a limb for us.

"Send me a signed book, and I'll consider it fair and square."

We exchange a few more details on the timing of how quickly this could come together, and I'm smiling like an idiot when we hang up. I need to call Chavez immediately.

"Flynn?"

I spin around, jolted back to the here and now by a warm hand on my shoulder. My eyes start to blink uncontrollably. I thought I had braced myself for this moment, but how do you prepare for the past to rush up on you like the sidewalk after jumping off a skyscraper? Cori searches my face, and her violet eyes are immediately familiar despite being rheumy behind thick glasses. She offers a tentative smile, waiting for me to return it. Low-grade panic buzzes through me. A sense of failure, too. Time is beyond our control—it marches on like a relentless soldier—and to see it marked in the liver spots on the backs of her hands and her slate-grey crown of curls that used to be brown drives home how much of it I have wasted.

If Cori didn't wrap me in her arms, we might still be standing there, the two feet between us somehow a mile long. Her warmth, how she makes me feel whole … words fail me. The world seems to shrink, and sounds disappear as I struggle to think of what exact evil I attributed to my parents, other than they were two people trying their best and doing what they thought was right.

I hug her back hard, never wanting to let go. She strokes my hair, every quiet touch stripping away years of anger and hurt. I promised myself I wouldn't cry, but her chest heaving against mine cracks my resolve.

"Oh darling," she says. "Welcome home."

Chapter Thirty

CHAVEZ

FRESNO IS A DIVIDED CITY, COURTESY OF THE SMALL-MINDED MONKEYS who established the area by slapping down a monster rail line that fostered social inequality that exists to this day. All the whites settled north of the line. And discriminatory tactics like redlining made sure all the browns, blacks and yellows remained south. And it happened in business, too. The dirty industries, like the slaughterhouses, lay south to corral all the low-income workers. I grew up in the southwest part of the city on the literal wrong side of the tracks. This town tried to set my fate early on, but I did not allow it. In reality, I only escaped in a physical sense. Today, Fresno gets banished from my mind, once and for all.

Westar Poultry is not a giant facility like some of the beef slaughterhouses, but it's big enough if you don't know your way around. I know exactly where I'm going. Forget parking in the employee lot a quarter mile away. I am a visitor to the executive offices and will not hang around longer than I need to. Earl hasn't made any upgrades to the place since my last visit, and I doubt the cheap bastard ever will.

He never bothered springing for security either, allowing me to waltz unannounced into the ghost town of the offices. Just like in tennis, timing is everything when it comes to Earl. The clock punchers are halfway home at 5:15 p.m. on a Friday.

Fury had me by the balls the last time I stormed through these doors. Today, my sneakers are in no hurry. They are silent on the piss-yellow linoleum that's older than Eisenhower. I empty my thoughts and let go of the endless confusion this place has created, wound tight like DNA threads in my memory. But a cold crackle of trepidation creeps on my skin as I approach his office. I can see him through the sliver of the open door, head-down, busy pushing paper. He never seems to age. Or I should say, he's looked like a pissed-off lizard who swallowed a cow for as long as I can recall.

I toe the door open and let that creaky old thing swing wide. Earl glances up, and it feels like time stands still. I swear he's wearing the same shirt and bolo tie he always wore, along with a cold smirk spreading like an ink stain across his face. Funny how he looks unhappy even while smiling.

"Look who's back," he says, jawing on a toothpick. "And still walking around like he owns the place."

I walk in slowly and deliberately. Earl does not move—it looks like nothing has moved in here for a decade—but I feel the rake of his eyes, on the hunt for the bulge of a gun in my waistband or the evil shine of a butterfly knife hidden in my palm. My Dior dress shirt from Monaco is overkill for a dump like this, but I want to plant a giant WTF in his brain. I drop my ass on a plastic folding chair where employees probably sit and grovel.

But I smile.

"I came here to say thank you."

He rolls back in his chair, eyes narrowing. He shouldn't trust me, not after I stormed in here months ago like a crazed baboon. And not surprisingly, he asks, "You expect me to believe that?"

"Nope."

My smile widens, and a flicker of assessment washes over his face. He is not expecting this, which is kind of the point.

After a long beat, he says, "I get it. You think you're all that now that you've upgraded? Your mama must be crying. What does she think of her only son dipping into the white world?"

This is where I would normally lose it. My fingers know it too. They twitch, itching to curl into a fist. But I manage myself, for once.

"I don't know where all your hate comes from Earl, but I feel sorry for you." I look around his sad office empire, the home of a million dead chicken souls, and see exactly nothing, as my girl Flynn would say. "Rumor has it you're married, but no one has ever seen your wife. Hell, you don't even have a photo of her in here. Can't imagine there is a lot of love. Not when you spend all your time hating."

My new world order is calm, and Earl is not happy with the changing of the guard. He stands without saying a word, hitches his belt, and spits the toothpick onto the floor. He slides a desk drawer open and lays the cold, deadly steel of a pistol on top of the ratty old Bible he likes to quote from. A moment of silence passes.

"This is a new addition," he says. "Courtesy of your last visit. Can never be too safe, right?"

He picks up the pistol and rounds the desk, boot heels clicking on the floor and sounding like a requiem. I could lick his pot belly when he comes to a stop in front of me.

"Get up, kid."

I think it was Mark Twain who said a man who lives fully is prepared to die at any time. Flynn would know, if I get the chance to ask her. The hardest thing I have done in my life is to stand without flinching while a cold gun barrel presses into my heart. I'm surprised I can hear Earl because the roar in my ears is deafening.

"I don't need your sympathy, kid," he says. "I don't need anything from you other than for you to hightail your brown ass out of here."

Up close, his face looks like a road map to hell. Deep trenches and watery eyes sunk into their sockets. If I rapped my knuckles against his forehead, I bet he would sound hollow, because he is the emptiest man I have ever met.

"You're going to pay Mama every cent you owe her, plus her legal bills. And you will do it with a smile on your face because you have no choice. The ruling is going in our favor. Heard it today, hot off the press."

His jaw squares. He heard the news too. "If forcing me to pay out on a lie makes you feel like a man, that's your burden to bear and not mine. Heck, I don't even notice she's gone. I had a hundred other applicants who wanted her job with even less pay. Your mama is one of the millions." He cocks the chamber, and the smartest part of my brain screams, *Run!* "No one will notice one less Mexican, so you better go on and git. Comprende?"

In another lifetime, I would consider this his victory. But I am done fighting. And he admitted to keeping tabs on me because how else would he know about Flynn? Maybe Mexicans are not so unnoticeable after all.

That is how I know he will never have the guts to shoot me.

"I said I wanted to thank you, so I'm saying it. Without all your anger and shitty behavior, I might have ended up here, under your rule with a bankrupt soul. And yeah, I will admit, you have haunted me for years. I didn't believe in myself because you gave me enough self-doubt to last a lifetime. But I found someone who does believe in me. And I would never have found her if it wasn't for you. So thank you, Earl."

Like all bullies, Earl has nothing when I extinguish his fuse. I push the barrel down and away, and there is no resistance because he is in shock. But he needs to save face and does so with a different weapon. The one he isn't scared to use.

"You will never win, kid," he says. "You want it so badly, to prove to the world that you are something. But you are nothing."

My fingers twitch and curl, but I find another smile. "You have a nice day, Earl. Go buy your wife some flowers on the way home."

The walk back to my car seems like a dream, something I can barely recall. It only hits me after I put enough distance on the place. I pull over in the nick of time. A lifetime of anger from deep inside me rots in a pile on the dusty shoulder of Highway 99, and good riddance to it. I can use the space for something worthwhile.

I drive back to LA with the top down and wind rippling through my hair. As far as Fresno goes, North or South means nothing to me anymore. God willing, I will never set foot in that place again. The memories are vivid enough. The feel of death bearing down on my chest will take a lifetime to forget, like the sound of the gun chamber cocking while the depths of my ass clenches in response. Or the eyes of another man, blind and unseeing, as he looks straight into mine. Big, flat Fresno is perfect for the Earls of this world who see all that flatness and convince themselves the earth can't be round. Our minds can limit us in ways we never imagine. But mine is finally free, and one woman is responsible for that miracle.

THE SECOND LEG OF MY TRIP FEELS LIKE A VACATION AFTER VISITING with Earl, but I am not busting out the umbrella drinks yet. No one ever said Mama Delgado was a walk in the park. I didn't rehearse any lines for Earl but have a script ready for Mama, just in case. As even Flynn realized, Mama can turn the most eloquent speaker into a tongue-tied mess.

A crescent moon hangs in the night sky when I walk through the front door. I hang up my jacket and notice Papa's is missing from his hanger. He should be home soon with groceries. I've offered to cook a late dinner, and Mama sees right through this obvious ploy to warm her up.

After a quick peck on my cheek, the first thing out of her mouth is, "Why didn't Flynn come with you?"

My short-term goal is for her to say Flynn's name without looking like she sucked on a lemon. I told my parents the whole story, even the awful bits, and Flynn being the cause of my suspension did not sit well with Mama, despite me explaining it was through no fault of her own. I mean, it's not like she dialed up 1-800-Rent-A-Stalker for fun.

"Her father had a stroke, and she's visiting him in Santa Cruz. What about dinner next Saturday?"

Her lips purse. I can tell she'd prefer not to bend too soon, but not even Mama can rain fire and brimstone down on a medical emergency. "Dinner here?" she asks, hoping for home-court advantage.

"Yo, Hermano."

Carmen strolls out of the kitchen licking a Popsicle, a punk cowpoke in baggy ripped overalls and shitkicker boots. Every other month her hair changes color or style, and I can never keep up, but something else is different about her today. I can't put my finger on it.

I duck her blue-lipped kiss. "What are you doing here? Mama said you had a party to get to."

She smiles and acts all coy. "Maybe there is a universe where I wanted to see you."

Apropos of nothing, Mama swats my arm. Hard. "Ow!" I say, rubbing at the sting. "What's that for?"

"For not saying anything."

Carmen adds cryptically, "Turns out, you are not the only one shitting the bed these days."

She stands tall with her chin up, her whole being lighter. Unburdened. I pick up on the energy between them. Holy shit. She's told them. I am genuinely stunned Mama isn't doing time at church praying in a pew right this second.

"Apparently, Flynn encouraged her," Mama adds, daring me to find some salvation in an abominable action such as this.

"Really?" I glance at Carmen, who confirms it with a shrug of her shoulders—a, *Yeah, she did*, gesture. Am I surprised? Not really. Why wouldn't Flynn help my baby sister? She helps everyone except herself.

"She's been a great sounding board," Carmen says. And because Mama's expression is still dour, she chastises her. "Don't pray for my soul in church. Throw more money into the collection plate and sing hallelujah because your son has somehow attracted the perfect woman. And," she adds, throwing a look my way, "if she has any hot, single friends, let me know."

Mama grumbles something under her breath, and I'm still trying to understand why this is not a Defcon 1 situation. Papa might be able to shed some light on it when he gets back. Mama being okay with this might involve him slipping her a mild narcotic.

"We're going outside to talk for a few, Mama." Carmen pulls on my shirt and pauses, fingering the sateen. "Nice disco duds, Chavelito. Still hoping for your boy band?"

I shove her toward the door. "Shut up."

We park our asses on the top step of the porch. The house needs a new coat of paint, and the neighbor's cat keeps shitting in Mama's flowerbeds, but tonight the place feels steeped in a certain kind of brightness. A black cloud has hung over this house ever since I forced my parents to move here, and Carmen's decision to live with them and not on campus or in the condo I offered to buy helped smooth and lighten the transition. Hard to believe my pigheaded sister is a beacon of selfless luminosity.

Or maybe, not so hard to believe.

"What's the deal?" I ask. "Did I miss the heart attack?"

Carmen laughs and stretches out her legs. "It's not as if Mama has called up all her friends. Papa said he figured it out already. His modern-day acceptance floored me."

I glance over. "How do you feel?"

She picks at her frayed denim. "Scared, which is like, totally dumb, because now they know. But now it's … I don't know." Her heavy sigh fits perfectly with how this entire day is going. Everything is changing. "It's a different kind of scary. Can't go back in the closet."

I throw my arm around her. "I'm proud of you. That took guts."

"I probably don't say this enough, but I'm proud of you, Hermano. You got cajones. You've always gone for it." Her voice becomes softer as she meets my eyes. "Maybe you even inspired me."

"Carmelita, bowing down to big brother." I smile. "It's about time."

She scoffs and untangles herself from my arm. "Uh, *no* bowing down here, so sorry. I believe *you* owe *me*. Carmelita, your sister, vouched for Flynn six ways to Sunday with Mama. You think she got where she is all by herself?"

I scrub her kneecap with my hand. Such a brat, but I love her. She's going to do great things, my sister. She follows my gaze skyward, and we stare silently into the starless cosmos. I inhale deeply and can smell spring in the air.

New beginnings.

"I have a ways to go before Mama's fully on board, but thank you," I say. "I'm nothing without Flynn."

She shrugs. "I could have told you that."

I laugh and kiss her cheek. Not everything is changing. "Fuck you."

Chapter Thirty-One

FLYNN

My Santa Cruz homecoming fills me with dread, but it's less jarring than I imagined. I'm amazed at how little my childhood home has changed. Cori's collection of garden gnomes still stands guard in the front garden bed. A painting of mine from fifth grade hangs by the hall closet, the red and blue streaks fading with age and convincing no one of artistic greatness. Every piece of furniture in my old bedroom stands where it once was, and Cori wrings her hands as I take it all in.

"We planned to change this into a guest room but never got around to it," she explains, almost apologizing for maintaining a shrine to her daughter.

"It's fine," I say, blinking away the tears that have been more on than off.

The fourteen-year gap shrunk somewhat during our drive from San Francisco. And we navigated beyond weather and traffic talk to more emotionally charged topics during dinner in town at a trendy cafe. But the most piercing memories hit me hard in the kitchen.

Cori sets the kettle on for tea and excuses herself to the bathroom and thank God she does. I'm suddenly eighteen again, morning sun threading through the trees in the backyard while Cori and Edgar talk outside on the back porch. All the things I wish could change bear down on me with an almost suffocating weight. The arguments that should never have happened, words of forgiveness left unspoken, and the shifting sands of time I can never reshape. I steady myself on the kitchen island, and just when I think my heart cannot wrench another time, Chavez calls. He had texted earlier saying things went fine with Earl, but when he shares the startling truth, it feels like the floor gives way beneath me.

"Are you kidding me?" I pace around the kitchen, a madwoman unleashed. "You should have told me earlier."

"You would have had a heart attack reading that shit in a text," he says in defense.

"I'm *still* having one. Jesus. How do you feel?"

"I dunno. Relieved?" He sounds at peace with it, but no one walks away from having a gun barrel pressed on their heart without a lingering lick of horror. "How are things going there?" he asks, diverting me.

I make my way to the bay window, resting one knee on the bench framed within it to stop my leg from trembling. "Okay."

"Is it weird for you?"

"A little," I admit. "It's like trying to squeeze into a pair of jeans from high school. Everything is familiar but nothing fits exactly the same."

He sighs. "I wish I was there with you. I miss you."

"I miss you, too. How is your mother?"

He chuckles, knowing damn well the subtext to that question. "Halfway there," he says. "I suggested dinner at their place when you get back. It will be four against one. Me, Carmen, Papa and you wearing her down."

"Approval by coercion?" I snort a laugh. "Awesome."

"Listen," he says, bristling. "If I gotta suck it up and let Brandon Dixler help my ass, you can deal with Mama."

I relayed the news of Brandon's offer earlier in the day, and Chavez had no choice but to reluctantly agree by saying, quote: 'Just my luck, it has to be him with the fucking solution.' End quote.

The kettle starts to scream and I wrap up our call. "I should run, babe. I'll FaceTime you later."

"Tell her I say hi, all right?"

I steep two peppermint teas and wander into the living room with outrage swirling hot in my belly. What Earl did today was so wrong. That he can get away with it bothers me the most. Cori clocks my shaking hand when I set her mug on the side table. Immediately after I sit next to her on the old love seat, she drapes a knitted blanket across my lap and tucks the blue wool under my thighs. She lowers the volume on the TV, blows on her tea and waits. Her general approach to mothering was to let me come to her if something was bothering me.

Eventually, the silence gets to me.

"Chavez says hello."

She smiles. "How was his day?"

"A little crazy."

"Everything okay?"

I fleetingly mentioned Chavez and the betting circumstances at dinner. And we spent a lot of time discussing my desire to switch career gears away from non-fiction. But I didn't share everything.

"There's a lot going on right now," I say.

Cori reaches for my knee and squeezes it. "I'm glad you found someone special. I wish you could see your face whenever you talk about him. Consider yourself lucky."

I slurp my tea and try to mask my upheaval. On the shelf beside the TV are all my books, shelved in publication order. Next to them is a photo of the three of us grinning, taken on the day my Stanford acceptance letter came in the mail. Cori and Edgar both look so young. The sting of lost time cuts deeply again.

"I'm sorry, Mom," I blurt out. "I'm sorry for everything."

Her lips press into a tight line, all the fine wrinkles around her mouth bunching. She sets her tea down and hugs me fiercely.

"I want you to know you are loved, Flynn. You have always been loved. The biggest regret of our lives was not telling you sooner."

Cori rocks me gently, sniffling between ragged breaths, and I have never needed the comfort of a mother more. When I pull back to cuff my nose, Cori reaches for a nearby Kleenex box. We honk loudly into our tissues, eyes bright with tears. The space around my heart widens with every passing second. I go for it, addressing the elephant in the room.

"I looked for her," I say, my voice barely a whisper. "Up in Oregon. In Madras, where she was living when you met her."

Cori stills. We have never had a rational discussion about my birth mother, Ava Reid.

"And?"

"Nothing, aside from her obituary."

Over two days on a stinking hot July, I had canvassed strangers on the street, in cafes, and at the supermarket. But either I came across as unhinged, or Ava had lived like a ghost. Whatever the case, no one knew anything about her. A clerk at the local newspaper office searched their online files and sadly informed me of her death five months prior.

"I am so sorry you never had the chance to meet her," Cori says quietly. "And I know you never believed what we told you, but I swear she was adamant about not keeping you. And honestly, she seemed mentally unstable. Not quite all there."

Ava had been part of a cult, is what they told me. Because I could never confirm this, I lied about her in *Pieces of a Pisces*. Shaped her into who I wanted her to be. She became a mother who had died in childbirth—a good and honest woman and not some cult freak who abandoned her bastard daughter. Considering my fame, I'm surprised no one has ever dug deeper into that lie. But what kind of heartless fool questions a mother dying so brutally and poignantly?

And no one ever did.

In retrospect, I think it was my way of testing the universe. To see if someone would come forward.

"My adoption records said the father was unknown, but ... did she ever mention anybody?" I ask.

Cori strokes my arm with a far-away look. "It's funny, the things you remember about people. For some reason, I distinctly remember that she spoke in the singular. Neither Edgar nor I sensed she was involved with anyone. And she insisted she never knew who your father was. Why do you ask?"

I chew on my thumbnail. With the topic of Ava broached, it feels like the right time to bring up the stalker. Maybe Cori can offer some insight or recall a lost detail. Remember something.

When I finish my story, her stricken expression makes me second-guess my decision to tell her.

"Oh my God," she says. "How awful for you. And Chavez was dragged into it as well. Has this stalker ever mentioned Ava?"

"No," I say. "But there is a connection. I know it."

"And this Brandon fellow can help?"

"Hopefully."

She leans back, and there is something going on there, behind those eyes. "Now that I think about it, she did mention a place called Shaniko. A nothing town, thirty or forty miles north of Madras. Abandoned, I believe. I doubt anyone lives there full time."

The grandfather clock in the hall chimes midnight, triggering dual yawns. Both of us are tired from the long day. "We should get to bed," I say. "I want to be fresh for Dad tomorrow."

Cori gets up slowly from the loveseat. "I left towels in your bathroom."

I smile, gathering both of our mugs. "It hasn't been mine for years."

Cori lays a hand on my cheek, her eyes soft. She still smells like baby oil, the cheap and cheerful moisturizer she always preferred.

"It will always be yours, Flynn."

And little tremors erupt around my heart, shattering it ever so gently.

A CHILL CREEPING THROUGH THE BEDROOM WINDOW IN THE MORNING wakes me from a deep sleep. I forgot to shut the blinds last night, but the wall of heavy fog blocks daylight like God draped her own curtains. Only my cell phone screen shines bright in the dim, still lying beside me in bed after a late-night FaceTime session with Chavez. Stacked on the screen are two unread texts.

CD: I love you.

BD: Call me. Urgent.

I sit up so quickly all the blood rushes to my head. Like everyone else, I don't expect a miracle to happen on a Saturday morning, but maybe my luck is changing.

Brandon answers on the first ring. "Morning," he says.

"Good news?" I ask. There is no time for small talk, sorry.

"Yes," he says, "and I wanted to clarify what my friend could and could not provide. At this stage, he was willing to share an email address and a name. Off the record, he did confirm the name on the credit card used to set up the account is the same name I am sending you. You didn't hear any of this from me."

I shut my eyes, dizzy with relief. "I won't tell anyone, I promise. But what about the ITIA? Have they tried to reach this person?"

"I'm sorry, Flynn," he says. "Those are the only details I can share."

"Yeah, of course, I understand. And you've already gone above and beyond."

After a pregnant pause, Brandon clears his throat. "If you don't mind me asking, how is it looking on his end?"

"They found nothing incriminating on his phone or laptop, but they are still dragging their heels and not officially absolving him."

"This is a highly unusual situation," he says, telling me nothing new. "They have to cross the T's and all that jazz. I'll send you what I have, and hope it helps. Good luck."

A physical ache seems to flow through me, starting in my neck and radiating to my chest. I have a strong premonition that whatever Brandon is about to send is the missing piece of the puzzle. When the text comes in, my heart beats wildly. My stalker is no longer nameless.

But what a name.

Jerry Linkley.

Better suited to a Baptist preacher or a used car salesman than a loser who fancies himself a criminal mastermind. A year's worth of aggravation shimmers under my skin as I type his name into the browser and hit search. Other than a Facebook account with no activity or photos, nothing else comes up under that name.

A ghost. Just like Ava.

When the second text lands, air flutters deep in my lungs. I try to slow down the cascade of my thoughts.

_shaniko_monkey@hotmail.com_

Holy Toledo.

Holy shit!

I kick the covers off and rush out of bed, almost tripping my way down the stairs. After rounding the corner into the kitchen, I smack hard into Cori, alerted by my thundering steps and on her way to find me.

"What is it?" she asks, steadying us from the crash. She looks like an Easter grandma in her pink bathrobe and matching fluffy slippers. "It looks like you've seen a ghost."

I'm breathless, my heart jack-rabbitting all over the place. "Does the name Jerry Linkley ring a bell?"

She shakes her head, confused. "Is that him?" I flash her my phone screen, and her eyes balloon. "Oh my lord."

Chapter Thirty-Two

For better or for worse, humans are creatures of habit. I suppose I should count my lucky stars for this. Without thousands of souls stuck trying to break their bad routines, my career as a motivational agent of change would have fallen flat pretty damn quickly. Predictable patterns make us feel safe, but they can also bite us in the ass in more ways than one. Two weeks after my return from Santa Cruz, the police apprehend Jerry Linkley in Shaniko on his daily noon walk. For a man who has been a toxic apparition in my life for the past year, that they find him living in a ghost town doesn't surprise me in the slightest.

The call comes while Chavez, June, and I are feasting on homemade tacos in the cabana. I recognize the Oregon number and immediately feel my throat constrict. After I greet Constable Watson, Chavez sits up, his radar pinging on high alert.

"Yes, I can talk," I say, and leave the table for some privacy. My heart beats so fast that I worry it might blow up. Constable Watson is the lead officer assigned to this case in Madras. When we first spoke, I said if his team had any success finding Jerry, I wanted them to ask if he was my father.

After bringing me up to speed on the details surrounding the arrest,

Watson says, "He claims to not be your father. Apparently, he found your mother pregnant and homeless, sleeping under a motel heating vent when she was eighteen. Did you know she was involved with the Rajneesh cult up in Antelope?"

"My adoptive parents mentioned something about that."

What Cori had told me sounded like a groaner plot for a movie of the week—Ava Reid, a teen runaway, joins a cult that eventually infiltrates the small Oregon town of Antelope and creates havoc. She lived on the compound until the cult disbanded, at which point she and several other members scattered to Madras. The forty-odd group lived commune-style on an old farm off the city grid. Ava, pregnant with no idea who my father was, fled the commune after the mood turned militant.

Watson confirms that the outrageous story proves true after all.

"Jerry says that to protect her from the 'kooks and browns,' as he calls them, he took her to Shaniko and told no one. Out of sight, out of mind."

I've been pacing in circles on the lawn and come to a full stop. "So, they lived together?"

"Until she died, is what he says."

Died.

I know it's true, but to hear it…

The next question squeaks out. "How did he find me?"

"By fluke," Watson says, and his tone suggests he didn't believe it at first. "Says he saw you being interviewed on TV at a bar in Portland. Claims you have the identical curly hair and green eyes that Ava did. When he figured out your age, he knew it had to be you."

My mind cycles through the details of last year's tour. I did make an appearance on a local Portland network to promote my event. Did Jerry show up at that talk? I shudder thinking about it.

Watson continues in a grave tone. "Full disclosure, Miss Dryden, Jerry is an unmedicated schizophrenic known for delusional behavior. For now, take what he says with a grain of salt."

I let out a deep breath. Chavez watches my every move from the cabana, and I can feel anxiousness radiating off of him. "What happens next?"

"Depositions," he says. "You can read the transcripts and decide how you'd like to proceed."

"With a restraining order?" I clarify.

"You can file for a temporary one immediately. Down the road, a judge will weigh in on whether the situation warrants a permanent one. In the interim, you can decide if you want to press charges."

"Did he say anything about Chavez and the betting?"

"All we know is he placed the bets, but we're not sure if the intention was anything more than to get your attention." He clears his throat. "As I said, he's a little unstable. Keeps talking about how the browns are the downfall of society. We think it stems from your mother's involvement with the Rajneesh cult. I'm not sure how familiar you are with them, but the leader was Indian and so were several key members."

A few years ago, Netflix released a series that documented the rise and fall of the Rajneesh cult in Oregon. I watched it five times, scanning through all the faces to see if any of them looked like me. What a crazy group. Dangerous, in the end.

Watson and I go back and forth on a few more items and when we're done, I struggle to place how I'm feeling. Not delighted, in any event. The denouement lands without fanfare. It just is. I join June and Chavez back in the cabana and he immediately squeezes the life out of me in a bear hug.

"I heard," he mumbles into my ear. "Thank fucking God."

"And it's a good thing they did catch him," June chimes in. "For Christ's sake, luv! You could have been in real danger."

I confessed everything to my besties this week and it wasn't pretty. Vandana had a meltdown that I kept this secret from her. June slapped me across the face when she arrived for lunch today, albeit in a gentle way. But she was pissed.

"You see?" Chavez says. "I'm not the only one thinking you are crazy for keeping this to yourself."

Logically, I understand how crazy it was not to deal with this back in December, but I wasn't the same person then.

After sharing what the police told me, Chavez hops on his phone to Google Shaniko, Oregon, a deadbeat blip on Highway 97, population thirty-six. It might as well have been Antarctica when I consider how futile my search was for my mother years ago. Ava and Jerry lived together like dysfunctional hermits for eighteen years in his double wide that is being searched for evidence as we speak. Watson told me Jerry came quietly, perhaps anticipating the moment.

"And Jerry is *not* your father?" June reiterates.

"I guess not," I say.

"Then why the fuck? If you're not his child…"

"We'll never know," Chavez says, "because the next step is to slap a restraining order on his sorry ass."

I press a hand onto his shoulder—a gesture to settle down. But it is the million-dollar question I would like an answer to as well.

"Is he going to jail?" June inquires. "I don't know all the legal backend to a case like this."

Chavez has become a near expert on the topic in record time and provides a short overview. The legal arena around stalking is like all law—labyrinthian and subjective. The offense can be a misdemeanor or a felony, depending on myriad factors. If Jerry is convicted, jail time varies from one year to five, but defense lawyers have multiple ways to disprove any claims, which is why Chavez wants a restraining order. Violation of a RO is a bona fide crime and can fast-track a jail sentence.

"What a bloody bizarre puzzle," June muses, lighting up a Marlboro. Smoking means her stress level is running high, but you'd never guess it because it looks like she stepped out of the spa—her alabaster skin glows, set off by her favorite aquamarine Givenchy blouse. "How does this affect what is going on with you?" she asks Chavez.

We data dumped the betting scandal details while prepping lunch to bring her up to speed. With Jerry's arrest, I hope we can tidy this up and get Chavez back on the court for April. March is definitely out.

"Nothing is guaranteed," Chavez admits. "But it's pretty obvious

I'm clean. I'll tell them that Jerry got arrested, and they can go after him."

June blows out three perfect smoke rings. "It seems a bit grasping that a man living in a trailer in the middle of nowhere had sufficient funds to pull something like this off."

"Who knows?" I say, although I agree with her. "Maybe he gambled his life savings."

"If you need material for your next mystery, doll, look no further," June says. "Truth is stranger than fiction, right?"

"Don't encourage her," Chavez warns. He knows the crumbs of information from today are enough to put me hot on the trail. Maybe I should have been a detective.

Hearing his protectiveness, June smiles. Today is our first proper visit since I returned from Europe and her first time meeting Chavez. She has given me her full approval via our tried and true shorthand signals. Mind you, Chavez has played right into her degenerate hands with his cargo capris dangerously loose on his hips. Never mind that he's commando. Or how smoking hot he looks shirtless in his aviators. All that notwithstanding, they hit it off immediately, gabbing about finance and the markets. Every day he surprises me with how much he knows.

After churros and espresso, June hits the road to beat afternoon traffic back to Malibu. I'm suddenly exhausted, weary with relief if that can be a thing. Chavez wastes no time getting me into bed. It is his number one skill, aside from bashing a ball on the court. Snuggled together under the duvet, he brings my head to his chest.

"I like June," he says, fiddling with one of my curls. "She's down to earth."

"Wait until she has a few drinks in her and you hand her a pool cue. You'll see a very different side."

"What do you mean?"

"She's a ball-buster pool shark. I'm warning you now, don't put any money down."

He laughs, as anyone would who believes that a petite and voluptuous finance powerhouse could slay at a pool table. "I forgot to bring it up, but if she wants that intro to Dallas, let me know."

Oh boy. I am not going to relay her thoughts on Dallas. I did a quick Google scour on him a while back, and he is definitely the king of the money hill, but also, per June, a rogue running ruthlessly amongst the LA babe scene. He is a stunner, for sure, if I was into the macho finance types. But I would not want to sit across a table from him while those eyes undressed me. There is no doubt he would get his way. Guys like Dallas always get their way.

"I think she's okay for now. But I'll remind her again."

He cradles my head and then shifts his body so we can curl inward and face each other. Entire conversations pass between our eyes.

"I'm so relieved they got him," he finally says. "You must be too."

"It feels strange," I admit. "I suspected he knew my mother somehow."

"But you're okay with it? Not digging deeper?"

"I know it sounds ridiculous, but I would like to talk to him."

He nudges his knee into mine. "Don't you dare. There is no point in getting a restraining order if you plan to walk right up to him."

"But you understand why I want to, right? The same reason why you went to see Earl."

"The circumstances are completely different," he counters. "And I gave myself time before I went back. You have to let things settle in here." His palm presses against my forehead before the warmth of his hand moves to my heart. "And here."

I could argue him into a corner on this issue, but he makes a valid point.

"Take some time," he reiterates. "You will have your day with him in court and hear it all. Focus on getting back in sync with your parents and sort out the crap with your agent."

Ah, yes. Good old Nathaniel. Still making life miserable for me. He and my lawyer square off again next week.

"I know," I concede. "You're right."

His voice turns softer. "And I want us to spend more time with my parents. Last week was a good start."

Compared to round one, the Delgado dinner last Sunday was a walk in the park. Gloria made an effort not to make me feel like a clown showing up at a birthday party with a sawed-off shotgun. Judging from the pointed glances between her and Chavez when we arrived, he laid down the law in advance. And throughout the night, he kept tabs to ensure she remained on the right side of it. Now that Carmen has come out, the other tightrope of tension in the house slackened, and dare I say, I enjoyed myself. The wine helped, as it always does. And I do like Rodrigo. We share a special bond, battling his son with varying degrees of success.

"My parents want to meet you as well," I say. "And you have a rabid fan club at the hospital who would love a visit."

Edgar was the one who encouraged me to take tennis lessons. He played for years with his fellow teachers from Santa Cruz high school. As it turns out, his day nurse, Maria Hernandez, loves tennis. Her husband is from Veracruz, the same city Rodrigo grew up in, and she told me during my first hospital visit that Chavez is a bona fide celebrity in Mexico. She treated me like one, too, practically curtseying.

"Let's do a road trip," Chavez says, perking up. "I have the time for now."

"That sounds like a great idea. On the way back, can we swing through Fresno?"

His brow furrows. "What for?"

"I'd like to see your hometown," I say. "The house you grew up in, the courts where you taught yourself how to play."

The corner of his mouth twitches. "Nothing to see but some beat-up courts and a beat-up house, but if you want to go, we will."

I weigh the tone of his comment and understand the hesitation. "We stay far away from Earl, okay? I never want to lay eyes on that man."

Earl threatening him at gunpoint still makes me ill. If we ever cross paths, I can't be held responsible for what might happen.

Chavez kisses me softly. "I will do whatever makes you happy, all right?"

He traces a finger over my lips and follows the curve when I break into a smile. My finger traces his stubbled jawline, and his next sigh is deeper as I feel my way tenderly underneath the duvet.

"Flynn baby," he murmurs. "I will always keep you safe. I promise."

I slip my tongue into his waiting mouth, and he groans, two fingers sliding deep into my wet velvet. His skin is hot and smooth against mine as I arch into him and reach for his rear assets, twin handfuls of hard muscle. He nips at my lower lip, sucking it into his mouth, and works me until my body shivers with growing urgency.

"Cógeme," I whisper into his ear.

He pulls back with a chuckle. "Figured you would know Spanish swear words. How hard does my girl want to be fucked? On a scale of one to ten?"

"Ten."

"You sure?"

His body draws taut against mine, and his cock thrusts against my flat belly with little pulses that match my racing heart. I am ripe and swollen and hungry, so hungry for him.

"Someone once told me they like even numbers."

Even or odd, it makes no difference in the end. I lose track of time, my brain is mush, all of me becoming a gelatinous mass of conflicting and colluding sensations from the insistent pressure on my clit. I feel dizzy like I'm chasing, losing ground, happy, and he slides between my legs fucking me with his tongue next, that opulently nasty beast that feels like a whip cracking wildly in a dark tunnel. I hold him tight with my thighs and move against his mouth, higher and higher until the world splinters into patterns of light. The walls of his room start to shake, and I am so hot I think I must be burning. Or it's just my nipples on fire as he turns them into bullets with his supple fingers.

"Chavez, please," I moan. "I want you inside me."

What I want is end-of-the-world sex. A stone-hard knight to plunder me so we can close rank and slam the castle door shut, forgetting about everything and everyone, safe knowing the crowns we need to bear are the ones we give each other.

"Okay," he says, catching his breath. "Hold on."

He does what he needs to do, and the thick, tangy smell of him rises as he sinks inside me. With slow, pulsing strokes and wearing the smile of a conqueror, he's overjoyed to watch his captive squirm and moan. I can smell myself, salty and sweet, the scent of wanting something badly. My fingertips dig into the solid flesh of his back. I pull him closer like I plan to do a thousand times in the future, and we rise higher and higher again.

Sweet Jesus, he is the best afternoon lover, a demigod of lust, if such a thing exists. And because he's also Chavez, give him a target and away he goes.

So he doesn't just fuck me.

He transports me to the depths of an emerald erotic jungle tangled with palm trees and wet dirt and wild-eyed savages desperate for sacrifice. In heavy, dark silence and slippery, thick bliss, he leaves me howling, aching, and clawing at nothing.

MAY

Chapter Thirty-Three

FLYNN

Jesus once said: The truth will set you free. Whether he is my savior remains to be seen, but full credit to him for memorable quotes that ring true centuries later. And truth be told, I might be thinking about higher powers this morning. Something in me has changed. I read all the transcripts from the March and April depositions, and Jerry filled in so many blanks about Ava and her tragic life.

But one question remains.

I hopped on an early flight to Portland today and drove to the Jefferson Country courthouse in Madras, determined to get my answer. If Chavez knew I made this trip alone, he would blow a gasket, so there is some small mercy he is busy in Italy. Only one more tournament in Rome before we reunite in Paris next week for the French Open. He hates that we are apart, as do I, but I needed time to process everything and get my head in order, just like he said.

And if all goes as planned today, my heart will also be at peace.

I arrive early at the courthouse and freshen up in the restroom to kill some time. My face is bare, with zero make-up, and I look like a gangster in an oversized hoodie borrowed from Chavez. The point is not to draw attention to myself. This afternoon, a judge will decide on upping the temporary restraining order served on Jerry a few weeks ago to a permanent one. During the hearing, Jerry gets the opportunity to defend himself, and if he does so successfully, the chances of a jail sentence become slim. I plan to slip into the hearing a few minutes after the proceedings begin and observe Jerry from a distance. After I get a feel for him, I will figure out how to get my answer.

I have it all organized in my head, but fate has other plans.

On a warm morning in May, I am face-to-face with Mr. Linkley in a hallway painted a very uninspiring beige. I exit the restroom just as he finishes drinking at the water fountain. Although I have never laid eyes on him, instinctively, I know who he is. He cuffs water from his chin and we stare at each for a good five seconds before he smiles. He has a pleasant smile for someone with very few teeth.

"Flynn," he says, in a spellbound voice I imagined would sound foreboding.

Nothing about him is what I expect.

Instead of a twitchy computer nerd with calculating eyes, he could double as a lumberjack. Barrell-chested and tall with meaty hands. His big, square face would do well on television if he had his harelip operated on, and it seems that in Shaniko, mullets never go out of style. After a year of worrying about what would happen if we ever crossed paths, safety is not an immediate concern. Not because a restraining order is in place or because the courthouse is crawling with law enforcement types. Jerry Linkley, in the flesh and standing before me, loses all his power.

But my stomach somersaults as a reminder not to get too close. His brown eyes are lively and inquisitive but also carry a sheen of madness.

"You look just like her," he says.

At his last deposition, Jerry described the moment of seeing me on TV as though God was speaking to him. The way he looks at me right now is evidence we both have ghosts haunting us. Jerry had begged Ava to consider adoption over abortion in the hopes a full-term pregnancy would change her mind. He had always dreamed of having children—a monkey of his own, were his exact words.

He became obsessed with reuniting with me.

If only he had approached things differently.

I take a deep, wavering breath and move on to the task at hand—my freedom moment.

"Did she ever love me?" I ask.

Jerry blinks as if the question is beyond his comprehension. As if it mingles in his memories in another time and space. Then his eyes dim with sadness.

"She refused to love you," he says. "You were part of a past she wanted to forget. And once Ava made up her mind, good luck in changing it. Although she never breathed a word, deep down, I know she regretted giving you up. She turned to the bottle for that very reason. Every day, I wish she had kept you, Flynn."

The guard chatting up one of the admin girls catches wind of his charge in my proximity and immediately steps in to restrain Jerry. No more than twenty-two years old, he needs another thirty pounds of muscle to be menacing, and he is no match for the solidly built Jerry who flips from Jekyll into Hyde in the blink of an eye.

"Get your hands off me!" he shouts and shoves the guard with enough force that all work stops in the surrounding cubicles. Phones ring without answering. Every wary face behind plexiglass protection has eyes on Jerry.

But he only has eyes for me.

"That brown boy will never love you like I can, Flynn. The browns are crazy. The browns fucked your mother up. You—"

The guard swiftly pins Jerry's arm behind his back with icy authority. "Get a move on," he growls and shoves Jerry down the hall.

"I tried to save you, Flynn," Jerry yells, resisting every step of the way. "I tried. I tried my best."

They disappear through a set of doors, and in the awkward silence left by their departure, I must look like death warmed over because one of the clerks rushes up to me and asks if I am all right. For someone who probably sees this sort of thing regularly, she is far more skittish than me. But I am not unaffected, not by a long shot. Nausea courses through me. My rattled mind is in desperate need of fresh air. And the time has come to leave.

Forget about the hearing.

Jerry gave me what I needed.

Outside, the hot noon sun feels good on my face, but the chill in my bones persists. Before I leave the parking lot and Madras for good, I survey the town and surroundings as my mind skips from one thing to the next. There are years of residue to mop up, and emotional sludge will pour in daily as I sift and sort through the backlog of what I've learned in the past two months.

Truth be told, I feel a little sorry for Jerry. A mentally challenged man who spiraled into a crazy mission he believed would heal him. A man who bet on tennis matches in the hopes Chavez would lose, and he could win enough money to fly to Europe and rescue me. A man who knew nothing at all about tennis or how his actions would threaten Chavez's career. Jerry has not revealed how he got my phone number, but I have a sneaking suspicion about who gave it to him.

And that is another chapter for another day.

For now, I say goodbye to Ava, the life I never had, and head home to my new life. The one I never thought could be this good.

I'M LOUNGING IN THE CABANA WITH A MUG OF CHAI TEA WHEN CHAVEZ FaceTimes me at midnight. He flips out when I tell him about the day, and only after I explain what this has given me does he settle down. I am still dealing with Chavez, however, lest I forget.

"When you get to Paris, there might be some disciplinary action," he warns.

"I am counting on that," I say. "After five weeks…"

He laughs, a losing-it kind of laugh. "You have no idea. I am walking around with a permanent hard-on. People are starting to talk."

He angles his screen downward, and sure enough, he is swollen, thick and ready. What a tease. I asked once before, but he is not into the phone sex thing, aside from flashing his massive erection like it's no big deal.

"Maybe you should thrill the Italian ladies with that thing," I say with a sly grin. "Stand in Trevi Fountain and pretend to be one of your pool cherubs."

"I can hear them tinkling in the background."

"They keep me company. Every night I come out here and think about you."

"Flynn baby," he whispers. "I miss you so much. I loved our road trip. Let's do another one after Paris."

In March, we drove up to Santa Cruz, and the joy on his face watching Cori and Edgar fuss over us is something I will never forget. We toured my childhood haunts, and a week later, we toured his in Fresno. I found it hard to place him in that city because Chavez today is a million experiences different from who he was there. We will never visit again because, like Madras and me, Chavez and Fresno are finished. But I can see him on those run-down courts, banging balls against the crumbling concrete wall with the tenacity and fearlessness that shaped him into the man I know.

The man who ends our FaceTime by kissing his phone screen and wishing it was me.

I am the luckiest woman in the world.

After we hang up, the fatigue of the long day catches up to me. The night air has cooled, and I head inside for bed. A strange peace settles over me as I lie in the dark, thinking of Ava. To feel grateful after all these years is like wishing for something you never think will come true, and then it does. I used to believe my life would have been better had we known each other. In reality, I dodged a major bullet. To rot away in a ghost town with an alcoholic mom and a slowly dementing father figure is a story best told as fiction.

Only you can make yourself happy is Flynn Dryden's Truth # 9. Ava might have been heartless for giving me up, but she knew enough about herself to make the right decision. I can't fault her for her wisdom. Yes, it hurts, and it will always hurt that she never loved me—never gave herself a chance—but it is the truth, and I am no longer a prisoner of it.

Chapter Thirty-Four

CHAVEZ

Welcome to Paris in May.

Infinitely fucking better than Paris in February.

Instead of my career looking as bleak as the winter skies, I'm in the semi-finals at Roland Garros with Flynn back at my side. March and April flew by in a hurry, and my brain spins at what changed in those eight weeks. It only took the rug being pulled out from underneath my life and hers to make me realize how much of a self-centered and toxic shit I've been. The valuable stuff becomes pretty damn clear when you take away everything a man has.

Moving forward, all Flynn and I want to do is make up for the lost time.

With the Linkley loser snapped up and nothing dirty on my end, the ITIA had no choice but to admit they were wrong and reinstate me. It was too late to get a wildcard for Indian Wells, but I snuck into the Miami tournament and made it to the quarters. Not bad for my first pro tour match in almost a year, considering I had to readjust to a stark reality. Python bit the bullet and unretired for a few weeks while Flynn hung tight in California. The better move for her was to stick close to home so she could bond with her parents and let the stalker shitstorm pass without traveling around and adding more stress.

With a restraining order in place, we both breathed easier.

Then she gave me a heart attack, sneaking up to Madras.

Of course, she ran into Jerry; that destiny felt pre-ordained. She never believed the stories Cori and Edgar had told her about Ava, but to hear the truth come from the mouth of a stranger who knew her mother the best, well, let's just say it was dark times for my baby in the days that followed.

The early weeks back on tour were disorienting for me, as well. Python did his best and helped smooth my rough edges with his usual sarcastic charm, and I am forever grateful he helped me during the transition, but Flynn is my special sauce and I missed her. (Papa stepped up to the plate and offered to help, but that ship has sailed. He has sacrificed enough for me.)

My main goal in returning to the pro tour was to put in a decent showing during the clay court season, and I have aced that, homies. I won the Monaco Masters in April, and my man Morgan never admitted anything, nor did I ask why the tournament offered me a wild card when it's typically the French players who get them. I suppose being tight with Prince Albert is handy since he rules over everything in that place, including the tennis tournament. The Monaco win boosted my ranking points enough that I could play Madrid and Rome without wildcards. And those two events brought me closer to my secondary goal—to kick Arlo Märklin's ass on clay.

He and I have snarled at each other for the past six weeks, both in the locker room and from the other side of the draw. We have not crossed paths yet and it's my fault because I lost in the semis in Rome, and he was waiting for me in the final and went on to win it. We are the hottest players coming into Roland Garros, and today, we both play our semi-final matches. I am one tantalizing step closer to my dream of a Grand Slam. If God looks down on me and decides now is my time, I will suffer through cramps and match-ending blisters to give me a shot at beating that douche.

I am not surprised he and Vanya are back together. They are two peas in a skanky pod. Flynn saw them in the hallway outside of the locker room last week, and I could tell Vanya circling bugged the hell out of her.

The Velvet Vagina is a stain we would both like to wash out of our lives.

If I could subtract from my tally of conquests, Vanya would be the first one vanquished. Who knows what was going through my mind last year? First of all, I have never been a club guy. But it was a Saturday night and a bunch of the players were going out, and I tagged along. Bored senseless after twenty minutes and not wanting to let my peeps down with an early exit, I showed off my moves on the dance floor. Soon enough, Vanya was grinding behind me, half-dressed and half-cut. I should have ignored her, but I was lonely and feeling a little lost, and a pair of giant boobs in my face could make the time fly faster.

The sad thing is, she set me up. Arlo had fucked around on her, and she was a vindictive bitch. Her friends were slinking around and filming us kissing, but she denied it when I brought it up and said to stop being so paranoid. The club doors slammed shut at three a.m., and by then, her friends had disappeared—gone to upload all the footage to piss Arlo off. She invited me back to her hotel, and I had nothing to do besides walking in the rain back to my room for a night of bad European TV, so I caved, plain and simple. Sex isn't the worst way to end a night.

And then the horror show began.

She already proved to be a shitty kisser and could not give a blow job to save her life. My options were to have my dick scraped raw by her evil veneers or dive for cover into the velvet vagina and make it out quick for the walk of shame.

Long story short, Vanya was my number eighty-three and I needed to bounce off that number hard. And now I have to beat Arlo to not only prove to myself I can do it, but I am not going to have Vanya smug and looking down her plastic nose at Flynn from her perch beside a guy who has just beaten me.

Hells to the no.

My girl deserves a win, and I have plans to accommodate that in more ways than one. Every man should be so lucky to have an angel like Flynn drop into their life. I have had a lifetime's worth of disposable sex crammed into a decade, and when God looks down on your pathetic ass and graces you with the real deal, you lock that shit up. This is one of the reasons why I am so out of it today.

The other reason is, well, I am in my first Grand Slam semi.

And here comes Flynn now, pretty as the day I first met her. She likes to kiss me in the locker room before a match, and most of the players have finally stopped harassing me about it.

"What do you think?" she asks, eyeing me with those fierce green pupils that never let me get away with anything.

We spent most of last night watching YouTube videos of my opponent Alex Turner. A seasoned American player without much to show for it, he's had a dream run in Paris. He played two qualifiers in the early rounds, and his opponent retired during their quarterfinal. Neither he nor I have ever made it this far though, and we are guaranteed to be a bucket of nerves on either end of the court.

"I know," I say. "Watch out for his drop shots."

"Not that, silly. How do you feel about playing an American? ESPN won't shut up about it."

Oh, yeah, *that.*

The United States media is crying in their milk because two American players have never faced each other at Roland Garros in the semis, and an American spoiled their party. Last month, I switched countries and now play for Mexico. All I can say is it was time. Papa wept on the phone when I told him. My new agent, a firecracker named Tony, is knee-deep in brokering a bunch of sponsorship deals with Mexican companies, and even the president of Mexico sent me a letter. He also wished me luck this week through my agent and hopes to see me play at Wimbledon. Not having the pressure of a president watching me in the stands suits me just fine. I've got Papa to contend with and Flynn's friend June has been here all week. Morgan and Vandana fly in on Saturday, regardless of whether I win or lose. Come

Sunday, if I'm still standing, my player box will be the fullest it has ever been.

"I feel like this is meant to be," I say.

Flynn kisses me one last time, and I can taste vodka on her breath. I would start drinking in a heartbeat if it could help calm me down.

"You can do it," she says. "We both know it. Go."

A voice crackles over the loudspeakers, calling Alex and me to the stadium. A match official escorts us through the hallways and up the final flight of stairs that lead to the holding room before we step onto court Philippe Chatrier. The lower-ranked player always walks on first, and Alex bounces up and down like a hot potato in anticipation.

"Hey," I say. "Good luck."

He turns around and smiles. Very few players speak to each other at this moment. "Yeah, you too."

I stretch out my arms and my pecs. Twist my back until I hear the crunch. The officials radio each other on walkie-talkies to let everyone know the players are ready.

I close my eyes and try to control the rush of adrenaline.

Focus.

Right.

When I step outside onto the court and the roar of applause swallows the sound of my name still ringing from the announcement, focus is borderline impossible. All I have are my routines to keep me on track—what I eat and drink in between sets, making sure I look at Flynn, and changing my shirt if it gets too sweaty. Alex and I have never played together, so I don't know the tricks and psych-outs he might deploy to keep me unsettled during the match. The bathroom break. The mid-set fade. The grunt-fest on an important point or an injury time-out if he is tanking. Legit or not, these things disrupt rhythm, and I win matches only if I can find the rhythm zone.

And today, I am not just in the zone. I *am* the zone.

I am pure force, ability, and energy, free of the crushing doubt in my head.

Winners scream off my racket in every direction because the ball is ten times its regular size. I see numbers—15, 30, and 40—always identical numbers, and in the final minute, when the roller coaster takes me up, up, up to a height I have never ascended to, and the air is thin, I can barely breathe through the tightness in my chest. I toss the ball, arm straight, and go through the motion that was once upon a time fueled by rage.

White chalk flies up from the center service line, and I see Alex lunge, miss, and then the ball smacks hard against the back wall.

Now the sky is above me, a brilliant blue bubble so far away for a guy flat on his back in the hot red clay. Am I not hearing the crowd, or can I not hear anything beyond my heart exploding in my ears? Flynn jumps and down in my box like she won the lottery, the sun glinting off her auburn curls and that tight body in a dress I plan to rip off in the locker room if she doesn't stop me. June stands beside her, both hands raised and encouraging me to get up.

But I can't move.

A hundred memories squash me all at once. The stifling summer heat of Fresno and shitty courts with asphalt chunks missing. Me and Papa fighting. The flights and countries, days and months. All the time I thought I had wasted. I wipe away the sweat dribbling into my eyes, only to realize I am crying.

Shit.

This moment is so much bigger than me.

Punch-drunk and weaving, I stagger to my feet. Suddenly, my ears pop, and the roar of the crowd sets every hair on my body on end. The stadium is awash in Mexican flags, and I bet Mama is calling everyone who will listen with the news. Alex waits for me at the net, head bowed, his opportunity missed. I know that feeling. I have been on the losing end more times than I count, so I need to get my ass in gear and congratulate my opponent.

But I need a minute longer to absorb it all.

Just a minute to comprehend I am in my first Grand Slam final.

Chapter Thirty-Five

FLYNN

THE FACILITIES, PERKS, AND THE SENSE OF OCCASION ... WELCOME TO a Grand Slam where everything is bigger and more amplified, including nerves. Chavez slept well on the days before the final but tossed and turned for most of last night. I left him in the locker room a few minutes ago with both legs pumping up and down like pistons.

It's showtime.

The final.

There is nothing more I can do or say at this point.

Team Chavez waits for me in the players' box, and I hug everyone before taking my seat in the front room. Rodrigo flew here yesterday, as did Vandana and Morgan. June has been here all week. The only ones missing are Gloria, who never watches her son play live, and Carmen, up to her eyeballs in exams. And my Mom and Dad. They are watching from home, and Dad is shitting bricks he's so nervous. Vandana is like a kid in a celebrity candy store, scoping out the glamorous crowd for famous faces.

"This is so exciting," she says. "It's like the Superbowl but with better food and everyone is dressed well."

Morgan leans across her lap to ask me, "How is your man? He looked great during practice."

"Christ! He hits the ball so hard," June marvels.

"He's ready," I tell them all. "As much as he can be."

"Win or lose," Morgan says, "we celebrate in style."

Is there any other way with him? His ensemble today is a chic white suit and breezy black dress shirt, and why not add a Panama hat and look like a million dollars while every man wonders who his supermodel girlfriend is? Dressed to kill in a body-con Valentino jumpsuit, Vandana is primed and ready for a global TV audience. June went for an elegant, simple sheath, and I splurged on a cute V-neck Miu Miu dress that strikes the right tone between coach and girlfriend. (Little did I know the benchmark for this combo would fall on my shoulders.) Behind me, Rodrigo squirms in an ill-fitting blazer and looks as comfortable as a prisoner in the cargo hold of a tanker heading for Siberia.

"Chavez sends his love," I say. "He says he'll do you proud. He wouldn't be here without you."

He bows his head. "Gracias, Flynn. For everything you have done. All we can do now is pray."

God certainly turned it on in the weather department. Rain yesterday forced officials to close the roof for the women's final. The buzzy crowd today is pumped for a final played in picture-perfect conditions. The media hype for this event has been off the charts. Arlo comes into this match with a strong tiebreak record and the best return game of the year. But Chavez has better hands at the net and a more consistent serve. I never want to hear betting and tennis in the same sentence again, but the pre-match analysis pundits all say the odds are pretty even.

"What is that rubbish?" June lowers her Prada sunglasses to gaze across the court. "Did she put her dress on backward?"

Vandana and I follow her sightline, and my stomach twists into a tighter knot. Vanya slinks her way to the other player's box with gravity-defying boobs held in place by what might be dental floss.

"That's Arlo's girlfriend," I say. "She inhales cigarettes like they're food."

"She is smashingly trashy," June muses.

Vandana leans in to whisper, "Is that the one?"

"Yes," I grumble, having told her the details. I hate Vanya irrationally and forever. We bumped into each other at the start of the tournament and have thrown virtual daggers at every opportunity. The Arlo entourage of physio, trainer, coach, agent, and some European actor guy get a fine view of her double zero body as she squeezes past them. With nothing else on her agenda but to show up courtside flawlessly airbrushed and pouty-lipped, she takes a seat with an air of casual boredom before getting to the most important business at hand: snapping a selfie.

To get my brain off her, Vandana asks, "How does it all work during the match? Do you and Chavez talk?"

At that, Rodrigo breaks into wild laughter. I shoot him a smile over my shoulder before I answer.

"I can communicate with him when he's on this side of the court. But he can't say anything to us."

With Rodrigo still chuckling, Vandana, sensing she's missing something, asks, "What's so funny?"

I am about to explain when the air turns electric. The players are ready to come on the court. A surprising number of Mexican fans rise to their feet and wave their flags with chants of *Chavez, Chavez.* I glance at Rodrigo, choked up with a hand on his heart. What a moment for him. A roar of approval greets his son as he walks onto the court, and we all rise to our feet, clapping and shouting encouragement. Chavez unpacks his gear at the bench and sorts out towels and water bottles while Arlo gets introduced. Chavez wears his usual head-to-toe yellow outfit, and Arlo looks like a ninja in all black. The bumble-bee rumble. Get your stingers ready.

My mind shuts down during the warm-up and remains a swathe of emptiness as the crowds settle and Chavez steps up to the baseline to serve.

Across the red dirt of court Philippe Chatrier, Vanya smirks at me.

I smile back, gritting my teeth.

Please, Chavez, I say to myself. You have to win.

This is not just a final. This is personal.

EXACTLY ONE HOUR AND FOURTEEN MINUTES LATER, CHAVEZ WINS THE first set tiebreaker with a daring stab volley that has no business being a winner. It's been dog-eat-dog with no breaks of serve and both players firing on all cylinders. Fans disperse for the small break with a gigantic sigh of collective relief.

"Oh my God," June says, slumping back in her seat. "That was so intense."

Vandana tugs on Morgan's blazer. "Babe, take a seat."

I stand corrected on Morgan. There is a universe where he is less than perfect. He turned into a raging hooligan, on his feet at every opportunity to fist pump back at Chavez or shout "Vamos!" on every changeover. He smooths his hair and plants the hat back on, happy as a puppy with an entire yard to poop in.

"That was unbelievable!"

Vandana shoots me a look, equally surprised Morgan has not jumped on the court to high-five Chavez, who sits on his bench in a zone, legs pumping as he eats a banana and hydrates. In a minute, he'll change his shirt, currently smeared with clay from a few crowd-pleasing dives. Rodrigo and I huddle to do a quick recap of the first set. In general, clay court tennis is grueling, a moving chess match that requires stamina as much as skill. But the ball moves quicker on dry clay and if Chavez takes some spin off his forehand and flattens it out, it can pay dividends in the surprise department.

But Arlo is all over that tweak, and the first service break comes at the beginning of the second set. Three forehands sail long and *boom*, Chavez is in the hole. Dammit. Rodrigo nips more frequently at the flask of vodka he smuggled in as the set progresses, and I would pound that down in a heartbeat if all the cameras weren't focused on our box. (I've done all my drinking behind the scenes.) Chavez is playing well, but Arlo isn't going anywhere. The Hungarian beast maintains his cool and the lead to win 6-4 in a brisk forty-five minutes. During the break, a different energy hums through the crowd. This is shaping up to be a five-set classic.

My girls and I take a bathroom break between sets, and June glances at me gnawing on my thumbnail as she applies a fresh coat of powder-pink lipstick. "It's tied," she reminds me. "He's still in the running."

"I know. I hate this part."

"How much does he get if he wins?" Vandana asks, touching up her blowout.

"2.2 million Euros."

June raises a brow. "Not bad for a day's work."

If it only was a day and not years of grinding it out. When I think of how fragile I was at ten, what Chavez has achieved from the same age is remarkable. The fortitude to teach himself and navigate up the tennis rankings is a lesson in determination and commitment. He never went to college, but he understands real life and is hell-bent on proving he can be the best in the world at something. I know one of them will have to lose today, and even if he is runner-up, I'm so proud it hurts. But Chavez will not settle for runner-up.

Unfortunately, Arlo isn't willing to either.

He wins a lopsided third set 6-2, and Chavez shoots me a brooding look on the changeover. Arlo, the stupid lunk, is reading the Chavez serve while mixing his up brilliantly. So I signal Chavez to start doing the same. Sometimes your game and style of play will not win you the match, and the mark of a great player is the ability to change it up on the fly. Roger Federer was brilliant at this during the late stages of his career, adding new tools to his arsenal to keep opponents guessing. Chavez and I discussed what plans B and C might be today if he needed to dig himself out of a hole. He better be prepared to turn his racket into an excavator.

Because of the dry temperatures, the ground crew sprays water on the court between sets to keep the dust at bay. The clay gets swept, the white lines are brushed clean, and the pristine court of orange granules seems to pump Chavez up. He bolts to the service line long before the umpire calls for the end of break time. At least he's serving first. It's a psychological advantage when your opponent must win their service game to stay alive in the set. Team Chavez all lean forward as the play begins. The fourth set is a make-or-break situation, and no amount of deep breathing will relax me.

Holy Toledo, does Chavez dig deep as ever.

In the first game, he spins every serve viciously into the body of Arlo, catching him off guard. Then Chavez drops shots on every other point in game two and goes for huge second serves in game three. The disruptive rhythm rattles Arlo, and he loses 6-3. The first break of his serve the entire match. The Mexican fans whip the stadium into a frenzy.

Chavez! Chavez!

A fifth set is what they wanted.

It all boils down to this.

Very quickly, it gets nuttier.

After an epic display of clutch serving from both players all match, every game in the fifth features a break of serve. Poor Rodrigo sweats bullets with his blazer long since ditched. Morgan goes off the rails with Vandana slouching, somewhat embarrassed, in her seat.

Me? I am losing my mind when we go into a fifth-set tiebreaker.

The first player to reach ten points with a two-point lead wins, and I pray for Chavez to sweep Arlo. But the agonizing see-saw back and forth comes to a head when a brutal dribbler, a ball falling just over the net onto Chavez's side of the court, sets up a match point for Arlo. On his serve.

The quiet in the stadium is louder than anything I have ever heard. Vanya and I share a mutual gaze of disdain, although hers trumps mine because her fool man is in the driver's seat. With the sun behind him,

Arlo bounces the ball. Five times. Ten times. Fifteen. The multiple bounces of stress. A player once described the pressure to serve out a Grand Slam as akin to being on top of Mount Everest, where the oxygen is non-existent and your cells are slowly dying. It is the ultimate finish line, and the path to tennis glory is littered with the names of men and women who never successfully crossed it.

Just before he serves, Arlo glances up to clock Chavez stepping left and farther away from the baseline.

No, I want to scream.

Stay close. You're giving it to him!

Arlo has been catching him with the short and wide serve on the AD court all match.

Rodrigo mutters something in Spanish that rings with quiet desperation.

Morgan's lovely manicured fingers turn white as he clutches the railing in front of us.

June and Vandana each lay a hand on my leg, both women eerily still.

I bury my face in my hands.

I know it's just a game—there will be more matches and opportunities. But there have been too many losses. The lost years with Cori and Edgar; the loss of the tennis career I chose not to fight for. Losing Hamilton, and the final, painful loss of knowing the truth about Ava. Positives are on the horizon, more than I can count, and that should be enough, but after five exhausting hours and enough acid in my throat to fill a bathtub, I cannot watch Chavez lose.

Chapter Thirty-Six

"D**ID YOU SEE IT?**" V**ANDANA SQUEALS.** "I**T'S** *SOOO* **CUTE!**"

"Hold on," I say, juggling my coffee, phone, and hotel key card. "I just got back to our room."

I shoulder the door open, set my coffee aside, and am floored at how many new texts have landed since I last checked. Chavez and his incredible comeback win yesterday set the world abuzz. His phone must be spewing flames.

I open Vandana's text and burst out laughing. "Oh my God. Chavez is going to love this. I'm sending it to him right now."

What to say when you become a trending GIF on Twitter? Chavez scrambled into the player box post-win yesterday and went to town with me. Full dip kiss with tongue and an ass grab. File under *Aww*.

"How did today go?" Vandana asks. "He must be exhausted."

Last night's celebration rolled into the wee hours of the morning, and Chavez was up early for a full day of press commitments. I joined him for the first leg, being shuttled around Paris to be photographed with the trophy. He's finishing up the last of several interviews, and I'm back at the hotel to chill.

"He's running on fumes, so I expect a full crash."

She slurps into my ear, and I'm putting ten bucks down it's a Red

Bull. The beverage of choice for hard-partying socialites. "Last night was such a blast. I've never seen Morgan so drunk."

We raised a few eyebrows in Pur', an elegant, Michelin-starred restaurant. They expected a monied group of well-behaved citizens and not a rowdy celebration party. Rodrigo, Vandana, and I danced like teenagers; June downed champagne like it was water; and Morgan paraded around with Chavez, three sheets to the wind and handing out cigars like Chavez was his firstborn.

"Is he conscious?" I ask. "He and June must have swilled three bottles of champagne between them."

Vandana cackles. "Barely. The plan is to lay low tonight and give you two some private celebration time. But let's do lunch tomorrow before we fly home."

Home. I look out the window with a smile. For Vandana, Monaco is home now. Something June has slowly come to terms with. Which reminds me…

"Did June say anything else to you before she left?"

We both received a cryptic text from June early this morning. She flew back to LA to deal with a work emergency, and when we pressed for details, she said she couldn't talk about it.

"No," Vandana replies, and I can hear her concern. "But I suspect it has to do with her business partner in this new deal. He sounds slimy."

We devote the next ten minutes to unpacking what may or may not be happening. Her latest project has taken a toll on June mentally, and it might finally be the thing that encourages her to slow down. She is a multi-millionaire who doesn't have to work anymore, but the thrill of a company succeeding is her version of cocaine addiction. Chavez and I fly back to LA tomorrow night, and I promise Vandana to get the full scoop and report back.

After we hang up, I grab my laptop, get comfortable on the bed, and comb through two day's worth of unattended emails. Most surprising are the congratulatory wishes from fans via my Flynn Dryden website who have been following my path with Chavez. I never knew how many of them were such rabid fans.

And there is one email that my lawyer, Jax, sent on Friday. No subject. I open it, breathe hope into my lungs, and skim the few lines.

Flynn,

Lots to gossip about but long story short, Nathaniel got fired! You are good to go. I know you are busy in Paris, but call me when you have a minute.

Jax

It isn't beneath me to fist pump with a, *Yes!* Nathaniel wanted the rights to my mystery, claiming it as the book I contractually owed. Jax pushed back, insisting a fiction book did not fall under the same terms. A drawn-out court battle was the last thing I wanted, and now that Nathaniel got the boot, I'm free to start shopping my finished novel. Chavez will be thrilled. But where the hell is he? His interviews were supposed to wrap up at one, and it's now half past two. No texts. No nothing. But I'm not going to be that girl, creeping on him on the biggest day of his life, so I go back to reading and purging emails.

Brandon sent a note of congratulations, and I will pass it along, but I delete his email right away. That chapter is over. It took a lot of pushing on my part before Chavez thanked him for his assistance, and he did it on his terms. Text only, no call, and after, he requested that we forget all about Brandon. To be fair, I did send him an autographed book. Without his help, Jerry might still be running loose and Chavez would not be the current French Open champion.

And speaking of that.

It still boggles my mind how badly Arlo misfired on match point. He served underhand and Chavez ate that cheap shot for dinner. It pissed him off to no end that Arlo would pull a stunt like that and he channeled his anger the way we discussed. Arlo never even came close to touching the winning serve. Blown off the court was more like it. While Arlo wore a look of dejection during the trophy presentation, Chavez dropped jokes during his winner's speech and endeared the French crowd to him when he attempted, and botched, a few lines of their language. Everywhere I turned today, he was headline news. The first Mexican player to win a Grand Slam since Rafael Osuna. Apparently, we might get invited to Mexico City to meet the President. It's crazy! And it will only get crazier for him. Winning a Grand Slam is a game changer.

I surf all the new articles written about the match, even though I know every detail, and thirty minutes later, the long night, early morning, and too much alcohol catch up to me. I shut my laptop and put my head down to rest.

A gentle kiss rouses me from a deep sleep. Chavez has slipped soundlessly into the room, and he looks so dapper in his dress shirt and slicked-back hair a la Morgan. The photos snapped of him with the Eiffel Tower in the background and the French Open trophy in his arms will send hearts racing when they hit the internet tomorrow.

"Hi," I say, propping up on both elbows. The light has changed outside, and I have no idea what time it is. "Did you have fun?"

He sits close to me, the mattress dipping with his weight. "I sure did. But I'm done talking about myself. I've said the same things twenty times in both English and Spanish."

I tip my head to the bedside table. "I bought every newspaper today. For mementos. Oh, and did you see my text?"

His eyes sparkle as he laughs. "That GIF is ridiculous. But I love it."

"Your mom is going to love your hand on my butt," I say with a playful roll of my eyes. I can joke around now because the ice has melted between Gloria and me.

Chavez tucks an errant curl behind my ear. "Mama loves you, but not as much as I do."

"Why are you smiling like a buffoon?" I ask. He has an ear-to-ear grin getting bigger every second. "What have you got up your sleeve?"

"I'm smiling because I'm happy," he says. "And I don't have anything up my sleeve. But…" He moves off the bed, and down onto his knees. Or one knee, I should say. "I do have something in my pocket."

With a grand flourish, he presents a scarlet Cartier box and pops the lid. The glittering mass sends my brain into a complete tailspin. I've never seen so many diamonds on a single band. Not this size.

"What!?"

Chavez reaches for my left hand and slides the heavy band onto my ring finger with a gentle push past my knuckle. A perfect fit.

"It's not what or where or how or why, Miss Flynn," he says. "The question is, *will* you marry me?"

I can feel my face struggling to contain all the emotions coursing through me, and I do the sensible thing and burst into tears. Wet dribbles of happiness fall faster than I can wipe them away, and I can't believe I'm wearing ripped jeans and a T-shirt for such a defining moment. Can't win them all.

"Oh my God," I say, blubbering. "Yes, dummy! Of course I will."

His mouth is an endless pleasure no matter where it falls on my body, and this is not our first kiss, but in many ways, it remains one of my favorites, marking the transition between the old and new me. And he never breaks the kiss, even as he climbs onto the bed to sit beside me. When we do come up for air, I hold up my hand to admire the craftsmanship of what must be six figures of platinum and jewels. I need to call Mom and Dad and my girls. Vandana and June are going to flip out!

"And this…" I pause, frozen with the sudden fear of losing it. But no, that will not happen because I am never taking it off. "It's stunning."

"I told them I need a ring that shines as bright as a star. Because you are my cielo, Flynn, and I needed something worthy of shining in your sky."

Is this why he was late? Ring shopping? Who knows and who cares? He's here, and that's all that matters. I plant the sloppiest excuse for a kiss on his mouth. "I love you so much."

"I love you too," he says, running a hand through my curls. "And you can't change your mind. You're committed."

"If you're worried, we can consummate this right now."

He winks back. "I already planned on that. Give me a sec."

I reach for his wrist, holding him in place.

"The gear's in the bathroom keener," he explains with a smile. "I'll be right back."

I shake my head. "We don't need it."

The conversation on when we would try has never happened, and his face is a complete blank, nothing but blinking eyes in the throes of processing.

"Seriously?" he says.

I grin and nod, in spite of the butterflies. I don't know if I'm ready for this, honestly. But are we ever ready to go down the path to being someone else?

"But … you know what this means, right?" he asks like he needs to make sure I'm of sound mind.

"I do."

Now it's my future husband's turn to wipe his cheeks, and I can tell he's a little embarrassed with the flood of emotion. "Flynn, baby, I will never let you down. I promise. It's you and me. Forever."

He hugs me furiously in a long and gratifying embrace. I feel the heat in my face, the prickling of my nipples. I will never stop wanting him.

There is no X-rated strip tease this time around, but articles of clothing do get flung around the room. He undresses both of us, our skin radiating a crackling electricity. He is my erotic hotel, his body heat a roaring, welcoming fireplace in the lobby, his tongue the consummate front desk clerk encouraging me to relax, tending to my every desire until the general manager arrives. A serious length of wicked fun, rising hard from a tangle of curly hair blacker than my Better Than Sex mascara and determined to leave his guest satisfied and not leaving the room anytime soon.

Hair falling loosely around my shoulders, I nestle into the duvet, ready for our brand of sustained lovemaking. He nudges my legs wider with his knees, and then, just like the Chavez I once envisioned, he spits into his hand. Strokes himself. No need to slather me up however, because I am always ready for him.

"What's so funny?" he asks.

"Nothing. I can hardly wait to feel you inside me."

"I can't promise anything. I'm so damn tired and once I'm in you bare…" His weak smile dissolves into something more self-conscious. "This might be over before you know it."

"Really? June said a twenty-five-year-old should be able to fuck me to the moon."

I tweak my nipples, pink and hard and ready, and then tweak his. Cute little things poking out like nails from a slab of muscle. He starts to laugh and finds it hard to stop, his cock bobbing up and down like a fishing lure in the waves.

"I'm twenty-six next month," he says. "An old man, in tennis years."

"A Grand Slam champion never gives up. Not with the prize in sight."

Maybe he hears the challenge in my voice. Or sees it in my eyes. I know it's the best way to motivate him. Chavez Delgado loves a good challenge. And he's challenged me right back. I'm off the pills, reunited with my family, embraced by his, and we're about to start our own. It's only taken thirty-three years to get my life in order, but at last, it's my time.

"You know what?" Chavez says, staring down at me with his usual authority. "I think it's time to ditch the coach part."

I laugh and pull him closer. "Firing me after a taste of glory? I don't think so. I just need you to focus. One last time today."

And focus, he does.

He draws slow circles of sweet agony on my clit with the tip of his cock until the pleasure rises like a wave, and the only way to shut it down is by closing my eyes. As I do, he yanks my hips high, and the air rushes out of my lungs in one glorious gasp as he buries himself. He whispers for me to wrap my legs around him, and with the bubble cheeks of his ass firmly locked in place, our eyes meet in a single, defining moment.

"If you want the moon, Mrs. Delgado," he whispers, "you better hang on for the ride."

And with no distinction between my sex and his, we start to rock at a perfect tempo I could only ever dream of—the rhythm of two lives merging into one.

Creating life.

Always enjoy the journey is Flynn Dryden's Truth #10, and how fitting to end my story with that. I never guessed I would end up with a wild and wonderful man who takes no shit *and* no prisoners. One that dragged me kicking and screaming into a better place. We both have mountains to climb and demons to slay before we lay down our swords, but we have brought out the warriors in each other and that is the greatest gift of all. Yes, we will have challenges—I am marrying Chavez after all—but my confidence is high I can veer us onto the right path if we ever get lost.

When you feel safe, anything is possible.

Thank You and Free Bonus!

I hope you enjoyed *The Challenger!*

Reviews are the lifeblood of an indie author's success. I'd be honored if you took a moment to post a review on any of the sites below. If you're not comfortable putting your thoughts into words, a star rating works just fine.

Amazon

Good Reads

Book Bub

What's the song that Chavez does his strip tease to? I know y'all wanna hear it! Scan the QR code below for *The Challenger* playlist.

The Challenger Playlist

What to read next? Dive into book three of The Hustlers Series or fall in love with the fabulously sexy Trenton brothers in The Trenton Troublemakers series! Save 25% on all eBooks by buying direct through my Rowan Rossler Shop. All eBooks delivered immediately through Book Funnel. Signed books also available, mailed with love & bonus swag!

Scan to Shop!

Also by Rowan Rossler

The Hustlers Series

The Cruiser (book 1)

The Challenger (book 2)

The Closer (book 3)

This jet-set romance series stars three BFFs navigating dreams, desires, and all the beautiful complications of falling in love. Glamour, spice, and sexy drama. Pack your bags and follow your heart!

The Trenton Troublemakers Series

My Grape Crush (book 1)

My Cherry Duet (book 2)

Book Three (coming soon!)

Three brothers and the fiery women who tangle with them star in a trio of interconnected but standalone romances brimming with sibling drama and shameless fun. Trouble always comes in threes…

Acknowledgments

No author writes a book alone. *The Challenger* started as a love affair for my favorite sport but quickly evolved into a layered story requiring specific expertise to flesh it out. Gracias to all the fine folks below who shared their time and knowledge.

For his help on things related to the Challenger Tour, thanks to Ryan Borczon, Director of Professional and National Events at Tennis Canada.

In the UK, special thanks to Adrian Bassett, Head of Communications at The International Tennis Integrity Agency. He provided insider details on how match-fixing is flagged and handled within The Challenger and ATP Tours. Players do get suspended, and some receive lifetime bans if they get caught match-fixing. Since the ITIA has never adjudicated a betting case that involved a stalker, I took creative liberties in fleshing out that part of the story. Any mistakes are my own.

In Oregon, big hugs to Kendra Morris-Jacobson, Director of Oregon Programs at the Oregon Post Adoption Resource Center. When I started to write the character of Flynn, she kept telling me she needed to feel safe. I knew adoption was part of her backstory, although the full scope of how it impacted her only materialized in the second draft. When Kendra and I connected, she provided some excellent resources that sent a chill up my spine. Specifically, a common issue that manifests for adopted children is their inability to feel secure—not with who they are or where they are. Identity crises can result, especially in cases where a child finds out later in life they are adopted. The subconscious correlation between what was going on in my brain with Flynn and what happens in the real world with adopted children is part of the writing process that never ceases to thrill me. My characters inevitably tell me their story long before I understand it.

Special thanks to Diego De la Torre for his valuable insight into Mexican culture and family life and for making sure the correct Spanish words made their way to the page.

I am immensely grateful to Amanda Garcia for her thoughtful and insightful sensitivity read.

A big shout out to my editors at Two Birds Editing—Andrea and Meghan. Your feedback always makes my work better.

And for all the beta readers who weighed in with their notes, you know how grateful I am.

Wild, Wild Country is a Netflix documentary on the controversial guru Bhagwan Shree Rajneesh and the Rajneesh cult in Oregon. This fascinating series stuck in my mind for months after watching it, and I knew it would somehow, tangentially, wind its way into one of my stories. Check it out. It's a crazy one!

And I imagine the super nerd tennis fans might call me out on this, so I'm owning it before they do. The player boxes on Court Philippe Chatrier are on the same side, not across from each other. But it makes for a better story the way I had it!

Last, but definitely not least, thanks to all the booksellers and readers! You're what it's all about.

About the Author

Rowan Rossler is an Amazon Top 100 bestselling author and travel junkie living in Vancouver, BC. She loves bringing bold and flawed characters to life in her contemporary romance tales. If you're a lover of sultry moments, sexy drama, and heartfelt emotion, Rowan is your one-click author.

A lifelong book lover and former financial planner, her pivot into TV production inspired her to put pen to page. If she's not writing, you'll find Rowan stage left at a concert, cooking, whipping her abs into shape, or enjoying la dolce vita on one of her many travel adventures.

CONNECT WITH ROWAN:

27

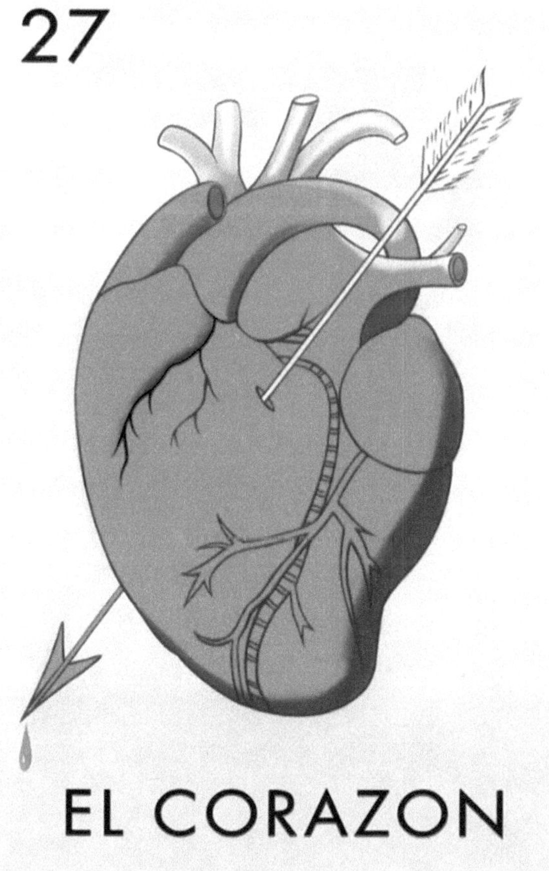

EL CORAZON

PIECES OF A PISCES

Breaking into Better

FLYNN DRYDEN